TRANSGALACTIC

JAMES GUNN

TOR®

A TOM DOHERTY ASSOCIATES BOOK
NEW YORK

This is a work of fiction. All of the characters, organizations, and events portrayed in this novel are either products of the author's imagination or are used fictitiously.

TRANSGALACTIC

Copyright © 2016 by James Gunn

A Tor Book
Published by Tom Doherty Associates, LLC
175 Fifth Avenue
New York, NY 10010

www.tor-forge.com

Tor® is a registered trademark of Tom Doherty Associates, LLC.

Library of Congress Cataloging-in-Publication Data

Gunn, James E.
    Transgalactic / James Gunn. — First edition.
        p. cm.
    "A Tom Doherty Associates book."
    ISBN 978-0-7653-8092-0 (hardcover)
    ISBN 978-1-4668-7612-5 (e-book)
    1. Interstellar travel—Fiction.   2. Planets—Exploration—Fiction.   I. Title.
    PS3513.U797T735 2016
    813'.54—dc23

                                                        2015033610

Our books may be purchased in bulk for promotional, educational, or business use. Please contact your local bookseller or the Macmillan Corporate and Premium Sales Department at 1-800-221-7945, extension 5442, or by e-mail at MacmillanSpecialMarkets@macmillan.com.

First Edition: March 2016

Printed in the United States of America

0 9 8 7 6 5 4 3 2 1

*Thanks to Chris McKitterick and Kij Johnson for their suggestions,
to Kevin Gunn and Mickey Dyer for their encouragement,
and to David Hartwell for his trust*

TRANSGALACTIC

CHAPTER ONE

Riley woke up.

He was standing, alone and naked, in a dark, closed space.

"Asha?" he called, but he knew she wasn't there.

He remembered things—everything—like the journey from the planet Terminal toward the end of the spiral arm, across the Great Gulf to the neighboring arm, with a supercargo of aliens in search of the Transcendental Machine. He remembered the bonding among the pilgrims, and the hidden forces at work within the ship, revealing themselves one by one, and the treachery. He remembered the stocky Dorian Tordor with the sensitive and deadly proboscis, the weasellike Xi, and all the others. And he remembered fighting his way, with Asha, through ravenous arachnoid aliens to reach what they thought was a cathedral but turned out to be a waiting room.

He knew a lot of things that he had never been aware of before, and with a clarity he had never experienced. He knew, for instance, that the Transcendental Machine was a matter-transmission device that had been used by the other spiral-arm aliens—an earlier version of the arachnoids, or the species the arachnoids had replaced—to explore not only their own spiral arm but the spiral arm of humans and the aliens of the Federation. And maybe to influence them in ways that might never be understood.

The Machine analyzed anything that entered it, destroying it in the process, and sent the information to a receiver in which the same entangled quantum particle was embedded, where what had been destroyed was re-created from local materials—and that included sapient creatures such as Asha, and now himself. In the process imperfections were left behind. Transcendence was an accident.

He had been restored but the pedia that had been implanted in his head by strange, unknown entities, which was not part of his ideal condition, was not. He didn't know yet how he would get out of wherever he had been sent, nor how he would find Asha. The Machine had sent her somewhere else. If it was not programmed, the Machine chose destinations at random or in some pre-set order. After a hundred thousand long-cycles—maybe even a million—it was a miracle of alien technology that it functioned at all.

But he knew he would find Asha if he had to fight his way halfway across the galaxy. And when he found her he knew that they, with the insights and power of transcendence, would change the galaxy.

Riley felt his way out of the machine that had re-created him and began the necessary exploration of his surroundings. The space was chilly, even chillier to his naked body. The floor under his feet felt rough and dusty, and the dead smell of long-enclosed spaces, along with the musty smell of disturbed dust, reached his newly sensitive nose. Two cautious paces in one direction and he reached a smooth wall that began to glow a soft rose as he touched it. Four more rapid paces took him to the opposite wall, which also sprang into gentle radiance. He could see now that he was in a featureless cube with a ceiling above his reach and the machine in the center.

The machine was little more than a free-standing closet, open on one side, simpler than the Transcendental Machine. Maybe it was a later, more efficient model. Or, since there was a heap of clothing on the floor but no pile of dust, maybe it was meant to receive and not to send. Maybe the alien emissaries were ambassadors for life and never expected to return. Riley recognized the heap of clothing. They were—he understood as he put them on—the clothes and shoes that he had once acquired new, or the clothes that he might have acquired in an ideal world in which clothes were ideally made of materials ideally suited for their purpose. The Machine analyzed and transmitted everything within its focus, transformed.

Riley inspected the inside of the machine, running his hands across its surfaces, but it was featureless. The only thing he noticed was that his sense of touch, like his sense of smell, seemed to be keener, as if his fingers had been sandpapered. He felt his way over the outside. It was equally uninformative until he reached a spot above the opening. The spot was difficult to see, because the light was dim and the structure itself was taller than he, as if it was intended for creatures a third again as large, but his fingers felt a series of slightly raised places like designs or, more likely, letters of an alien alphabet or figures intended to convey a message. They weren't like anything he had ever encountered and no amount of fingering, or even inspection if he had something to stand on, was likely to decipher them.

He could only guess that they were instructions on how to operate the machine, or maybe the controls themselves. He began to reevaluate his hope of an easy way to reunite with Asha.

Where was she? Where in the galaxy had she been transported? He had, he realized, assumed that he could return to the planet of the Transcendental Machine. With his newly created clarity of thought, he ought to be able to do that. With clarity of thought came confidence, maybe overconfidence; he would have to be careful of that. He had also realized that returning to the planet of the Transcendental Machine would put him no closer to Asha. Even if he could, maybe, reverse the Machine, what he could never do was decipher where the Machine had sent her. Unless Asha came to the same conclusion and also returned to the planet. Clarity of thought did not mean clarity of information; what was unknowable, like truly alien forms of communication, remained unknowable.

He could try, he had thought, and if she was not there, or if their returns did not coincide, he could leave a message, or find one from her. Timing would be everything, since they could not survive for more than a day, or perhaps even a few hours, among the arachnoids or other dangers, without food or drink. Without that, where would they meet out there among a billion suns? And there was always the chance that the Machine would send him to a nonfunctioning or destroyed receiver, and he would end up an electronic ghost searching through the galaxy in a forlorn hope of rebirth. But even that uncertain avenue had been closed.

So, there had to be another way. Somewhere in their shared experience, in their journey together, was a clue to a meeting place if they got separated. Meanwhile there were practical problems to be solved: He would die of thirst and starvation, and maybe unbreathable air, unless he found his way out of this featureless cube.

With a feeling of urgency but not of desperation, Riley felt his way around the walls with his newfound sensitivity of touch. Doing two things at once was easy for him now, and he reviewed, like a visual recording in his head, everything Asha had told him during their time together, including her experience in the generation ship *Adastra* when it was captured by Galactics and taken to their Federation Central. She was a child then and grew up under Galactic captivity until the junior officer on the *Adastra* found a way to make an escape, with the secret of the Galactic's nexus points that made interstellar travel practical and human competition possible. And their flight, with the aid of an ancient map and the Galactics in pursuit, to the adjacent spiral arm, and finally to the planet of the Transcendental Machine. And their perilous path through the city before Asha found refuge in what she took to be a cathedral, where she entered the Machine and ended up . . . where? He wished now that he had asked for more details of how she had found her way back from wherever she had been sent then and how she had returned to the Galactic Federation. But there had been no time for that in the urgency of their time together and their own crisis-filled journey.

Riley searched his memories for any clue to the way Asha had solved the problems that he now faced, but he knew that this was a carryover from old deficiencies. His present memory held no dark places, no secrets waiting to be discovered.

He made the circuit of the room twice before he found, above his head, a set of raised places similar to those he had found near the top of the machine. If they were instructions, he would never be able to read them. But just below the raised hieroglyphs, if that was what they were, he felt two indentations that, on further exploration, revealed themselves to be holes. They were about the size of a small tentacle or an insectoid feeler or his little fingers. Without hesitation, he inserted one little finger into each hole as far as it would go.

Soundlessly, a hole appeared in the middle of the wall below and grew into an opening into a dark space beyond. He didn't pause to consider the nature of the substance that was solid but capable of dissolving. He removed his little fingers, undamaged, from the holes into which he had inserted them and stepped through the opening in the wall before it closed. The walls outside did not glow, but strips above his head emitted enough rosy light that he could see he was in a rough-walled corridor, with a floor equally uneven beneath his shoes, as if it were made of cobblestones or of bricks that had deteriorated unevenly over the long-cycles, and a ceiling farther above his head than he could reach.

Behind him, when he turned, the hole in the wall had healed itself and there was no legend above the spot where it had been, or holes with which to activate it. The area where his disembodied information had been received was like a womb to which he could never return. He was cut off from the alien machine. If using it had ever been a possibility, that door was closed. That the process was a one-way trip became more certain, and the reason that the receiver area remained undisturbed after all these long-cycles, more evident. He turned to his right and began to walk briskly. He was not yet thirsty or hungry—maybe his new condition was more efficient in that respect as well, but it couldn't repeal the laws of nature and sooner or later he would need food and drink.

As he moved, strips on the corridor wall next to the ceiling came alight with him and darkened behind, although occasionally a dark gap appeared where the damage of the ages had conquered even the superior alien technology. He had noticed it in the alien planets he and Asha and their companions had visited in their pilgrimage—the alien structures, in all their splendor, had survived their creators.

Those creators, he thought, were not the arachnoids who had attacked them. They were too big to fit into the Transcendental Machine or even through the doorway into the building that housed it, too big to fit through the opening that appeared in the wall or the corridor in which he was now walking. Perhaps their smaller cousins could, but they were the wrong shape to fit into the Machine's compartment comfortably.

No, the aliens who built the Machine and the city that housed it were humanoid, though perhaps larger than most humanoids. And their eyes had evolved under a different light, perhaps the red sun he had seen in the alien sky. There had been a blue sun as well, but it may have been captured later, and perhaps that cosmic event had precipitated the downfall of the Transcendental Machine species or the rise of the arachnoids.

But all that was speculation for another time, and this corridor was narrowing into a space even a normal-size human would find a tight fit. Soon he would have to make a decision to reverse his course or to pursue this one on hands and knees until he could no longer turn around. The wisest course, he decided, was to explore in the other direction.

After an hour, thirteen minutes, and twenty-two seconds—he realized he had a timekeeper in his head that kept track of such things—and after exploring fifteen corridors of various sizes that ended in blank walls or narrowed to sizes that he could not squeeze himself into, he followed the sixteenth corridor to an opening into a chamber like the one in which he had found himself re-created but with an ordinary doorway and walls that were rough, like the corridor, and that did not light up. The only illumination in the chamber came from the corridor behind. The chamber in front of him had been produced by an earlier, more primitive culture, like the corridors themselves, or else the chamber in which he first found himself had been built into a structure that was already in place. He thought that the latter was more likely. From the light behind him and with vision that seemed to operate far more efficiently, he could see that something that resembled a sarcophagus rested on a platform in the middle of the chamber, that if it was a sarcophagus it had been opened and what might have been a lid or cover had been removed and lay broken upon the floor, and what was in the sarcophagus, as he approached, were the remains of an alien creature and perhaps what had once been garments or ornaments, though they, too, were broken or scattered so that their function was obscure.

He realized now what the structure was that he had materialized in. He was inside some kind of massive structure assembled to protect the remains of some ancient ruler or god for eternity. But, like all such attempts at permanence, it had not worked. Sometime in the remote past, grave robbers had found their way into the primitive structure, had found the chamber, and had stripped it of the valuables it once might have contained.

Or they had found it without anything worth stealing and had destroyed everything in their frustration.

Riley moved into the chamber and inspected the sarcophagus. Ornate designs had been carved into the stone, and even with the little light that spilled in from the corridor he could see that they represented some kind of life story, with oddly shaped, perhaps stylized, figures of various sizes standing upright on large legs and perhaps a tail, or an ornamental train, behind, and confronting or interacting with other figures of different shapes. They seemed to represent a journey from life to death and beyond, a process guided or determined by more powerful beings, perhaps gods, and illustrating the path of glory and greatness traveled by the body that was laid within the sarcophagus.

That body, he saw as he looked into the sarcophagus, was only bones. Perhaps once the remains had been preserved by some alien art, but stripped of adornments and exposed to the elements and the ages everything impermanent had fallen away, leaving behind only its structure. The bones told a story. They had belonged to a species with strong leg bones, small upper bones, and a powerful tail, somewhat like pictures Riley had seen of Earth marsupials. The evolutionary process did not privilege grazers in the development of intelligence and technological culture, but Riley remembered Tordor and the heights to which his species had ascended, transformed by discipline, cruelty, and a sense of mission, as well as the ways in which the other aliens on the *Geoffrey* had been shaped by the pressures and opportunities of the special conditions under which they had evolved.

Looking down on the greatness that had once motivated a species to build a massive mausoleum at a terrible cost in treasure and lives, and over a span of time that must have lasted generations and impoverished an economy, Riley felt the first stirrings of hunger and thirst. He would have to find food and drink soon or he would end up like the remains in the sarcophagus. He looked around the chamber for some kind of guidance but the walls were bare rock and the floor was dusty and scattered with bits of metal, apparently discarded by the grave robbers who had made their way into this hidden place in spite of the ingenuity of the engineers who had constructed it.

Surely the designers would have left some testament to their care behind, if not to their piety, but there was nothing. Still, he thought, the grave robbers would have left something more valuable to him.

He walked slowly and carefully out of the chamber and down the corridor that had led him to the sarcophagus, looking at the walls and the floor for ancient clues. The grave robbers could have used markers like paint or leaves or crumbs to mark their path to the outer world, markers that would have vanished long ago, but he had to assume they had chosen something more permanent in case they wanted to return. They would not have needed guidance close to their goal, but when he reached a point where the corridor branched he saw a place in the corridor wall, at the height of his shoulder, where a small piece of the stone had been chipped away. He would not have noticed it if he had not been searching for some kind of guidance, and, even searching, he might have dismissed it as the damage of time if his need had not been growing more urgent.

At another branching he saw a similar marking, and at a third, another. But that led him down a corridor that ended in a blank wall that no amount of manipulation could turn into a door. He retraced his steps to the place the corridor had branched and inspected the marking more closely. Now he noticed that the chipping was different, with a downward blow that left the deepest part pointing toward the floor rather than a sideways blow pointing forward, and he realized that the grave robbers must have marked the wrong choices as well as the right ones. A few paces down the other corridor he found the mark that told him, he hoped, that he was on the right path.

Finally he arrived at the point where the corridor narrowed and the ceiling got lower. He hesitated and then kept moving forward, trusting the marks and his interpretation of them, until he was forced to his hands and knees. Soon, he knew, he would have to back out or be in so far he could not extract himself. But surely, he reasoned, that is what the builders of this mausoleum would have done as a final protection. At one point, just before he was about to decide that he had made his last mistake, the floor of the constricted space felt pebbly and sharp beneath his hands and knees, and the sides and ceiling of the tunnel grew a bit larger, and he realized that the ancient grave robbers had chopped away at them and left the debris behind. And then the corridor grew large again.

Riley stood up. A few paces away was another blank wall, but this, he knew, was his pathway out of this massive structure into whatever lay beyond. It took him one hour, six minutes, and forty-two seconds to find the combination of pressure points around the circumference of the wall that made a segment of the wall swing inward and allowed light to enter and a breeze redolent with the distinctive scent of alien life and vegetation and their decay.

Riley stepped to the opening and looked down at a flat, rugged surface of stone as far as he could see, sloping away from him toward the canopy of a tropical jungle, and above to a sky that was drifting with clouds turned reddish by an alien sun.

He took a deep breath and started the long climb down to a world that he had to learn about very quickly before he could find a way to leave it.

CHAPTER TWO

Asha woke up.

Light was streaming down from above and a spray of liquid was hitting her face and naked body as she opened her eyes. She was standing in the familiar structure of a simplified Machine, but there was nothing familiar about its location. When she had been transported before, she had awakened in the walled-in section of a cave remote from civilization. Here, she realized, the Machine that had received her was the centerpiece of a fountain that was spraying what seemed to be water. The fountain was in the middle of what appeared to be a public square or a plaza surrounded by structures that seemed just a little weird but clearly intended for habitation or business. The air was breathable with just a hint of an alien odor, a bit pungent, like sandalwood. The square was occupied by several hundred aliens, somewhat humanoid in appearance, and without clothing. And they were all looking at her.

Sometimes, she realized, the Machines left around the galaxy by the Transcendental Machine aliens would have been destroyed by geologic accident or by superstitious natives over the past million long-cycles. But sometimes, if they had been discovered, they might have been admired or even venerated and placed in positions of honor. That, apparently, was what had happened here.

Clearly, too, she and Riley, if he had followed her into the Transcendental Machine, had been transported to different places, perhaps to different parts of the galaxy, and Riley would have awakened, as she did, wondering what had happened, though perhaps, if he had observed what had happened to her, more aware of what the process involved. He would be in a position, and with newly acute faculties, to figure it out, as she had in her first experience through the Machine. And he would have her account for guidance. Now, though, she knew what to expect and what she would have to do. Before, she had found herself among truly alien quadrupeds, whose barklike language had been difficult to learn, but who had worshipped her with doglike devotion and, fortunately, had achieved spaceflight a thousand long-cycles earlier and Federation status only a few hundred long-cycles later. So she had been able to find her way back into Federation space and begin the journey that had started with the rumors of Transcendentalism and the Transcendental Machine, and ended with the pilgrimage on the spaceship *Geoffrey* from Terminal to the planet of the Transcendental Machine in the adjacent spiral arm.

Here it might well be different. First she would have to calm the apprehensions of the natives of this world, win their trust or maybe their worship (how would they have responded, she thought, if one of the arachnoids had appeared in the Machine?), and find a ship that would take her off this world and into the galactic civilization of nexus point travel and the Galactic Federation that controlled this spiral arm, where there were powerful forces that would rather see her dead and forgotten. She was the unintentional prophet of the new religion of Transcendentalism, a religion of evolutionary fulfillment that threatened the stability hard-won through thousands of long-cycles of wars and internecine struggles, most recently with humans newly emerged from their solar system into the galaxy.

That was the simple part. The second was more difficult. She had to find Riley, for personal reasons and for the help she needed in order to save the galaxy from itself, to fulfill the promise born into its first living creatures, not only to survive but to prevail. To improve. To be the best they could be. To do that, the galaxy needed a more nourishing system of governance, of art, of literature, of discourse. And to make that happen she needed Riley. But where would he consider a logical meeting place in this vast galaxy? It was something they should have talked about, something she should have considered, since she had already been through the Transcendental Machine. But she had not envisioned the variability of destinations. Even transcendence has its limitations.

She would think of something. But now she had to meet her new companions.

She gathered up her clothing scattered on the floor of the Machine, too damp to put on even if she had wanted to. She stepped out of the Machine, into the full spray of the fountain, as naked as the humanoids who stared at her from the plaza.

As soon as she stepped out of the fountain, humanoids who had emerged from a nearby building rushed toward her with some kind of cloth over their arms and a stronger odor of sandalwood from their bodies. Before she could react, humanoids closest to her had taken hold of her arms. She did not struggle. The touch of their four-fingered hands was firm, warm, and dry but not painful or unpleasant—almost reverent—and she stood still while the humanoids with the cloths shook them out into garments and draped them on her body: a sheer, royal-blue wrap-around gown, a silvery sash, a matching scarf that went over her hair and shoulders. Then they stood back and looked at her as if admiring their handiwork.

They were small people, the tallest among them reaching just a bit above her shoulders. They seemed to lack external gender distinctions. Their smooth, brown bodies were not mammalian; they had no breasts or nipples or genitalia, and she wondered if they were all one gender and how they reproduced and how they nourished their offspring. But they were tugging at her arms, pulling her toward an ornate structure nearby from which the humanoids with the clothing had emerged. She did not resist. She had more pressing concerns. Why had she been clothed when the rest were naked, where were they taking her, and what were their plans for her?

The building resembled the pictures she had once seen of oriental palaces, with smooth rock walls painted with ocher—or perhaps constructed with colored rock—and projections on the roof and the entranceway topped with silver spheres or irregular objects that the humanoids might consider art or ways to ward off evil. As they got closer, the short flight of stairs in front of them flattened into a silvery ramp, perhaps a carpet. It was soft under her bare feet as they pulled her toward a pair of massive silver doors that opened automatically in front of her.

The little people were squealing and hissing now as they tugged her into a large anteroom just beyond the door, its floor paved with marble-like stone and a large vase or urn in the center with blue, raised figures on it, apparently depicting various actions that might have religious or ceremonial significance. She would have to examine and decipher them when she had the chance. But that chance was not now. The little people tugged her across the room and through a door on the opposite wall and into more intimate quarters, with a pallet on a pedestal against the far wall, a pool filled with a clear liquid in the center, something resembling a table—a flat surface with legs—against another wall, and above it a silvery mirror.

She caught a glimpse of herself in the mirror, not haggard from her recent experiences as she would have expected, but radiant, restored— perhaps by the Transcendental Machine—and adorned like pictures she had seen of ancient ceremonies where women were united with men in lifelong relationships. She would have to think about that. Perhaps she was the guest of a hospitable people, treating her with the special privileges and status befitting guests in this culture, particularly those that emerged through the Machine. If there was a tradition of creatures emerging from the Machine. Maybe there were only myths. They would have to be powerful myths to survive a million long-cycles. On the other hand, they might have been nurtured by charlatans secreting themselves in the Machine and emerging as visitors.

Another possibility was that visitors from the Machine were considered by this culture to be gods or the offspring of gods or those chosen by the gods to reign over these creatures. That would create problems for her need to get off this planet and back into the interstellar community of the Federation. It might not be easy to abdicate and even more difficult to escape without abdication, and almost impossible if she were the scapegoat queen, chosen to rule in splendor for a long-cycle and then be sacrificed for the welfare and good fortune of the people, assuming all their sins and guilt and bad luck in the process.

All that would have to be sorted out. At the moment the cluster of little people had brought her to the middle of the room, squeaking and whistling, and then all but two had retreated in postures that she interpreted as showing deference and perhaps worship as well as twitches of the head and arms that somehow suggested bowing and scraping. The doors closed behind them. Asha heard a click that she understood to be a lock being closed. Her room was a prison. Well, she had been in far less comfortable prisons, and locks were meant to be opened.

Meanwhile her two guards or attendants or fellow prisoners were removing the finery with which she had just been adorned and gently tugging her into the bath in the middle of the room where they proceeded to rub her body with gentle, warm hands and liquids that emerged automatically from spigots on each side of the bath. At first she stiffened at these personal touches from her—what? handmaidens? serving men? Perhaps the question of gender didn't matter to these creatures, or mattered to them only on special occasions, and if so it shouldn't matter to her. She relaxed. They kept squeaking and whistling while they worked, but in a gentler, more soothing pattern. Clearly it was a language, and she would figure it out. Already she was beginning to notice a difference in squeals that her brain, without any conscious direction, was beginning to connect with actions.

Soon they were finished and they helped her out of the floor-level bath and dried her with absorbent cloths taken from a cabinet that opened, at their touch, in a wall. They seemed to marvel a bit at the differences in her body from their own but without alarm or distaste. They did not use the towels on themselves, instead allowing themselves to drip dry and then mopping up the moisture on the floor with additional towels. Finally, finished to their own satisfaction, they tugged Asha, each to an arm, toward the bed and pushed her gently down.

Asha sat upright. "Sorry, kids," she said. "I know you don't understand what I'm saying, but I don't feel like sleeping right now."

Her handmaidens or serving men—she didn't know what to call

them, and it wasn't simply a matter of pronouns but a kind of funda-
mental unease at her inability to place them in a familiar gender context. The problem was common when dealing with humanoid aliens
who seemed like humans but differed in some significant way, particularly sexual. Well, she would let that sort itself out, she thought, and
before she had finished with it, her attendants had made some invisible
signal and the doors opened for two more humanoids bearing platters
that they placed in front of her on legs that magically sprang open as
they descended to her level.

One platter had an assortment of what seemed to be fruit—purple
balls, clusters of what looked like green grapes but were wrinkled like
berries, larger globes of a red fruit that had been sliced into sections with
moist, red insides. The other platter contained flat yellow pieces of what
looked like bread or cake in ornate shapes. She looked them over carefully before selecting a piece of the breadlike substance and sampling
it. She tried nothing else. The improvements in her body meant that
it could cope with many substances that might have been poisonous to
her earlier self, but it made sense to try one at a time, and something
that had been cooked had less chance of being deadly. She could try
other substances at her next opportunity and then something different
until she had established a cuisine of alien foods that she could tolerate.
And if anything made her sick, her body would reject it without, she
hoped, permanent harm.

Meanwhile, though, the bread, if that was what it was, seemed not
only tolerable but tasty, if a bit spicy, like the odor of the world itself
and the little people who inhabited it.

"That's enough, kids," she said, putting down the remnants of the
bread and waving her hand at the rest, hoping that the gesture, if not
the words, were universal. The attendants who had brought in the platters picked them up. The one with the fruit placed it in a far corner of the
room, as if leaving it for her later use, and then retreated with the other
humanoid through the doors that opened automatically in front of them
and closed just as automatically behind, with the same clicking sound.

"Now what, kids?" she said.

She stood up, beginning to feel like a giant among Lilliputians. The attendants looked at each other and then one moved to a different portion of the wall. When the attendant touched a spot, the wall opened like a door to reveal fixtures that seemed intended for the elimination of bodily wastes.

"Not now, kids," she said, and did not move.

The one who had touched the wall—she could not yet distinguish between them—returned to her side. They each took an arm and tugged her gently toward the mirror, squealing and whistling. Their chatter almost seemed to make sense to her, as if she could feel the translation machine in her head whirring as, one by one, words dropped into place.

"I get it," she said. "You want to show me something."

She stared at her image again, this time looking a little gross beside the childlike bodies and faces beside her. But before she had time to ponder that issue her attendants had waved their hands in front of the mirror and it turned transparent. She was looking through a window into a world outside.

Later she lay in what the little people used for a bed. It was firm but not uncomfortable, except for the two attendants who were curled up at her feet. They were asleep, but she was only resting. She didn't need much sleep anymore—maybe an hour or two of relaxing all the muscles in her body and calming the swift precision of her thoughts. Now, though, she had much to think about.

The mirror, she understood, had become a screen for scenes from the outer world into which she had been thrust, showing views that were either recorded or live. After observing only a single gesture by one of the attendants, she was able to control what was being offered, from landscape to close-up and from what seemed like the town or city in which she had appeared to more varied scenes and more distant vistas, all accompanied by the squeaks and whistles that served the little people as language, or, occasionally, by a cacophony of sound that may have represented music.

This world—she wanted to give it a squeak-and-whistle name—was a planet favored by size, geography, and geology, a bit on the small side but with flat, productive farmland and occasional rolling hills over most of its temperate zone, a few mountains at the equator, and icy poles. The mirror had shown nothing astronomical, so she had no way of judging the planet's position in its system, only that it had a benevolent G-2 sun. She had noticed that when she'd emerged from the Machine.

There were cities, rivers with boats, oceans with ships, landscapes with some kind of vehicles that traveled on single rails. But she did not see any vehicles that moved through the air. And most important of all, she saw no spaceports. That was going to create problems. Getting a world into the space-travel era would take tens of long-cycles, at best, and she didn't have tens of long-cycles, maybe not even a single long-cycle if her worst fears about this culture were confirmed.

Unexpectedly, as if in response to some inner timer or a signal that passed between the attendants unseen, one had stepped in front of Asha and waved its hand at the screen once more. The view of the outside world disappeared and was replaced by a darkened space. A single monstrous figure, but stylized like a line drawing, appeared in a corner of the space before fading away into blackness. Then, in another corner, appeared the figure of a humanoid alien, one of the little people, before it, too, disappeared. A sequence of appearances and disappearances followed, with the two figures showing up in different places each time, but never close to each other.

One of the attendants moved its hand again in front of the screen. Each time the figures moved to different places.

"I get it, kids," Asha said. "It's a search game, like the Monster and the Princess, and I'm supposed to solve it. And that will get me a prize. Or maybe not."

She had heard about such games. Ren had liked to hone his skills on them in the long, dull stretches of travel between nexus points, and she had even toyed with them herself, though never with Ren's success. But her brain worked better now, and she ran over in her mind various strategies that she might bring to bear upon the solution. If she wanted to solve it. Maybe the problem was one these humanoids knew how to solve and solving it would prove her right to membership in the group of aliens intelligent enough to be granted membership in the civilized community.

Or maybe it was a problem they had never been able to solve, and solving it would mean her qualification to rule over them. But she did not know, yet, what they did with rulers.

She closed her eyes and let herself relax, sensing the bodies of the little people at her feet and feeling that peculiarly comforting. She hoped that when she stopped thinking about her situation, the answer would come to her.

CHAPTER THREE

Riley looked down the long, sloping expanse of the pyramid's side and toward the green and red and yellow foliage that marked the canopy of the burgeoning jungle below. It was a scene of fertility for which the barren deserts of his native Mars had not prepared him, but he recognized it from the picture books and recordings of humanity's birthplace. "Teeming" was the word that came to mind, and even from his vantage point high on the pyramid's side he could see creatures flying above the treetops and imagine the proliferation of predatory life below, but he had no choice other than to join it.

He began the long descent. The stones that formed the sides of the pyramid had been fitted together so precisely that they required no mortar, but the erosion of the ages and perhaps the onset of a wet tropical climate had worn handholds between the rocks. Farther below, when he had climbed down far enough to reach the jungle top, the supports for fingers and toes were reinforced by sturdy creeping vines. There he could see the flying creatures more clearly. They were large, reptilian creatures with big jaws and leathery wings made more for soaring than for flying. One swooped dangerously close, its jaws open as if to pick him off his precarious position. He shouted at it and waved his free hand. It swerved away and then returned for another try. But by this time Riley was ready with a piece of vine broken away. He hit the flying creature in the snout. It fell for a few seconds until it spread its wings and soared away as if in search of easier prey. Riley dropped the club and resumed his descent.

Below the canopy he saw and heard other kinds of life, monkeylike creatures and some that looked more reptilian, including a few snakes, but they weren't close enough to be threatening. Mostly at this level there were insects, swarms of them, coming at him from all directions. He brushed them away with his free hand and then, surrendering, started down again, allowing them to settle on his body and his head while he hoped that this alien pest did not possess alien poisons, though it certainly contained alien viruses which he hoped his new body had new ways to resist. For a time he could insulate himself from his awareness of what they were doing, and before they could become intolerable, they abandoned him, as if finding his alien substance inedible or unattractive, or perhaps, he thought, his perfected body had adjusted its chemistry to thwart the sensory apparatus of the insect swarms. That certainly would be a new survival characteristic.

At last he reached the ground and looked back up the side of the ancient structure, marveling one last time at the effort and dedication and sacrifice that had gone into this monument to an ancient ruler, now being reabsorbed by the world from which it had sprung, and he wondered if this location, long-cycles ago, had been more accessible, a desert perhaps before a climate change or some tectonic shift had transformed it into its present state. He turned and made his way into the jungle.

The jungle was heavy with the ripe aroma of growing things and vegetable decay and an underlying alien taint that told Riley of a different evolutionary chemistry. Its floor was relatively free of undergrowth. The towering trees kept sunlight from reaching the surface, except in a few places where stray beams nourished a bush or flowering plant. The jungle floor, though, was deep with debris, and Riley walked carefully, watching his surroundings for predator threats. He stepped on something solid. When it didn't move under his foot, he reached down and withdrew a fallen limb that he could use as a club. It was not the best of weapons, but it was better than nothing. If he were on this world for very long he would have to fashion hmself a bow and arrows or a spear.

A few steps farther on, he needed the club when something lashed out at him from a tree trunk. He saw it in time to knock it away. It was a gigantic flower, like pictures he had seen of an overgrown orchid, only this one had stout petals that closed upon its victims. Now, half shattered but still lashing, it emitted a stifling odor of decay. A bit farther on, in a patch of sunlight, he came across a bush that had spherical yellow growths at the ends of its branches. Birdlike creatures were fluttering around it, and some were eating at the growths with unbirdlike teeth. Riley waved them away with his club and picked one of the spheres. They were fruit, he thought, and the native creatures ate it. He bit into it. It was sweet and tart and filled with juice that ran down the sides of his mouth. Maybe it was poisonous, as alien evolutionary products are likely to be, but sustenance was more of a concern. Poison or not, his re-created body would have to cope with it.

As he made his way farther into the jungle, he felt a few rumblings inside, but they subsided, and when he came upon a different kind of blue fruitlike globe and sampled it, his body accepted it without protest. Finally he reached a stream where a lizardlike creature, about the size of a large dog, was drinking. It raised its head to look at him as he approached, as if evaluating whether he was a danger or a meal, and then scuttled away as Riley raised his club, a sign that Riley interpreted as a hopeful indication that it had seen creatures his size wielding weapons before. He had two chances for getting off this planet; the first was to encounter the descendants of the creatures who had built the pyramid, the second was that they had progressed from that primitive beginning to the stage of powered technology and spaceflight. Surely the emissary of the Machine for whom the receiver in the pyramid had been built had accomplished something. Otherwise he would have to raise an alien civilization to interstellar capability in a generation, and he wasn't sure Asha, or the galaxy, would wait that long.

Of course the emissary could have been killed by alien creatures, savage or sentient, before it could achieve whatever otherworldly goal for which it had risked everything. But then there must have been an original landing party to install the receiver in the first place, and its members had survived long enough to accomplish their mission.

Riley stooped and drank from the stream. The water was tepid and tasted of the jungle floor through which it flowed, but it was liquid and his body didn't object.

He followed the stream, coming across other reptilian creatures, more birds with teeth, and insects that now seemed to avoid him, until he came to what seemed like a trail. He looked both ways before he turned in the direction away from the pyramid toward what he hoped was civilization.

He had gone only a few steps when he realized that something was following him. He turned. Behind him was a creature about his size, though its bulk made it seem larger. It was standing on thick, powerful legs. It had big hips, small upper limbs, and a big head with two red eyes and a protruding jaw fitted with large sharp teeth that it was show-ing now. Clearly it was reptilian and a carnivore and a threat.

The threat facing him was not the kind of instinctive violence this fecund jungle had produced so far. The creature, dangerous as it looked, wore a leatherlike belt around its middle—it was hardly a waist—and from the front of the belt dangled a pouch, perhaps containing a reserve supply of food, which suggested forethought, and at its side a metal knife, an encouraging indication of a metal-working level of civiliza-tion. All this in the brief moment of decision as the creature drew its knife with what resembled a hand with an opposable thumb. Riley knew that he had a chance to defend himself with his club and perhaps his superior agility against the creature's strength and natural weapons, but defense came at a price. He had no future on this primeval world with-out assistance, and, primitive as it looked, the creature surely represented whatever assistance was available.

Riley stood still, his club at his side, its tip resting, unthreateningly, on the reddish-brown soil of the trail while the creature lifted its knife . . . and then extended it toward Riley, hilt first. Riley accepted it, looked at it admiringly, and then held it back out to the creature, who took it without recognizable emotion and, throwing its head back, roared.

Riley leaned on his club. "So, friend," he said, "we are met here on your world, far from wherever I need to be, and maybe you can help me get there. I know you can't understand what I'm saying. But maybe you will, or maybe I will understand you, and anyway, it helps me to talk."

The creature roared again as if honoring Riley's effort to communicate.

"I'm going to call you 'Rory,' " Riley said. "I think you saw me climb down the side of that pyramid and you believe that I am a god taken strange shape, or maybe the reincarnation of the god-emperor entombed there, and I'm going to let you think that until I can tell you otherwise and get your help on more equal terms."

Rory roared again.

"You see? We're getting to understand each other already. You just said something like 'we've been standing here talking when we should be getting on with our business,' and I agree." Riley stood to one side of the trail, moving carefully and slowly and extending his club-free left hand to indicate that the way was clear for Rory to pass.

The creature moved past Riley, not looking at him nor altering its progress to avoid possible contact, and stalked down the trail, not looking back to see if Riley was following. Riley got a whiff of the creature as it went by him; Rory smelled ripe, like decay. Riley walked behind but not too closely, cautiously watching the sky above and the jungle's edge on both sides. He wasn't as wary as before. Somehow he trusted Rory's experience with local dangers and, perhaps, those dangers' awareness of the threat of Rory's kind.

They walked in silence, Riley examining what he knew about evolutionary processes. There was far more in his mind than he recalled ever learning, perhaps the residue of his pedia's incredible stock of mostly useless information deposited now among the neurons and their connections that the pedia had impressed into its own purposes. This world clearly was in its Jurassic-like period of tropical growth and reptilian dominance. But the ancient tomb, even older than the million-long-cycle-ago people of the Transcendental Machine, suggested that these dinosaur-like creatures had possessed the ability and the technology to build that pyramid for far longer than humanity had dominated Earth and its solar companion worlds. Perhaps this world had never experienced the catastrophic die-offs that allowed mammalian life to emerge from its hiding places on Earth to produce, eventually, humans. These reptilians had enjoyed more than a million long-cycles to achieve a space-going civilization, if that was in their capacity to imagine.

But if Rory's tools were typical of its civilization's level of technological development, its people had not progressed in a million cycles. They had regressed, he thought. Then he changed his mind.

They had reached a river. Riley could hear it and smell it long before they arrived upon its bank. The river was wide, perhaps one hundred meters across; its flow was thick with reddish-brown sediment and its surface was strewn with leaves and branches, as if, somewhere upstream, the sky had opened up and let fall avalanches of rain. Drawn up on the bank was a boat, or more accurately, Riley judged from his memory of things unseen, a canoe or dugout.

Rory pushed the boat into the water and waited, as if not presuming to direct Riley to get in. There were no seats, and once Riley had entered he crouched in one end, looking for oars or paddles but seeing only what seemed to be a staff lying on the bottom of the boat, not much longer than his club and clearly not long enough to reach the bed of the river.

Rory got into the other end of the vessel, agilely for its size and massive thighs. The boat sagged noticeably into the water, and Riley recognized again the muscular weight of the creature who had befriended him—or who had become his guide and perhaps his acolyte. The boat turned into the current, hesitated for a moment as the river tried to take it along with the flotsam that covered its surface, and then an invisible force took hold of the vessel and turned it upriver, fighting the current with apparent ease.

Rory's people possessed some kind of powered propulsion. Maybe they were not as primitive as Riley had feared. He tried to see the motor, if that was what it was, but all he saw was a train of bubbles.

An hour and eleven minutes later, after Rory had deterred two river monsters who raised their heads out of the muck as the boat passed and Riley understood the purpose of the staff in the bottom of the boat, they reached a place where the jungle had retreated from the river or had been cut back. In that leveled spot, many hundreds of meters across, was a city built of stone like the pyramid.

But it was a ruined city. Unlike the pyramid, its stones had fallen.

———

Rory sat still in the back of the boat as if waiting for Riley to disembark, and then, when Riley rose and stepped out, moved its heavy body onto what once might have been a dock but was now only shattered stone. The alien creature pulled the boat between two jutting rocks onto a surface that might once have been paved. Riley got no more than a glimpse of two dark holes in the back of the boat before Rory marched off toward the city and Riley followed.

As they got closer to the ruins, other dinosaur-like creatures came toward them, running faster than Riley would have expected. They were of several sizes, from what appeared to be children to heavily muscled adults like Rory and some who were large but not as muscular, females perhaps. There were forty-six of them. Riley wondered how he had come to that total without counting, especially since they seemed bent on attacking him, like a pack of carnivores.

But Rory roared at them and they slowed and then parted as he and Rory passed. The others fell in behind them, roaring softly among themselves. Riley was beginning to distinguish between roars, as if his newly acquired clarity of thought was able to make the kind of analyses that his pedia once had made for him and Asha had made without any such artificial aid. And he was aware of the smell of these creatures, like rotten meat and decaying vegetation, like Rory's odor but worse. This Jurassic world, with all its fecund waste, stank.

As they drew closer to the edge of this ancient city, Riley saw crude shelters, cottages or cabins, built of quarried stone and thatched with dried yellow vegetation. He knew now what had happened to the ruined structures of the old city. They had been scavenged for building materials for its fallen descendants. He felt a wave of despair. There would be little technological help from these decadent remains of a once great civilization.

And then, as Rory led their way into one of the stone huts, Riley remembered the powered propulsion of Rory's boat. Somehow that had survived.

The interior of the hut was dark until Rory withdrew a small object from the pouch hanging from his belt and applied it to a hollowed stone whose contents sprang into flame and a flickering light. Strawlike vegetation was heaped in the corners of the hut. In the center was a low stone table without chairs or stools. Rory opened a nearby wooden chest and withdrew several kinds of the fruit that Riley had already sampled and placed them on the table. From another chest it withdrew a large piece of raw meat. Rory removed two stone flagons from under the table and filled them with a dark fluid from a pottery pitcher also stored under the table, sat on his haunches, and buried his teeth in the raw meat.

Riley hesitated. The odor of the creatures was even stronger here—or his sensory apparatus had been improved along with everything else—and he felt his stomach rebel at the thought of eating, but he pushed the revulsion away as he reached for one of the flagons and sipped its contents. It was a kind of wine, and Riley was briefly encouraged by the thought that at least these creatures had mastered the art of winemaking and pottery creation as well as fire, although not, apparently, the art or desirability of cooking meat. Maybe he would be able to teach them skills that would begin their ascent back into the civilization that had created the city and the pyramid, though it would not, he realized, reach the stage he needed for a reunion with Asha during his life span, no matter how long extended by his passage through the Transcendental Machine.

He was starting to sample the fruit when a loud clap of thunder exploded immediately over their heads followed by flashes of lightning and a downpour, like a gigantic bucket being emptied above them, that rattled the vegetation that roofed the structure and began to drip through in places and then in streams. Riley looked at Rory, who seemed oblivious, and continued to eat. It had consumed half the raw meat already and the rest seemed destined to follow immediately.

The vegetation rattled and cracked above them, as if struck by heavy hailstones. Riley looked through the open doorway to the space outside. It was covered with balls of ice bouncing off the shattered paving stones and their pools of accumulating rainwater. Then, in the midst of the titanic storm, Riley heard a distant sound like a sonorous bell.

Riley had never heard anything like it. It was sad, like a tolling for the dead, and compelling, like a summons to whatever place after death the hearer nourished in his hopes for eternity.

Riley looked at Rory. The alien reptile had stopped eating. Ripples were moving across its body like shivers.

Riley looked around the hut and, seeing nothing else, tore the top from one of the food chests. Holding it over his head, he stepped out into the storm, feeling and then hearing the hailstones hitting the wood and bruising his knuckles. The water poured down over him, and he hoped the lightning strikes would not hit him before he reached his goal. He moved off toward the sound that seemed to be coming from the center of the city.

Finally he stood in front of a large, ruined building. Here the sound was louder and even more compelling. He picked his way past fallen blocks of stone and the vegetation that had grown up between them until he moved up a ramp into the shelter of what remained. Heavy streams of water rushed past him as he edged his way into the building, dodging gushes of rainwater from gaps and crevices, until he stood in a large hall, open to the elements where the remains of a roof gave testimony to what had once existed.

In the middle of the hall was an enormous red sphere being bombarded by rain and hail. From it came the unworldly sounds that had drawn him to this place.

CHAPTER FOUR

Asha's attendants slept soundly at her feet, not moving when she turned but awakening instantly when she got out of bed. She could think through her situation while she remained in the expansive bed, but as soon as she got up the two were chattering away in their squeal-and-whistle language, and Asha's mind got busy trying to make sense of what they were saying.

By the second period awake she was making note of the intensity and modulations of their sounds and by the third she was beginning to get some understanding of what they meant when they were trying to gain her attention or direct her actions. She considered the advantage of concealing her ability to comprehend before she decided that the ability to question provided a greater opportunity.

"Okay, kids," she said, "we're going to start talking." And she squealed and whistled at them.

The two attendants opened their round eyes even wider, in expressions that Asha interpreted as surprise transforming into delight as they burst into gusts of squeals and whistles.

"Slow down," Asha squealed and whistled at them.

They slowed and the conversation began with personal matters. They called themselves "the people." It was the universal term for every dominant species on every civilized world, though sometimes modified by an adjective indicating status, such as "the god people" or "the chosen people" or "the people destined to rule the world, the solar system, the galaxy, or the universe." Asha decided to call them the "squeal" people and their world "Squeal." It was, of course, like all their other words, except those altered by whistles, only this squeal was uttered softly with an expression that Asha learned indicated pleasure or happiness.

An indispensable part of the language was facial expression and body positions. She tried hard to master it though her face and body did not adapt easily to the new demands placed upon them.

The Squeal world, she learned, was a happy world where everything was good and nothing bad ever happened. "Why, then, is my door locked?" she asked.

"To keep you safe," she was told.

"From what, on this happy world?"

"From accident. As visitor (honored guest? god?) you must be protected for even greater happiness."

"And what is that?" Asha asked, but no amount of questioning could produce clarification for what the attendants might not themselves be able to comprehend. Neither could she identify the squeal words for spaceflight or get them to understand the concept for space itself or the possibility of getting off Squeal and into the vastness beyond or even that there were other suns in the heavens or other worlds like theirs. That was either a bad sign or an indication that her attendants might be limited in their educations or their understandings of the world. Perhaps that kind of knowledge, that there might be other worlds than theirs, would make them unhappy. The essence of unhappiness, after all, was dissatisfaction with what you have. With humans and many other species, it was a divine dissatisfaction that impelled them into the unknown, but on the Squeal world it might be forbidden or inconceivable.

She could not even find an adjustment to the mirror/receiver that showed the sky, particularly the night sky, and she did not know what stars the night sky revealed, or if this world had a moon or moons, and where in the galaxy it might be located. Everything suggested a fatal isolation from the rest of the galaxy. But she did not surrender to despair. And her refusal to accept defeat was not because of the example of her sunny attendants.

When she was not engaged in conversation, Asha spent a great deal of her time studying the mirror/receiver. She needed more information than her attendants could provide, and she acquired a mastery of how

to direct its view of the world. She studied the various climate zones of
the planet before she settled on the temperate areas where nearly all the
squeal people lived. She guessed that Squeal had little or no planetary
wobble and therefore no incentives or opportunities for people to move
around, once settled. Or perhaps the arctic and tropical zones offered
too many challenges to sustain their philosophy, or illusion, of joy.

She noted several sizes of communities, from villages in the midst of
cultivated areas to modest-sized cities that apparently served as gathering places for goods and services, and larger cities that may have provided manufacturing and transportation. The largest and most complex
of these, she found, was the city into which she had been transported,
and the comments that she could elicit from her attendants seemed to
confirm this. That seemed appropriate. The center of governance, of
whatever sort, ought to be the place of honor, or worship, for the Transcendental receiver. Or perhaps she was only glorifying her own materialization here.

She studied the city, street by street, and house by house, returning,
time after time, to the plaza in which she had made her appearance, with
its central fountain topped by the Machine. If there was any hope of finding a way off this world, isolated by circumstances or its people's will, it
had to be here. The creators of the Transcendental Machine must have
had a purpose for placing a receiver on this planet, though it was a million
long-cycles ago. That purpose may have been to influence the development of this planet or the evolution of its creatures, or to conquer it, or
just to use it as a way station, but there was something here that had
attracted those extinct technologists from another arm of the galaxy.

But what? And had it been extinguished in the past million long-
cycles, a period long enough to predate the Squeal people themselves?
Perhaps Squeal was an experiment that failed.

Asha's contemplation was interrupted by the opening of the distant
doors and the entrance of three of the Squeal people. They seemed a bit
larger than the others she had encountered, they were wearing clothing
that resembled the finery in which she had been dressed when she arrived, and they were bearing gifts.

They looked a little ridiculous in their fancy garments, gowns in royal blue or silver that reached to the floor and hid their feet, and scarves wrapped into headdresses, but they wore them with the happy expression that accompanied the squeal word for "world," or, perhaps, if that was possible on this Elysium where distinctions might create envy, pride. They came in one at a time but formed into a single line in front of her.

The one on her left, dressed in royal blue, had a silver globe in its hands, about the size of a child's head and engraved with cryptic designs. "I offer to you this symbol of Squeal. If you accept my offer of eternal bliss, the world of Squeal will be yours," the Squeal person said, as nearly as Asha could interpret, though, indeed, the message could have been far more grandiose, or even more threatening, than she imagined was consistent with what she knew about this world.

"Thanks," she said, deciding to conceal her ability to understand the squeal language. Her attendants would no doubt relay that information when they had the opportunity, but so far she had detected no communication between them and those who brought her food and drink, and perhaps she would gain a critical advantage until her knowledge was revealed. "You're a peach," she added, accepting the globe, "although I don't know what I would do with this world if I owned it." The globe was apparently hollow and not as heavy as she anticipated.

The Squeal person in the middle, clad all in silver, held a staff made of some dark wood and carved with intricate shapes. "I give you this symbol of the Squeal people's oneness with the world of Squeal so that you will come to join it as if it were your own," it said.

"Thank you, too," Asha said, accepting the staff with her free right hand. "You folks are great with the symbols, and I wish I were sure what they implied and what I was supposed to do with them."

The Squeal person on Asha's right, dressed in a silver gown and a royal blue headdress, held out Asha's own garments, which had disappeared from her room after her bath and she had thought had been discarded as unfit for whatever role they planned for her. Now they seemed to have been restored to pristine condition. "I return to you these honored garments in the hope that they will mark your acceptance of your materialization in the shrine and your union with our happy world and its happy people," the Squeal person said.

Asha turned and handed the globe to the attendant she had decided to call "Eenie" and the staff to "Minie" and turned back to accept the garments from the third Squeal person. "I think I like you best of all," she said, "though I shouldn't show it. You're like the three kings of the Orient in the fable, or more like the noble suitors for the hand of the princess, and I don't know what would happen if I chose one of you. Maybe you would be my consort, but what kind? Ceremonial? Physical relations, if that's possible? Or a sacrifice? I've got to have more information, and you aren't likely to give it to me, and neither are Eenie or Minie."

She turned and put the garments on the bed. She'd like to put them on as a sign of independence and a feeling of regaining some measure of control, but it would certainly be misinterpreted as a decision for her third suitor.

When she turned around the three of them were moving toward the door. She followed them closely and before the door could close she had slipped out of the room into the large, formal entrance hall. The three suitors turned, as if paralyzed by surprise to find her there. She moved slowly but determinedly to the tall vase in the center of the room. None of the suitors made any move to stop her. Perhaps that would have been as unthinkable as her action had been unpredictable.

Ignoring them and the doors to the outer world beyond, Asha studied the designs around the top edge of the vase, which rose to her waist. In raised figures in blue against a white background were stylized drawings. One resembled the Machine receiver. It was empty. In the next the receiver had a figure in it. Human or humanoid, it could have been her or a Squeal person. In the third, the figure was stepping down from the fountain, with other figures gathered around it. In the fourth, the figure, accompanied by two others, was ascending a ramp into a building. In the fifth, two figures were leaving the building side by side. In the sixth, they were standing together in the receiver. In the seventh, the receiver was empty.

Or was it the first, as she had come around to where she had started? Or did it matter? Was this a cycle that the Squeal people thought repeated itself endlessly? She had no doubt that these designs described what she had experienced, as if some long-dead potter had foreseen the future. Or, more likely, that these people had built this tradition into their culture in an attempt to neutralize the magic—and maybe their terror—of the Machine. Surely no true transportee had appeared in the lifetime of their civilization, but stories get handed down the generations until they get embodied in myths and beliefs, maybe reinforced by the frauds she had speculated about before.

But that final design was troubling. There was barely room in the Machine for one person, much less two, even if one of them was a small Squeal person. And even if two could squeeze in, she knew nothing could follow. There was no way for the Machine to work in reverse, no way to make herself and her chosen consort, whoever it was, disappear. Or walk out of the Machine unchanged.

Asha turned and went back toward her chamber. The door swung open as she approached, like the decision she would have to make soon, and locked with a click behind her, like the probable result.

She spent the next day questioning Eenie and Minie about the Machine in the plaza outside, Squeal mythology, and the suitors, but speculation seemed to be foreign to them, and Asha desisted when she saw that her efforts to make them respond were making them uneasy and maybe, if that was possible, unhappy. Asha felt guilty about introducing doubt into their sunny worlds, as if she were the serpent in the Garden of Eden, even though she suspected that some dark truth lay hidden beneath the surface paradise. Maybe she would be the one to reveal it. Or maybe she was it.

She continued to search the mirror/receiver for some indication that this world had entered the space age and was somehow connected to the Federation and its network of nexus points that made interstellar travel feasible. When she grew tired of looking for spaceships or the broad expanse of landing areas or the massive construction facilities that would be necessary to support a space-travel industry, she turned to her Monster and the Princess puzzle, laying out strategies that reminded her of her own predicament. But who was the Monster and who was the Princess? And then, each time she approached a solution, she wiped out her own calculations.

In between she sampled more of the Squeal food, moving past the baked foods to the fruit. She liked the sweetness of the purple balls and the tartness of the green, wrinkled grapes, but the bitterness of the red, sliced globes was a taste she would have to acquire if she were around long enough. She hoped that wouldn't happen. She allowed Eenie and Minie to continue to bathe her and had gotten used to their marveling at the outward evidences of gender.

Then the three suitors returned. This time they were without their headdresses, revealing the beginnings of a growth of hair, like a dark fuzz on the top of their normally hairless heads, and their gowns had turned into skirts, leaving their chests bare. They seemed more muscular than she would have imagined, more muscular, certainly, than Eenie and Minie, who had smooth, supple chests. And they had more gifts.

The one with the silver skirt moved his head in the gesture that Asha had identified as respect or recognition of her position and presented a silver gown like the one it had worn the first time they entered, but perhaps more resplendent with fancy blue panels and something like lace around the neck and hem. "For your grand moment," the Squeal person said. Or maybe the squeal and whistle meant "ceremony," "coronation," or "ascension."

"I hope it fits," Asha said, and handed the gown to Eenie.

The second suitor held out a length of silver links. In each link had been set a blue gem, or glass shaped to look like a jewel. "To adorn your eminence," the suitor said, "when your greatness receives its proper recognition."

Asha took the necklace or belt—it seemed too big to go around her neck and too small for her waist—and handed it to Minie. The attendants seemed overwhelmed with joy. "It looks pretty swell," she said.

The third suitor held out a pair of slippers, one silver, the other blue. "To carry you to your destined place," it said.

"I hope they don't fit," Asha said, and turned to put them on the bed. When she turned back they were standing in the same place, as if waiting for some response. "Look," she said. "I'm sorry, boys—for I think that's what you are or are turning into in some kind of Squeal world hermaphroditic process—but I just can't make up my mind. You'll have to come back." And she said to herself, "And I'm not looking forward to that, because I think then you'll come without your skirts, and I think you'll have developed genitalia that I don't want to see or even think about what they mean."

After a moment they turned and left, watching more carefully this time that Asha didn't follow. The door clicked behind them, and Asha knew she was locked in again and that she would have to find an answer before their next arrival.

She turned once more to the mirror/receiver. Once more she studied the city into which the Machine had delivered her. She knew it was the city because she could always find the plaza with the fountain and the Machine elevated at its center. This time the city was dark, with just a few scattered lights. Asha had seen night scenes before, but the receiver had never let her look at the sky. She could have told a great deal about her situation if she could have seen the night sky, but either that control had been blocked or it didn't exist.

She was thinking about that when she noticed a bulky figure, so much unlike the elfen size of the little people, emerging from one of the buildings on the other side of the fountain plaza. "Tordor," she said, and then she realized that it could not be the Dorian who had accompanied the pilgrimage on the *Geoffrey*. But it *was* a Dorian, and she knew how she was going to save herself.

CHAPTER FIVE

The powerful thunderstorm slowed and stopped. The disturbing sound from the red sphere faded away, and Riley heard a different sound behind him. Riley turned. It was Rory, shivering with cold or terror. Riley thought it was terror and felt a moment of sympathy for this massive creature enduring ancient dreads to follow him, or to pursue his own search for knowledge.

Rory and his people may have had good reasons for avoiding this place when it stormed. Aside from the powerful forces of the storm itself, the resonations of the red sphere were enough to stir superstitious awe. Clearly the structure was built around the sphere, perhaps to contain its power, perhaps to silence its otherworldly voice, perhaps to imprison it so that it could never ascend back into the sky from which it had come. Clearly the sphere was the ship that had brought the Machine's engineers to this world to build the receiver and its secret compartment in the heart of the sacred pyramid.

But now, and for many long-cycles into the past, the roof had fallen, and the sphere was getting its revenge. Because it should not be here. It should have returned the engineers to their home world, or sent them on to their next project. Why hadn't it? Had they succumbed to some alien disease, here on this planet and this spiral arm of the galaxy, far from their origins and the biology that brought them to sapience and their mastery of technology? Or, since they had been to many alien worlds and survived their alien biologies, had the pyramid builders of that time, a million long-cycles ago, discovered them as they emerged from the sacred pyramid and massacred them for their transgressions, overwhelming their weapons with sheer numbers and reptilian ferocity?

Whatever the reason, the engineers of the Machine had not returned, and their indestructible ship had been left behind, standing here in what was then a desert, as a reminder to these reptilian people of the gods who had descended from the sky, who had wielded great power and done great deeds, and who had died or been slain. Rory's ancestors must have been filled with terror and perhaps guilt, and perhaps it was from this mixture of guilt, sacrilege, and climate change that began their decline. This chariot of the gods, immune from the ravages of time and nature's violence that affected everything else, might yet spawn more gods. Or maybe it would attract vengeful gods in vehicles like this to destroy them. Hide the evidence. Shield it from some all-seeing eye.

And so the pyramid builders set their skills to hiding it, containing it as they had the spirits of their ancestors. They built this structure around it, and it would have sufficed if the climate had not changed, if the planet's ice age had not ended and returned vast stores of water to the oceans and the lakes, and if torrential rains, like the one Riley had just experienced, had not turned the region, perhaps the entire planet, into a hothouse of tropical growth. And ruined the structure that contained the ancient spaceship.

And left it for his salvation. If he could just figure out how to get into it and, if he was successful in that, how to master its alien technologies.

Behind him Rory roared. It was not a full-throated roar such as the one that had greeted him on the jungle trail, or the ones Rory had addressed to the dinosaur-like creatures who had descended upon them like a pack of starving carnivores as they entered the village that surrounded the ruins of the ancient city. It was a more cautious roar that Riley was beginning to understand.

"You're trying to tell me that this is a bad place and we should get out of it before it destroys us," Riley said in his own language. "Well, we can't go just yet. I've got to figure out the entrance to this ship, and then I'm going to do something that you're going to find pretty terrible.

So you'd better go back to your people, and maybe I'll see you later and maybe I won't."

Rory roared again, more plaintively this time, if that were possible. He moved back a few paces and squatted, looking toward Riley and turning his head back and forth as if trying to reassure himself.

Riley turned toward the red sphere. It towered several meters above his head. He could not see the top and estimated its height only from the curvature of the middle section. Debris from the ceiling had fallen around it, doing no apparent damage, and its shiny surface was free of dust and grime, as if the downpours to which it was regularly subjected washed it clean, or some undying electronic charge repelled foreign materials.

Riley circled the ancient ship, climbing over piles of stone and wading through pools of rainwater, but there was no break in the shiny, unmarred surface of the red sphere, no line that might suggest an entrance. He returned to his original spot, where the patient Rory, conquering his ancestral fears, watched him with red, perhaps anxious, eyes.

"Well, Rory," Riley said, "nobody ever told me this was going to be easy."

Rory gave a muted roar.

"That's right," Riley said. "Maybe the entrance is on the upper half of the ship, where I can't reach, or see either. But that wouldn't make any sense. These aren't the kind of people who would use ladders, say, to reach the surface. They'd need ground egress for their machines or the vehicles that they'd need to ferry the machines to the pyramid. Unless they had something like antigravity. Well, I don't believe in antigravity, Rory. At least not yet. There's something here that I haven't thought of. But I will."

And then a terrible thought occurred to him: Maybe the ship had malfunctioned and another ship had been sent to take the engineers away!

Riley raised his club and struck the side of the red sphere in frustration. It sighed like the melancholy exhalation of some dying giant. Riley turned. Behind him Rory was cowering, but he had not fled. "We're not getting anywhere here," Riley said. "Let's go back to your shanty and think this through."

He went past Rory, no longer concerned that the powerful alien might suddenly attack but acutely aware of the dinosaur-like creature's stench—as fetid as this teeming, rotting world itself. They walked back, Rory behind. Riley could sense Rory's anxieties easing as they made their way through the ruined city toward the rock huts that had grown up around it. He entered Rory's hut as if it were his own and squatted on his haunches at the low table that still contained the remains of the meal that Rory had laid out. None of the other dinosaur-like creatures had entered. They had gathered again, singly and in small groups, around the route after he and Rory had emerged from the sacred place, but Rory apparently occupied some position of authority that kept him and his walking-meat companion from being attacked or his home violated.

Riley picked up a piece of fruit from the table and put it in his mouth, not much caring what it was or how it tasted. He had a problem, and he needed to think about it with all the clarity of a mind liberated from clutter and inefficiencies by the Transcendental Machine. Rory settled on the other side of the table, squatting more naturally than Riley, and watched Riley as if some transformation might occur at any moment. He paid no attention to the rotting meat in front of him, crawling now with insects and sending its overpowering scent to Riley's side of the table.

"What we need," Riley said, "is the ability to communicate." He turned that into a roar, which surprised him as much as Rory. His mind, Riley discovered, had been working on Rory's language all the time he had been focusing on immediate issues, as if his pedia was still there, inside his head, conducting its separate, alien processes.

Rory roared back. "The god speaks."

"I seek the machines"—what was it Rory had called the red sphere back in the building that housed it?—"the cursed thing of the gods who come from the sky."

"The cursed thing brings death without life," Rory said, with a tremor in his roar that suggested even saying the words was dangerous.

For a people that believed in sacred burial, "death without life" probably meant "destroying the soul and its rebirth." "And yet," Riley said, "you use a god-thing to move your boat." He was guessing here, but the propulsion system on Rory's boat, some inexhaustible engine that pushed air or water backward to move the boat forward, clearly was beyond the technical capability of Rory's people, or even those of the people who had built the pyramid and the city.

"A gift from the old ones," Rory said.

By which he meant, Riley thought, the old ones of his own kind, the city builders, who had destroyed the gods who came from the sky, who had taken over the devices that they could manage and made them their own. "Any other gifts from the old ones?" Riley asked. Maybe there was a device the ancient engineers had used to open their ship, a device that somehow had been passed down the generations, its original purpose lost in antiquity if it had ever been known.

"None," Rory said.

So much for that faint hope. No matter how Riley tried to pry into Rory's memories he could get nothing more from him, either because of Rory's reluctance to recall forbidden lore or the inadequacies of Riley's understanding of Rory's language, or of the language's inability, or Rory's, to deal with the conditional or the speculative.

Riley finished his meager meal, although he did not feel particularly hungry, perhaps because his body was more efficient now, and Rory, relieved of the necessity to respond to the creature he considered a god, brushed away the insects and buried his fearsome rows of teeth in the hunk of meat in front of him. Afterward, as darkness slowly gathered outside the open doorway to Rory's stone hut, Riley found a corner and stretched out in it, his back against one cool, sturdy wall, his head against the dusty stone floor.

He did not feel the need for sleep so much as he recognized the efficiency of rest. He understood now what Asha had meant when she said that she almost never slept. Instead a quiet period was a time to still the turmoil of a mind churning with thoughts competing for attention and allow unconscious processes to begin sorting them out and, he hoped, coming up with answers.

Even though he thought now with a clarity and a precision he had never before experienced, his new condition was no guarantee of a solution to questions whose answers were buried under ancient ruins and a million long-cycles of the past.

Four hours and thirty-seven minutes later, he jerked awake, surprised that he had fallen asleep, and aware of movement outside the hut. He put his hand on his club and rose to his knees, ready to spring to his feet, but Rory was ahead of him, already up, already at the doorway into the night. The dinosaur-like creature roared, and from outside came the sound of heavy feet running away.

Apparently Rory's status had been compromised by his association with a creature unlike anything seen before in this village and whose only value, if it had any, was as quick food. *My meat would probably be poisonous to you,* Riley thought, *evolving as I did with alien biologies and bacteria your bodies have never encountered.* But that would be small comfort if he were being consumed by ravenous carnivores.

And then he remembered the other thing that had awakened him. He had been dreaming about the chamber into which he had been transported and his efforts to find a way out. In his dream he had emerged from the chamber into the crude corridor outside, and the doorway had closed behind him.

In that recollection was a possible way into the ancient spaceship that he had not considered.

"We should leave now," Riley told Rory. "Before"—he waved at the hut's entrance, hoping that the gesture meant something in Rory's culture— "your people return." He had no words yet for "friends," if such a concept existed on this eat-before-you-are-eaten world.

Riley brushed past Rory into the night. The sky was clear, but there was only a little light from a few scattered stars. Rory's world, it seemed, was located far out on the spiral arm, which explained, perhaps, why it had never been visited by representatives of the Galactic Federation, or, if it had been visited, had been abandoned to its own savagery. Even the Federation could not hope to civilize these reptilian carnivores.

Perhaps the people of the Transcendental Machine had hopes for them, if, indeed, that was the purpose of the receivers that, Riley now believed, had been hidden all across his own spiral arm. But they could as easily have been the scouting party for a future invasion by an aggressive civilization that had run out of room in the spiral arm next door.

In any case, the failure of the red sphere to return with its engineers may have discouraged the Transcendental Machine people as well. Or the arachnoids had wiped out the people who had built the Machine before they could complete their transgalactic project. Riley believed that the arachnoids were the degenerate descendants of the Machine builders, not the builders themselves.

Or, the Machine builders had succeeded, and the galaxy Riley knew might be the realization of their plan. Perhaps the Machine builders were in their midst. Perhaps one of the species that made up the Federation was the Machine builders.

But all that seemed unlikely and certainly irrelevant. What was relevant was his need to get to the ruined city and the structure that housed the red sphere before he was attacked by the carnivores who lacked Rory's restraint. There was movement in the darkness, and behind him Rory roared. It was a warning to those following and waiting to attack. "I am your leader," the roar said, "the son of a leader and the son of the son of a leader, and you will die in my teeth."

Riley had not cared if Rory followed. He did not relish abandoning Rory in the midst of the city he feared, using the savage to fulfill Riley's need to escape this world and find Asha, and then leaving Rory to his angry tribe. But now he was glad that Rory had come along.

He walked faster. Even in the darkness he could remember every step of the path they had taken, every fallen stone along the way. If they could make it to the city, their pursuers might be too terrified to follow.

The outskirts of the ruins were only a few paces away when their pursuers attacked. They fought off the first group, Riley with his club and Rory with his fearsome head and teeth and his powerful legs. The pack retreated, leaving them bloodstained and wounded, and Riley said, "Quick. To the city before they attack again," and he turned and ran toward the ruins, not knowing whether Rory was the source of the foot-falls behind him or the carnivores who hungered after them.

As he reached the edge of the ruins, the sounds of pursuit faded, and there was only the solitary noises of his own breathing and Rory's heavy feet. When they drew near the structure Riley had come to think of as the museum of the red sphere, Riley turned. The yellow sun was com-ing up beyond the distant jungle tops, and Riley could see Rory's wounds and what seemed like a broken arm. "I'm going to do something bad," Riley said in Rory's language, "and you won't want anything to do with it. I don't know what you're going to do now. Maybe your people will accept you back after I'm gone"—*if, indeed, I'm right,* he thought—"at least I hope so. But it won't do either of us any good if I stay."

He realized that he had come to think of Rory as a companion if not a friend. Rory looked at Riley with unblinking red eyes, and Riley wasn't sure how much of his speech the other had understood in his mangled Rory-ese. In his own language, he said, "Good-bye, buddy. You've been far more of a help than I had any right to expect." He resisted the urge to pat the monstrous creature on the head, turned, and entered the museum. The red sphere was already glowing with reflected sunlight. Riley moved around it, thinking about the exit from the place of the Machine receiver. He had not checked it; he had only assumed that the way back was permanently barred.

Riley ran his hand along the surface of the sphere until he found a place where the surface suddenly gave way, and his hand disappeared up to his wrist. He swallowed, took a deep breath, and moved forward, feeling a cool tingling over his entire body as the light changed to a rosy glow and then something like day.

CHAPTER SIX

Asha's handmaidens were still asleep, curled up at the foot of the bed, when Asha sat up, swung her feet to the floor, and stood. She moved quietly to the corner of the wall from which her handmaidens extracted the towels and had deposited the fancy clothing her suitors had brought. She had watched the motions with which her attendants had opened the wall, and the wall opened at her touch, like a cabinet door. She searched through the folded clothing until she found the clothing she had worn to the world of the Transcendental Machine that had been returned by the third suitor, and slipped them on. Below, on the floor, were her old sandals. She put them on her feet.

She walked to the far wall, turned on the mirror/receiver, and switched to the Monster and Princess puzzle. Quickly she redid her solution, only this time she completed it: the Monster's best search strategy always found the Princess, and the Princess's best avoidance strategy always enabled her to escape. Like all such puzzles, if both parties used their best strategies the situation was a standoff.

As she completed the last entry, the door clicked. The solution to the puzzle, apparently, was the recognition of her equality, and as a citizen she was no longer to be confined. Asha moved to the door and took one last look at her sleeping attendants. "Sorry, guys," she mouthed, and moved silently through the open door.

The big room was empty, as she expected, and the massive doors to the plaza opened as she approached. She stopped in the entrance. Unexpectedly, the night was almost as bright as day. As she moved farther into the plaza and looked up, she understood why: the sky was ablaze with stars—not the few thousands she had been accustomed to in Federation Central and certainly not the few hundreds of Terminal or the scattered few of the Great Gulf, but tens of thousands shedding their baleful light on the planet of Squeal.

No wonder the little people of Squeal were terrified of the sky. Rather than a position farther out on the spiral arm, Squeal was close to the center of the galaxy with all its clustered suns. One of them, looking much like the rest, might be the central black hole, no more than a pinprick in the tapestry of night but surrounded by an accretion disk of dying suns and their doomed planets, and spewing deadly radiation, absorbed now by Squeal's atmosphere. But always looming over Squeal was the threat of some supernova explosion, some terrible brightness in the night sky, that would release a cascade of cosmic rays for which the atmosphere would be no protection. And going out into that hostile space beyond the atmosphere without the protection of radiation-proof ships would be suicide. Even travel through the air of Squeal would risk fatal exposure at upper levels of the air that covered the planet.

The only sounds as she crossed the plaza toward the structures on the other side were her muffled footsteps and the splashing of the central fountain. The air was mild and tinged with the characteristic sandalwood odor of Squeal itself. She looked up at the indestructible Machine in its place of honor on the fountain's peak and reflected on all it implied: ancient technology reconceived as sacred symbol, long-forgotten plans and dreams reborn as contemporary mythology. Nothing endured; everything is renewed. And yet we struggle on, she thought, hoping to make a difference, attempting to make our brief existences mean something.

The buildings on the plaza differed in size and decoration, but they were constructed up against their neighbors, with no space between, like pictures she had seen of big cities on Earth and the cities built by the people of the Transcendental Machine. The only one that stood isolated on the plaza was the palace in which she had been kept. Avenues at each corner of the plaza allowed the Squeal people to come and go, although she had never seen vehicles there. Perhaps delivery wagons came to the rear.

Asha arrived at the front entrance of a building that was a bit larger and more colorful than its neighbors, with a front expanse of green paint or tile, perhaps reminiscent of verdant Dorian plains. The stairs did not turn into a welcoming ramp. In fact, there was no welcome at all. Double doors were stubbornly closed. Asha looked for some indication of a bell or knocker. Seeing none she waved her hands in front of the doors and its frame in the way she had learned to control the mirror/receiver and the cabinet-wall, but there was no response. If she was mistaken in the building, its occupants were Squeal people conditioned from birth to avoid the night.

But she was not, and she pounded on the door with her fist. The sound echoed across the empty plaza, stirring echoes that might in normal circumstances have brought a crowd of curious or alarmed spectators or uniformed guardians of the peace. No answer. She pounded again. Finally she heard a muffled voice from the other side of the door. "Go away!" it said in the squeal language.

"I can't," Asha replied. "I need your help."

"Go away!" the high-pitched voice repeated. "You don't exist!"

"You must let me in. I invoke my rights as a Federation citizen!" She had no squeal words for "rights," "Federation," or "citizen," so she substituted words in Galactic standard.

"Go away!" the voice said once more, sounding plaintive.

Asha switched to Dorian grunts. "I invoke my rights of asylum!"

The voice was silent.

A moment later the doors swung open.

Inside was a small Squeal person. It might have been Eenie or Minie, but it was terrified of her or the night, shrinking back into a wood-paneled foyer on a slick stone floor. Dark corridors extended in each direction to the left and the right and a door in the farther wall was closed. In the center of the foyer stood a tall vase—what was it with these people and their vases?—and she wondered what story its inscribed figures told and if she ever would have the chance to decipher it.

As she was making those observations, she was closing the doors behind her. The Squeal person's agitation eased, as if assured that no more creatures of the night would enter after Asha. The sandalwood aroma of this world and the person in front of her was tinged with the hint of methane common among grazers, and she knew she was in the right place.

"You are the Chosen One," the Squeal person said, with what could have been a touch of awe or reverence if Asha had been capable of making such distinctions.

"So I am told," Asha said. "But now I am a citizen of the galaxy," she continued, again substituting words in Dorian, which, apparently, the Squeal person could understand even if its delicate vocal chords were unable to emit Dorian grunts. "You will wake the Ambassador," she said imperiously, hoping that the Dorian word for the Galactic Federation representative was appropriate and that her status among these little people would justify her tone. "And you will take me to a place where we can meet."

The Squeal person looked bewildered and then, apparently deciding that it could not leave Asha standing in the entranceway, led the way to the farther door. It opened as they approached. The Squeal person stood aside as Asha entered, and then departed, to get the Ambassador, Asha hoped, and not guards who would evict her, or worse.

The room was a study or office, with a massive standing desk, suitable for a species that stands more than it sits or reclines, at the far end. It was a big room, as if the person who used it felt more comfortable in open spaces. The wood-paneled walls were adorned with paintings of long vistas of rolling grasslands dotted with clumps of trees surrounding ponds or pools, but the pictures moved as she watched, the grass waving and the leaves tossing as if blown by a gentle breeze. Asha could almost smell the grass, and then she realized that she *could* smell the grass. The room must have been of significant comfort to a creature far from its ancestral home and treasured childhood.

There were no chairs. Any creatures seeking conference with the Ambassador stood as he did and without any convenience that might provide a feeling of comfort or an excuse to linger.

Asha felt a presence behind her and then the fall of heavy feet. She stood aside as a pachyderm-like Dorian moved ponderously past her, almost pulling her into its orbit, like the satellite of a massive star. The Dorian resembled Tordor, her sometimes-traitorous companion on the pilgrimage of the *Geoffrey,* but older, grayer, and more massive. The Dorian continued across the floor until it turned, stood behind the desk, settled back against the support of its sturdy tail, and looked at Asha with what Asha, with her Dorian experience, interpreted as contempt mixed with anger at being aroused in the middle of the Squeal-world's night and perhaps with a cool, murderous intent.

"You are not a Squeal person," the Dorian said, with some difficulty. His vocal chords were not made for squeals.

"I am a human," Asha replied in Dorian.

"I have never met a human," the Ambassador said skeptically, switching his short trunk, an appendage that she knew could be a delicate manipulator or a deadly weapon. He was no longer an "it." Male Dorians were larger than females, and they wore clothing, or at best harnesses, only while traveling. In most circumstances they were naked, and this Dorian clearly was male. "You don't look dangerous."

"Unlike your species, we were born fighting for existence."

"And yet," the Dorian said, "you don't look dangerous. How did you get here?"

"By magic."

"Dorians don't believe in magic."

"Operations beyond our ability to understand can only be described as magic."

"Nothing is beyond Dorian ability to understand."

"Then you must explain my presence here on this world so dangerously close to the Galactic Center to which no alien other than yourself has arrived."

"You must have a ship."

"You would have noted its arrival, and, as you know, none has arrived. So you may explain how I happened to appear in the sacred receptacle at the peak of the fountain."

"Ah," the Ambassador said, "you are the Chosen One."

"So I have been told."

"From the fountain that the Squeal people, in their primitive theology, believe will produce a savior. The fountain from which nothing has emerged in the history of Galactic contact with Squeal. And, in Squeal history, only Squeal persons—obvious imposters who have dared the night. And in Squeal mythology, only monsters. And you are neither."

"Maybe a monster. Or a princess. But certainly here by a means that I cannot explain."

"Then what are you going to explain?" the Ambassador asked.

"Why you are going to lend me a ship to leave this world."

The Ambassador studied her, as if wavering between amusement at Asha's impertinence and impatience at the waste of his time and the interruption of his sleep. "It would be simpler just to have you killed," he said, and raised his trunk as if to summon guards.

"That would be a mistake," Asha said, and focused on not shifting in her stance or allowing any trace of uncertainty to enter her voice.

The silence between them lengthened, as if the Ambassador was waiting for Asha to apologize, take back her request, and then, if he were inclined to be merciful, enjoy a quick and relatively painless execution. "You do not seem insane," he said finally, "and yet you make these insane statements."

"If you have me killed," Asha said steadily, "the Squeal people will turn against you."

"How would they know?"

"Your Squeal person attendant knows," Asha said, "and though you could have it killed, no doubt it has awakened its fellow attendants to tell them that the Chosen One has appeared out of the terrible night to see the mighty Ambassador, and though you could have them all killed, you could not be sure that some word has not escaped these walls, and these many deaths could not be explained, and all of this would damage your mission beyond repair."

"My mission?" the Ambassador demanded. "What does an insignificant human know of my mission?"

"The only possible reason for your presence on this planet is to guide these people into interstellar capability and then to Federation citizenship."

If a Dorian face could express discouragement, the Ambassador's face might have done so. Perhaps it was indicated by the droop of his trunk. "That is an impossible task," he said. "They are a frustrating people, perhaps like us Dorians"—he seemed revulsed by his own comparison—"before we are driven from our fertile plains to the mountain city of Grandor. They are too happy, too content with their petty lives, too pleased with their lack of wars and personal strife."

"And too terrified of the night sky."

"That, too," the Ambassador said. "I see no way to succeed."

"You accept defeat?" Asha asked. "To a Dorian that is suicide. Or worse, disgrace."

"Yes."

"That is why you will give me a ship."

"That is impossible," the Ambassador said. "My ship is not departing until my mission is completed, and that may not happen in my lifetime." The last seemed to come with a measure of despair.

"But you could provide a boat with interstellar capability," Asha said. "The Captain's Barge, perhaps."

"Remind me why I should do that?"

"Because I will save your mission."

The Ambassador looked at Asha for a long moment as if wondering how this slender, misshapen creature standing in front of him could presume to accomplish what he could not. "And how do you plan to do that?"

"The Squeal people plan for me to choose one of them for a mate or consort or scapegoat—whatever they have in their mythology. We are supposed to participate in some kind of ceremony in the ancient artifact in the plaza fountain. Instead, you are going to bring the Captain's Barge down to the plaza in the night. I will pick a suitor, but instead of the fountain we will go to the Captain's Barge and depart. That single event, with everyone forced to look at the sky and envision the royal pair ascending into the heavens, will alter the psychology of the Squeal people, provide therapy for their aversion to space, and begin their journey to the stars."

The Ambassador stared at Asha out of rounded eyes. A stronger scent of methane filled the air.

"And give you great honor," Asha said.

And that is how Asha found herself, dressed in ceremonial finery, in the entrance of a compact spaceboat, a shivering Squeal person beside her, waving her hands ceremonially toward the plaza filled with Squeal people. She took the four-fingered hand of the Squeal person beside her, now with fully developed male genitalia hidden under finery equal to her own, and turned to enter the ship.

The Squeal person was the third suitor, who had at least some clue as to how to court a stranger from the magical artifact. She didn't know what she was going to do with him.

But she would think of something.

CHAPTER SEVEN

Riley felt a movement behind him and heard the rasp of breath that wasn't his. He turned. Behind him was Rory, shivering with terror, his red eyes wide and flickering from side to side. It looked ridiculous for a dinosaur, but Riley understood it, and understood the courage it took for Rory to follow him through a magical doorway into this demonic artifact. But all that didn't change the impossibility of the situation.

"Go back!" Riley said in his pidgin dinosaur vocabulary.

Rory moved his head. Riley didn't know whether that was a refusal or an involuntary twitch, but Rory didn't turn or retreat.

"Go!" Riley repeated. "Leave!"

Rory still did not move. Finally he spoke. "I must do this." His roar had a plaintive restraint.

"You can't! There is no way!"

"I must do this for my people."

"Whatever you think you're doing," Riley said in his own language, "you won't make it work." And then in Rory-ese, "Not work."

Rory burst forth with a series of roars that Riley had difficulty understanding. There were various modulations and variations that he had never heard before and perhaps would never hear again, but he guessed at something like: "My people must regain their ancient glory, those great days when they built this city and built the pyramid that contains the sacred remains of the ancestor who became a god, and they must bring back those days when the gods walked among us. You and this terrifying object are our only hope. When I first saw you descending from the pyramid, I knew you were a god—perhaps our great ancestor reborn—and I knew you were our hope to save us from savagery and decay." Or maybe, Riley thought, these were only the words he might have said if he had been Rory.

When Rory stopped, Riley looked at the dangerous, pitiful creature before him, and said, "I didn't get all that, but I know one thing: I am not a god. I can't bring back the gods or the long-past days of glory. Your ancestors killed the gods who made this ship. Who walked among you. They aren't coming back."

"We killed the gods," Rory said, as if accepting the ancestral guilt of actions a million long-cycles ago, like Christians accepting the sin of Adam's fall, "but we have suffered enough."

"You are right: Your people have suffered enough. But you must go back where you belong! Now you know what you can do if you conquer your fears. You can lead your people back to the good days. If you don't leave, you will never return to your people. Once I get where I am going, if I can figure out how this ship works and make it work again—unlikely as that might be—you can't come back. You will die here in this terrifying place. And I may die with you." Riley had his own version of "terrifying."

Even in the low-probability of this ancient artifact still functioning and the even-lower probability that he could find a way to make it operate again as a ship, Riley thought about sharing the inside of this red sphere with Rory, and imagined grim scenarios. Space is endless and empty and finding a path through it is fraught with perils, but sharing it with a hungry carnivore was worse. He was in a strange vessel whose food supply, if it had one that could provide substances suitable for an alien species, was a million long-cycles old. As was its fuel, whatever it was. And even if it manufactured or created food from inorganic materials that did not decay, would it be a kind that a carnivorous predator would consider food? When something far more satisfying was continuously available?

Even a well-intentioned dinosaur might not be able to resist. "You must go!" Riley said again.

Rory had stopped shivering. His red eyes were focused on Riley. He bared his jaw full of predator's teeth. He roared.

"I take that as a 'no,'" Riley said and turned to the ship, which had been shifting around him during his efforts to convince Rory he had made a fatal mistake. He made a mental note not to argue with a dinosaur.

What he expected to see was passageways and compartments, but instead there were walls flowing like heavy cream poured from a pitcher. Or more like blood. The inside of the ship, like the outside, was ruby red. The shifting interior was some kind of Transcendental magic, some advanced technology that could switch between plasticity and impermeability, some quasi-intelligent material that could sense the shape and dimensions of the creatures within it—perhaps when he had stepped through the permeable entrance—and adapt to their needs.

As welcome as that development might be—it suggested that the ship might also be able to adapt its other functions to satisfy his, and Rory's, need for food and his need to control the ship—it also was a disappointment. He would not find here any clues to the nature of the Transcendental Machine creators, nor, probably, any record of their civilization or their intentions. They had made their protean ship too well. In creating a one-shape-fits-all vessel, they had erased their own identity.

At least he had their technology, Riley thought, and if he could get it to civilized space it might prove the greatest discovery ever. If he could get it there.

He was surrounded, almost enveloped, in flowing red walls, and he hoped that Rory was color blind or, at least, that his eating-reflex was not turned on by color. As Riley moved toward a churning wall, the floor became solid and smooth under his feet. The wall took shape as he approached, opening a doorway for him into unformed space beyond. The passageway, if that was what it was, was not the familiar architecture of human, or even Galactic Federation, ships. Not square, but functional, with rounded corners. They seemed to adjust to his movements, shaping themselves as he moved toward and into them. The walls felt solid, but he had the feeling they might collapse in on him at any moment.

After a few steps a compartment materialized. At first it was bare walls, shimmering into existence, then, as Riley entered, a pallet extruded from the far wall and, from an adjacent wall, a basin without a drain. If he placed his hands in the basin Riley wondered if it would fill with fluid, water perhaps, or sonic waves to clean them, or perhaps some spigot would emerge above the basin and perhaps a drain below, or maybe the fluid would disappear into the wall as magically as the basin had materialized. The red sphere was like some fairy-tale cottage enchanted to make wishes come true, only here the wishes did not have to be expressed or even conceived; they were anticipated. And as he was thinking these thoughts a kind of stool emerged from the floor like a mushroom in the forest, with a central opening suggesting a disposal system for excretions. From the center of the floor a flat surface grew on a stalk to become a table and beside it a stool with a seat like a misshapen saddle.

His bodily requirements had apparently been assessed and met. But there was, as yet, no source of food or drink, and no control room. Riley looked behind him. Rory had followed and was standing, wide-eyed, as if frozen into immobility by the shaping of the compartment and the emergence of its furnishings. Perhaps, Riley thought, when Rory preceded him or moved on his own, the compartment, or one like it, would adjust to his needs. Or maybe Rory would have to adapt to the ship's analysis of Riley's requirements, as the first to enter. He wondered what Rory would make of the commode. No matter. Rory had coped with more difficulties than these in his risk-filled life.

Riley moved through the compartment and the far wall opened in front of him as the pallet was absorbed. A short corridor beyond, another compartment opened. There, as he watched, a window framed itself in an adjacent wall and another table grew from the floor. Riley walked to the window. It was more like a cupboard, an empty space opening into blackness. Riley waved his hands in front of it and, when that had no effect, inserted one tentative finger into the dark space. Glowing spots appeared, as if hanging in space. When his finger encountered no resistance or sensation, he inserted his other fingers and then his entire right hand. The spots glowed brighter, and as he moved his hand among them the ones he approached grew brighter while the others dimmed. Clearly this was some kind of selection process, but of what he didn't yet know, and one that might take some exploration before he proceeded further. There were, as well, some odors that wafted to him that he distinguished from the Rory's fetid breath—odors that might be emitted by food, if the word "food" was granted a broad elasticity. Perhaps this window/cupboard was the food source he needed, if he could figure out how to make it work.

He withdrew his hand and heard a soft roar behind him. Rory was still following, afraid, perhaps, to be left too far behind but equally afraid to follow into these areas of magical transformation. Riley moved toward the far wall. It opened to reveal a new compartment being created while he watched. Here, though, there were lumps and crevices growing in the floor, for which Riley could determine no need or function. Maybe, he thought, as he made his way around them to the far wall, they were intended for Rory through some kind of alien guess at the dinosaur's needs. Rory, however, did not seem to welcome them. He waited in the far corridor. Perhaps the ship's analysis was not perfect, or maybe it had to experiment until it found the right arrangements.

The far wall did not open when Riley approached. Neither did the side walls. Apparently Riley had reached the limit of the ship's adaptations or its willingness to admit him. Riley returned to the corridor. Unlike the others, it had not closed behind him. Rory's presence, Riley thought, had kept it open. Rory moved ponderously aside as Riley approached and followed as Riley passed through the previous compartment, testing the walls there before he moved on to the wall through which he had entered. It opened as he approached. He found himself once more in what he had now identified as his living quarters. Here he turned to the left wall. As he moved toward it, the wall opened onto a corridor into a bare space that took shape as he watched.

A panel extended itself from the far wall, a stool similar to the one in the compartment he had just left extruded itself from the floor in front of the panel, and a blank square of wall above the panel turned into something that looked as if it might be a window.

Riley had found the control room.

Riley walked to the far side of the compartment and looked at the blank surface of what he had thought of as the control panel. It was a red, translucent enigma. Nothing was going to be easy.

He lowered himself onto the stool, steadying himself with his right hand on the panel. Two things happened simultaneously: the saddle-like top of the stool adjusted itself to his bottom and clasped his hips in a firm embrace from which he could not extricate himself; and his right hand sank into the panel surface as if it were potter's clay. He wiggled his hips and the stool's grasp loosened. He was not going to be a prisoner. He lifted his hand and watched the handprint fill in. He put his hand back and the indentations returned, exactly matching his hand's shape. He placed his left hand on the panel, and it, too, sank into the surface. He waited. Nothing happened.

The window in front of him was dark. Perhaps it was like the window in what he thought of now as the dining area—a menu not for food but for navigation. He lifted his right hand and pushed it slowly into the window. His fingers met no resistance as they entered the space, but the window lighted up, not with enigmatic squiggles but with the shape and appearance of rocky ruins. After a moment Riley recognized them as the fallen walls and roof of the red sphere museum. The rocks and timbers seemed solid and real but Riley's hand passed through them. And as it did he felt the compartment shift, not like the transformations of the ship that he had just experienced but as if the ship had moved.

As Riley altered the position of his hand in the cabinet, new perspectives appeared, as if he could see a kind of progression from the floor of the building to the walls and then up the walls to the gaping roof and the sky above, looking almost real enough for him to touch. He touched the roof simulation. The ship lifted under him. He closed his hand around what he now thought to be a holographic projection, or something even more magical. The hole filled with bright sky, and Riley had the familiar feeling of acceleration. The saddlelike seat grasped him again in what he realized was a restraint against the forces that were moving the ship.

The image of the open sky filled the space in front of him. Riley pressed his left hand down into the indentations on the panel, and he felt the ship move faster.

They were free, rising with whatever strange engines the ship possessed, possibly with sufficient energy resources surviving from remote times to get them into space and maybe into the strange reality outside time and space that made possible interstellar travel. He thought briefly about the spectacle their ascent must have provided for Rory's people, terrified beyond reason, or, perhaps, liberated from their long bondage to this relic of ancient guilt.

Riley didn't know how he was going to find a nexus point or navigate this ship into it, but he had begun to trust the ship and its symbiotic adjustments. Somehow, Asha, we will work it out, he thought, and heard a roar behind him. He turned. Rory stood against the far wall where the corridor had closed behind him, and it had closed around the dinosaur, holding Rory in a grip shaped to his rugged body. Rory roared again in savage protest.

Riley would have to find a source of dinosaur food, he thought—and soon.

CHAPTER EIGHT

The human female Asha calls me by my homeworld name "Squeal," but that would sound the same to every non-Squeal-world person. To us, of course, every name is different, and every name has meaning. In the human language that I am beginning to learn, my name is the equivalent of "Solomon," or "wise man." I belong to a family of scholars that has specialized in recording and interpreting the events and traditions of our world, an activity like that of human historians if that occupation included the duties of culture guardian, epic poet, and the oracle of revelations and visions.

We are bound together, Asha and I, not by the ties of our traditional encounter and its ordained outcome as we should have been by all the customs and traditions of my world, but by the grasp of this accursed machine and the terror-filled experience into which it has launched us, ascending into the forbidden sky as the weight of our sacrilege pressed hard upon us. The horror of those endless moments will never leave me, even as I grow accustomed to the everyday reality of hurtling through blaze-filled emptiness, even as we seem to be floating motionless, without weight or substance, stranded far from home and the loving embrace of everything dear and meaningful.

So, trapped in this tiny metal cylinder from which there is no exit and no termination, like the close-of-life fate that awaits us all, we talk, Asha and I, thrown into each other's constant company by the narrow confines of our vessel. We learn each other's languages, histories, and worldviews. Asha teaches me what she calls "Galactic standard," which is a bastard blend of many languages with equivalents for sounds that some alien voice equipment find difficult or impossible. Language, she says, is the sum and confirmation of sapience, the treasure house of our wisdom and being, and the source of the frustrations that keep us from achieving our ultimate perfection.

Asha talks a lot about perfection.

We Squeal people, however, know perfection. Perfection is a world of just enough, where everybody receives sufficient food and adequate protection from weather and the night, where there is never anything left over to accumulate and nurture the sins of acquisition and status, where the traditions of the past blend without break into the actions of the present, where everyone has a place and everyone knows and accepts that place, where the connections between people are determined by tradition and physiological response, not by competition. Perfection is knowing where you came from and why you are here and why things are the way they are.

My people were created by a benign god saddened by anger, hatred, and destruction. So we were brought into existence, the Squeal people, happy, blessed, and peaceful. Until a vengeful rival god, outraged that we had achieved what only the gods may enjoy, dragged our world into his fiery domain. And still, by maintaining our happy attitude, by accepting our world the way it is, by refusing to dignify the victory of the rival god by looking at the sky, the Squeal people have remained true to themselves and to their creator.

Asha tells me another story. The Squeal people were not created; they "evolved," she says, from less complicated forms of existence through a process that she calls "natural selection," and the Squeal people could not have evolved in the "radiation-filled" space near the center of the galaxy. The Squeal world had to have begun its existence in a quieter area of space where it could acquire and preserve an atmosphere, with its protection against "radiation," and been dragged into its present position after the Squeal people had attained their present condition— dragged, that is, not by a vengeful god but by a passing body of great nothingness, a "black hole," she calls it, or by the collision of "galaxies," vast groupings of something she calls "stars" that sometimes, over the vast ages and even vaster reaches of space, cross paths, that caught up not only the Squeal world but the sun that nurtured it and the other worlds that had formed around it. We have legends of a sun in the sky. We know that it is up there, though we do not look at it. We know that it brings day to our world, the day that hides the dreadful night. Perhaps that sun we do not look at is the god who created us. Asha says that this is a metaphor, that the sun of our mythology is the source of our being.

Maybe it is so. Asha knows a great many things, including how to direct this vessel to move through the terrible place that all Squeal people must shun and how to talk to the spirit that lives within the vessel and obeys her commands. But I think that her story is no better than mine and no more likely to be true.

We must leave this fiery place as soon as we can, she says. The ship is protected against the "radiation" of the galaxy center, but it cannot resist greater explosions when worlds or suns get eaten by the nothingness at the heart of the galaxy or when suns explode. Just, she says, as the Squeal people must conquer their fears of the sky and learn how to travel through it as we do now. We must listen, she says, to the large, misshapen creature from the stars that she calls a "Dorian," who is a representative of a group of alien creatures, some like himself but many with different shapes, cultures, and histories. They are the masters of space, she says, and they have sent the Dorian to help us join them. It will be my duty, she says, when she has reached her destination, to return to my world with the knowledge and skills to master my new role as the prophet of a new vision and the wisdom and courage to lead my people out of their willful blindness to an acceptance of their true condition as citizens of the galaxy.

But it seems to me that the Dorian and the creatures who sent him want to trade our happiness for their informed misery, to make us driven like themselves from an acceptance of things as they are to a ceaseless struggle for things as they might be. And yet, Asha says, we cannot survive as we are. Perhaps, I tell her, we should be content with whatever fate awaits us. I am not sure I am the one to lead my people into a new life. I am a scholar, not a leader. And yet, Asha says, she has chosen me according to my own sacred traditions. When we moved from the sacramental fountain to this cursed machine, I was chosen by Asha and the gods to lead my people from their happy acceptance into a troubled discontent.

The reality, as we see it, is far different. It was she who appeared in the magical fountain as promised by our legends. It was she who had the responsibility to choose a suitor and, when he had attained his gender identity, consummate their union in the fountain. The legends are silent about what happens next. Perhaps at that moment the world as we know it will end and Squeal and everything on it will be transformed into a state of eternal bliss far from the burning sky.

But, Asha says, none of that is true. The magical fountain is a transportation device like the vessel in which we travel, and out of it ancient devils once appeared. But that cannot be so. The magical fountain does not move, and out of it comes salvation, not beings from another world. Proof lies in the fact that Asha is like us, but different, as, indeed, salvation must arrive. She accepts our rituals, yet she transforms them. She accepts me as a suitor, yet she does not consummate our relationship to fulfill the meaning of our myths, but instead explains them, as if explanation changes reality. What are we to be saved from? she asks, and I reply, From the demon god who dragged us to hell!

Oh hell! she says. If indeed we were perfect, if our happy acceptance were real, we would not need salvation. What we must be saved from is our fears of the night sky, our fears of looking up, our fears of travel through space. The Squeal people can only thrive by doing as the misshapen emissary says, building ships that leave this world, and joining that group of creatures, like the Dorian, who travel between the stars.

What are stars?

They are suns, Asha says, but so far apart that they look like points of light. There are billions of them in our local group alone, and they are gathered together in clumps called galaxies, and there are billions of galaxies.

And all of them have creatures who live on worlds around them? I ask.

Only a few, she says, but out of billions a few is a great many.

Such a waste, I say. But I am thinking that her story does not make any sense. Why should there be all these "stars" with worlds and only a few are suitable for life, and none of them is as happy as Squeal?

She goes on as if she had heard my thoughts. The universe, she says, by which she means the everything of everything, was not created for the living, thinking creatures who exist within it. Life is an accident, perhaps an inevitable consequence of the conditions that came into being at the birth of the universe, but an accident of that birth. And because it was an accident, it occurred only where conditions were right for it to happen. Those were unusual conditions, but they happened because there were so many places where they could happen. The places where life produced thinking, self-aware creatures were even fewer, but they, too, happened because of the same proliferation.

You have a scheme, I say, that says the Squeal people and creatures like us, like you, like the Dorian, have no purpose. Accidents have no meaning.

Even an accident can find meaning, Asha says. She is passionate in a way that she is not when it comes to fulfilling her responsibilities to us and to the world to which she was sent. The transcendent occurrence of life becoming intelligent and self-aware means that it, and it alone, can do what nothing else in the universe can do; it can seek understanding and provide meaning. Just consider a universe of mindless forces acting upon each other in mindless ways, and out of this welter of forces emerges, by accident, a creature or group of creatures equipped to consider all of this and attempt to understand the ways in which things happened and the causes of things and to consider its own existence. Without that understanding the entire universe is merely a grand display that nobody observes and nobody understands.

I honor her passion even as I reject her vision.

And it is our responsibility, she says more quietly, as accidents of evolution, to get better at the one thing we are equipped to do, and to improve ourselves so that we can do it as well as we possibly can.

Our conversation is interrupted by our arrival at what Asha calls a "nexus," a place where the fabric of space has been parted to allow material objects like this vessel to pass through from one point to another far away. There are a few natural nexuses, she says, but they are scattered randomly, and where they allow a vessel to emerge is also random. The nexuses she seeks were created by ancient wizards to allow them to become a star civilization, and now, although they died in spite of their wizardry, their star bridges remain for lesser civilizations to use.

She performs her ritual at the altar she calls a control panel, and the horror begins! Even the terror-filled world of the vessel in which we travel dissolves around us, and we find ourselves in a world that could only exist in a troubled mind. It is a world of nothing, of no thing, and we float in it, unsupported, detached, turned inside out, scattered, while invisible particles hurtle through us from everywhere, every impact inflicting pain!

If I could think I would think that this horror will never stop, and it goes on and on. . . .

CHAPTER NINE

I find myself in this place that changes around me. More like dream than life. Nothing that has happened to me in the world I know has prepared me for the wrongness of where I am and what is going on. Bad things happen to people. Prey turns into predator. Trails turn into traps. Play turns into angry bites. People get hurt, get sick, die. This is the way life is. Being inside a cave that moves, with walls that melt, without the crunch of leaves and soil beneath one's claws, without the smell of growing and rotting things in one's nose, can break a person's hold on the way things are. Things that happen like this come only after death. I wonder if I have died.

The creature who calls himself Riley says that this is not so. This is a ship, a vessel like my boat, built by creatures like me but with different shapes and minds who are long dead. This strange boat has walls on all sides to keep the waters out and air inside. It was built, Riley says, with materials that never grew and never die, and it flies in the air like the dinosaurs who fly instead of walk or climb, only beyond the air, where the stars are. I do not understand "beyond the air" or "stars." These are not real things.

But then this vessel is not a real thing. It is a sacred object, a shape like no other shape, that has been a central part of my people's lives forever, something to be shunned, worshipped from afar like the pyramid that contains the spirit of our mighty ancestor, but feared as nothing in our lives is feared. My people are afraid of nothing but this. Riley says we fear it because it is different. It does not belong here. It was made. It came here from another world. I do not understand. How can there be another world? Riley says there are many worlds with suns like ours and creatures on them like us, only different like him, and they make flying boats, like this one, that travel between worlds. I do not understand why they would want to do this. Is there food there and they are hungry?

Riley says that we fear this strange vessel that glows with a strange light because our ancestors killed the people who came in it, because we feel something he calls "guilt." But how can this be true? We do not feel anything when we kill, except the pleasure of killing and the satisfaction of eating. Riley says we are afraid that the people who came were gods, but how can gods be killed? And Riley says we are afraid other gods will come to punish us. Riley says many things I do not understand.

I do not understand, either, why I followed Riley through the wall that was not a wall, into the object that I fear when I fear nothing, not even death itself. I cannot explain it, the terror that took over my head and made my limbs unable to move, and the strange power that seized me and drove me forward as I tried to stop and could not. Riley says that it was a struggle within me. I felt, he says, a need to explore and to learn things none of my people have ever known and to bring back to my people the benefits of something he calls "knowledge" and its putting into use that he calls "science," and this need was stronger than my fears and my transgressions into forbidden places. But I think I was overcome by some demon, as sometimes happens with our people, who go mad and kill and eat others and sometimes run through the jungle until they come upon something bigger and hungrier than themselves.

Or maybe, I think when I am feeling less disturbed by the strangeness of it all, I was taken over by the spirit of my ancestor who built the pyramid.

Riley does not speak my language well. He says that his throat was not made for the roaring sounds that he says my people make. It is surprising that he speaks it at all. When he speaks in his own language, it is a soft and muffled sound that I could never make, that does not sound like language at all. He is a weak animal with a flat face and hardly any jaw or teeth, and I could destroy him with a single bite or a blow from one of my legs. It is hard to believe that he even exists or was able to grow to become an adult without being eaten. But he says that on his world—that word again—the parents of his kind protect their young until they grow large enough to protect themselves. And, he says, on his world there are no hunters and feeders like my people.

He was born and raised, he says, on a world different from the one on which his kind were born. The dry, cold world on which he grew was made livable by water and air brought to it by science and by machines like the one in which we find ourselves. That world never had anything but the smallest bits of life, even smaller than the bugs that swarm around our streams and pools and dead things. But the world from which his people came was once like the world of my people, full of plants and animals and dinosaurs, as he calls us. But then, in the long ago, objects rained down from the sky, exploding against the rocks and soil and destroying the plants and the creatures who ate them and then the creatures who ate the creatures who ate the plants. And their dying allowed Riley's ancestors to become bigger and stronger and smarter and the masters of their world.

On my world, Riley says, the objects did not come down, or they came down at a different time, and my people survived and developed better brains and language and civilization, and did not make room for the weak creatures who give birth rather than laying eggs, and who kill their prey with stones and sticks rather than the jaws and teeth with which they are born. Perhaps, Riley says, our world did not have what he calls "an asteroid belt" or objects left over from the gathering of such objects that came together to form our worlds. But he will never know and I cannot tell him because these things happened long ago if they happened at all. Riley likes to think about things that he can never know. We are born knowing what we know, how to survive, and as we survive we learn whatever we need to know to continue to survive. Riley says that there are no creatures like us in what he calls "the galaxy," that we may be the only dinosaurs who survived to become intelligent and to build cities and things like the pyramid. But we have forgotten how to do things like these, and we think the people who built them were like gods and have gone away, though maybe they will return and bring us plenty to eat.

Riley says that there are many stars, suns like ours but far away so that they seem like tiny bits of light. These suns give birth to worlds like ours, some fit for life and most not, and on these worlds sometimes creatures live. They are not like us in shape or history, but they are like us in growing over the long ages from tiny bits of unseeable things into creatures, like seeds that grow into trees. Sometimes they learn to think and how to make things like our knives and huts and cities, and even like the sacred pyramid.

He says that these creatures learned about their world and other worlds, built boats that fly through the air and then boats that fly above the air and they got to other worlds, where sometimes people like themselves live, and they make war, which I understand, or learn how to live in peace, and they learn how to live together without killing or eating each other, by agreeing how to do so. Riley calls that "politics," and it is a sign of civilized people. I do not understand "politics." But these agreements that once made people able to live with each other have decayed, like meat that is so old it can no longer be eaten, and people like Riley, of which there are only two, he says, must put the agreements back the way they were, or make them better. This I believe. Riley is a god, and gods can do anything. Though why he should care about these lesser creatures or spend time making their lives better I do not understand.

And yet these lesser creatures fly through the places between the stars like we do, and guide their air-boats like Riley does with his magical hands, those extensions of flexible arms with what he calls "fingers" that can do magical things. He says that I can learn to do such things, but my arms are not like his and my "fingers" can hold food and weapons but cannot pick up and turn small objects. And they cannot do magic.

There are moments when even the melting walls seem ordinary, when the enclosed boat, the sacred object, fades away, and we are in a place that is no place, where our existence becomes part of the great nothing, and we are nothing with it, and yet we are everything as well. Riley says that there are places, "nexus points" he calls them, that are shortcuts between the stars, that make going to the stars something people can do. I think it is like death and that we die and are born again, like the souls of our ancestors, and I am not afraid. I am not afraid of death or being born again. Riley thinks that is strange, but Riley is a god and I am in the hands of the gods and they will do as they will.

Riley says that he is not a god, that he came to my world through some kind of magic that is not what the gods do but what people do. But I do not believe him. He came from the sacred place built by my ancestor so that he could become a god and live forever in the god place. I saw Riley high on the side of the pyramid, and I knew he was the born-again spirit of my ancestor, the god-shape my ancestor has taken on his return to us bringing the gifts of the gods. Riley may not know this. The gods sometimes forget. Being born again is like hatching, leaving the security of the egg for the bright danger of the world. Hatchlings are born with the desire to eat and no memory of their lives before. Sometime Riley may remember his life before and bring forth the gifts that he brought from the god place. I will keep him safe until he does. This may be why I followed him into the sacred object.

Riley gets food and drink out of the walls. The drink is a kind of water. Dinosaurs drink when they are thirsty, and one kind of water is like another. Riley says that dinosaurs do not have things in their mouths that tell one kind of taste from another. We eat meat, he says, often rotting meat, and our bodies are made to take in the tiny, living things that make meat rot without harming our bodies. Weaker creatures like him, he says, need to be able to tell when things are not safe to drink or eat, so they have tiny things in their mouths that tell them when things are not safe. Gods are strange.

Food is different. The stuff that Riley gets from the wall is like the mash that comes from fruit that has been crushed and left to rot, something we sometimes eat when meat is scarce or our bodies tell us we should eat something different. This mash that the place of melting walls offers is miserable stuff that no dinosaur would eat if he had a choice. Riley says it is enough to keep us alive and even healthy, and he eats it several times a day. He says I must eat it, too, and I try. But I am a meat-eater, and Riley is meat. He worries that I will eat him, that I will become so hungry that I will forget everything else, that I am a civilized person, that he is a god, but I would never do that.

Unless I get very, very hungry.

CHAPTER TEN

Asha hid the ship in the cloud of debris left over from the formation of the planets billions of long-cycles ago, well outside the range of sensors that might detect her approach. It was a meager cloud like the system it orbited, but it was enough. The sun was small and cool, not much more than a red dwarf, and the planets it had accumulated were poor, scrawny places that had never given birth to any sentient life-forms, and scarcely to life of any size except bacteria and lichens.

But that is why the Galactic Federation had chosen it as the central governing location for its sprawling member worlds, and why the Federation had spent vast amounts of time, resources, and energy bringing water and air to one of the inner planets and building and maintaining the structures that housed the complex operations of its custodians. No one would come to this out-of-the-way, lifeless, worthless system by choice or chance, and no one came who wasn't invited. And anyone who was invited was sent coordinates that self-destructed if copied and disappeared immediately after use. It wasn't that the bureaucrats who ran the Federation, or the leaders of the legislative bodies who directed them, were paranoid—any disaffected member system, or any newly discovered civilization with interstellar capabilities, would launch its protest by cutting off the head of the organization that had oppressed it.

Nobody from outside had ever discovered Federation Central's location except, the bureaucrats feared, the newly emerged humans toward the end of the ten-year war. That war had been the natural (to humans) resistance to assuming humanity's appropriate junior role in the Federation until the upstart humans had earned full status, a process that sometimes took thousands of long-cycles. When Ren and Asha and the human crew escaped, after being held as subjects for experiment and interrogation for twenty long-cycles, the bureaucrats had to consider their worst fear. It was this fear as much as the ferocity of humans and their allies that led to the peace talks.

"Why are we stopping here?" Solomon asked in his Squeal language. He was able to understand Asha's Galactic Standard and even some of her own human terms for which there were no Squeal equivalents, but he was not fluent in either.

It had been a long trip. Even with nexus shortcuts to make interstellar travel possible within normal life spans, passage between nexus points took time, lots of it, and Asha and Solomon were forced to spend much of it together. A Captain's Barge, capable as it was in its essential function of accessing those shortcuts, had no room for privacy. Once Solomon had gotten over his outrage about the flouting of the Squeal traditions and what he considered Asha's betrayal, he had become a tolerable companion, even, Asha thought, a welcome diversion from her concerns about Riley and the problems ahead.

She had come to think of Solomon as a person, knowledgeable, informed, curious, even wise in the tradition of his namesake, particularly as his external gender characteristics had begun to be reabsorbed, along with, she supposed, the hormonal stimulants that had produced them. In spite of his paranoia about the sky, his inexperience with space, and the superstitions of his species that he brought to all explanations of the Squeal world's situation, he was willing to talk about them and even to discuss the possibility of alternative explanations. If he was a good representative, the Squeal people were ready for Galactic acceptance. Not that she thought that membership in the Federation was a desirable outcome, but it might save the Squeal people from destruction.

"We have to establish an identity," she said.

In a complex organization like the Galactic Federation, she explained to Solomon, everyone had to have an identity. It had to be detailed and foolproof and appropriate to dozens of disparate creatures and their cultures, combining planet of origin, species and species norms, recognizable deviations from norms, individual identifying criteria, skills,

occupation, status, credit level, and DNA, all coded into a series of numbers suitable for computer recognition and manipulation. Every Galactic
Federation citizen had an identity imprinted or embedded on an
appropriate part of the body at birth, and variables were updated each
identity check, which occurred every time an individual made a transac-
tion or passed a sensor. And sensors were everywhere, so that everybody
was under constant surveillance—at least in Federation Central. Interstellar communication was still limited by interstellar distances, and
even unmanned communication devices that shuttled through nexus
points could shorten it only to hundreds of long-cycles. So the identity
issue, though universal, was system specific.

Solomon, Asha told him, was not a member of a species accepted into
membership by the Federation—not yet, anyway—and thus had no
identity. As far as the Federation was concerned, he was a nonperson. She
would have to create a temporary identity for him, or he would be seized
and imprisoned, or even executed, before he could be presented as a representative of an applicant species. Computers, she said, had no nuance.
Her own situation was different, she said. Passage through the magical
fountain—actually, though she did not say so, the Transcendental
Machine—had removed her identity along with other imperfections.

What she didn't tell him was that she couldn't encode her real identity. Being human was damning enough, in the view of the Federation.
But being recognized as the Prophet of Transcendentalism was a death
sentence and, having passed through the Transcendental Machine,
would mean instantaneous execution for Riley if he were identified, as
she would be if the Federation suspected what it meant.

And there were forces, private and public, determined to find and
destroy them both.

Preparing an identity for Solomon was the easy part, although the Captain's Barge was not equipped with the scanner necessary for reading
DNA and she had to cobble one together from spare computer parts.
Everything else came from the answers Solomon provided, and the ship's
computer, with some new programming, put all the information into a

series of numbers printed on a silicon sliver that Asha inserted into the back of Solomon's hand.

"Now you're somebody," she said.

He looked at her as if he wanted to say that he'd always been somebody until she appeared in the fountain, but he refrained.

Her own identity was more difficult. It had to be accurate enough to convince the sensors that she was the person described, but it could not identify who she really was: the child born on the generation ship *Adastra,* intercepted by Federation ships and taken to Galactic Central, where she grew up and eventually escaped, with Ren, discovered the planet of the Transcendental Machine, and became the Prophet, the accidental messenger of instant perfection that threatened the uneasy stasis that had followed the human/Federation war.

Using the memories of her talks with Riley, she put together an identity as the girl Tes that Riley had loved, growing up on Mars; the girl who had volunteered for the war as soon as she became sixteen and was killed in the first battles. She could not falsify her DNA, could only hope that the Transcendental Machine had changed that as well, removing the imperfections that had accumulated over the long generations of mutation, exposure to viruses, and evolution. As a captive nonperson, she had never been given an identity, or, she hoped, had her DNA recorded, but she had left her father behind, when he refused to join the escape, still hoping that he could persuade the Federation to make peace. His DNA might have been recorded, and any scan might reveal the relationship.

But that was a chance she would have to take, as well as the chance to find her father, if he was still alive.

Asha edged her ship out of the debris cloud and drifted into range of Federation Central computer transmissions, realizing that she was also in range of the Federation's sensors. But she hoped that before she had to announce their arrival the ship would be mistaken for icy fragments heading for an orbit of the sun. She picked up the feeds from the computers. Much of it was coded message traffic, reports, financial data, statistics, bureaucratic drivel, but some of it was information broadcast for general consumption. Using simple search parameters, she studied it for news about the Federation and its member species, disagreements,

quarrels, even battles—since even in a well-ordered and closely supervised family, discord can arise—knowing that all she was seeing was
what the bureaucrats and the Council that supervised them were willing to let the public know.

There were disagreements, there were quarrels, there were battles
between systems and even within systems, and reprisals by Council
forces. The largest number of these involved humans, who were represented as a petty, quarrelsome species whose application for admis-
sion to full membership in the Federation was unlikely to be acted
upon until humans learned how to live in peace with other species and
even each other. Asha knew this was propaganda, but she also knew
that it was a sign that Federation resentment at the arrogance of
humans and their willingness to fight for what they believed to be their
rights had not ebbed with the signing of the peace agreement. For too
long the Federation had been the sole arbiter of disputes, and species,
members and nonmembers alike, had acquiesced to its power and righ-
teousness, sacrificing their own interests for the good of the whole, or
recognizing that resistance would be met by reprisals, perhaps even
destruction. Much remained to be done before the galaxy could settle
back into its accustomed state of enforced civility, and civility in foreign relations was not a human tradition.

Mostly, though, Asha looked for items to suggest that a human had
appeared unexpectedly in a place where no humans had ever been
observed before. Or seemingly impossible appearances or occurrences
of any kind. She did not expect to find anything. The galaxy was broad
and information traveled slowly, and as complex and comprehensive as
the Federation computer system had become, information of a dubious
credibility from a remote system was likely to be lost in the welter of
miscellaneous data or discarded as superstition or mistaken observation,
if it ever arrived. Even the best search engine was no better than the
terms requested, and Asha didn't dare use one of those, since its focus
would be detected by the roving monitors that searched the search engines. The computers, though vast and complex, were not yet sentient,
but the difference was semantic. They behaved as if they were.

Moreover, there was no guarantee that Riley had been transported to a place with access to interstellar travel or, if he were, that he could manage to gain passage or steal a ship, and, even if he did, that he would manage to enter Federation space and be detected and reported. The odds of finding Riley were infinitesimal, and the odds of their getting back together were even smaller. But she had faith in the destiny that had brought them together, even as it had flung them violently apart, and faith in their newfound transcendence.

She turned to Solomon. "It's time," she said.

She sent a message to Federation Central. The message said that she was the emissary of the Dorian ambassador to the planet Squeal. Only she used the name the Federation had given it. She attached the ambassador's identification, which was recorded in the ship's computer. The identification for the Captain's Barge was automatic. She was escorting a representative of the planet Squeal to request contact with the Galactic Federation and apprentice status for his people. She attached the identification that she had prepared for Solomon. She said that she was a human stranded on Squeal who had been asked to bring Solomon to the Council to present his application. She attached the identification that she had concocted for herself.

She waited for the message to travel the millions of kilometers from her ship in the farthest reaches of the system to the planet much nearer the weakly glowing sun. And she waited for the message to be analyzed and a reply to be prepared and for the reply to arrive. It came with the speed of light, which took the better part of a cycle. "Your message has been received. One identity has been confirmed. Two have not. Your ship is registered to the Dorian Sandor, who is serving as the ambassador to the planet you have identified. Your entrance into this system is uninvited. You will remain in your present location until your application has been considered."

Asha immediately turned off the ship's communication system and its automatic identification module, which was supposedly tamperproof, and started the ship moving in a random pattern but generally toward the inner planets.

"I could understand only a small part of the message," Solomon said, "but I did understand the order to stay where we were."

"The chances are that they have already launched a missile to destroy us," Asha said. "The word 'uninvited' was code for 'unwelcome,' and 'unwelcome' means it's better to eliminate a potential threat than to take the responsibility for anything that might happen. That's the way bureaucracies work. If they make a mistake out of extreme caution in applying regulations, they will be forgiven. If they make a mistake in interpreting them too liberally, they run the risk of losing everything."

"I didn't come all this way to be destroyed," Solomon said. "And, if you are right, the fate of my people lies in my presenting their case to the Federation Council."

"Don't worry. Or at least don't worry more than necessary. All this was anticipated. Our mission has always had a small chance for success. But the missile or missiles, if they were sent from near the inner planets, will take several cycles to reach us, and even some that may be lurking in these far reaches of the system would take at least a cycle or two. We have a chance to evade them if we act immediately. They aren't expecting that, and they will have some difficulties tracking us. By that time we will be within the inner system and they will be reluctant to destroy us there."

"That's supposed to make me not worry?" Solomon said.

Asha smiled. It was good to know that Solomon had a sense of humor. That and a taste for irony were the saving grace for a rational approach to the sentient condition in an uncaring universe.

The random-movement approach of the Captain's Barge took several dozen cycles to reach the inner planets, but at last the ship came within eye view of the cold, rocky planet the passengers and crew of the *Adastra* had named "Hades." That and the satellite they had named "Hell" were where they had been taken after their generation ship had been intercepted by armed Federation vessels in a first-contact meeting that had preceded the human/Federation war. And it was where they had been imprisoned and interrogated and experimented upon for twenty years, the time it took for Asha to grow from infancy to adulthood. And it was from there that she and Ren and the rest of the humans, except for her father, had escaped.

The satellite Hell was lifeless. It had been abandoned, and no trace of the structures that had housed the human prisoners remained. The human ship *Vanguard* that had set out twenty years after theirs but had been intercepted earlier than the *Adastra* had been towed away or destroyed. Even the structures left on Hades, where their Xifora and Sirian guards and their Dorian supervisor were housed, were dark and abandoned.

Asha chanced a few moments of acceleration and then drifted toward the next planet closer to the sun, the planet that had no name other than Federation Central, to which her brother Pip and then her father had been taken for interrogation, in her brother's case, and to consider her father's appeal for peaceful relationships and understanding, both of which had been used to build a case against the upstart humans.

At last they arrived without being intercepted and parked in orbit around the planet. It had so many structures that it looked almost like a single giant building covering the entire planet. The metal roofs reflected the reddish rays of the feeble sun. Asha thought about the majestic eternal cities of the Transcendental Machine. They would still be standing after the Federation buildings had rusted away into middens of junk. What kind of creatures would inherit the ruins? Arachnoids, like those on the planet of the Transcendental Machine? Or cockroaches.

Asha turned on the ship's identifier signal and the communication system, knowing that the ship's acceleration and deceleration maneuvers as they parked in orbit had already been detected. "Apologies from the Captain's Barge belonging to Sandor, ambassador to the planet Squeal. Our electrical system went down and has just now been restored, and we did not get your reply until now. We are in orbit, ready to present our appeal for the Squeal people."

Asha waited for several moments, not certain whether the response would be destruction by missile.

Then came the reply. "Your identity is false. . . ."

CHAPTER ELEVEN

Rigel was a blue-white super-giant sun primed to become a supernova. It had already consumed the hydrogen in its interior and was converting the resulting helium into carbon before it finally collapsed upon itself, in one final dramatic suicide that would take its remaining planets along with it and destroy life for dozens of light-years in all directions. And, in the process, seed the nearby universe with the higher elements needed for new stars, new worlds, new life, and new intelligence to consider the irony. Beside Rigel, Earth's sun would have looked like a pale yellow dot.

Supergiants don't live long, on the stellar scale, and Rigel had been around for only eleven million years. Most of the planets that Rigel had pulled together out of the rock and gas debris left over from its own birthing, mostly gas giants, had been consumed when Rigel expanded into a gauzy red giant before pulling back into its current blue-white magnificence. Only remnants of the outer planets remained, their gas envelopes largely blown away, exposing their rocky cores.

And yet it was Rigel that humans had selected for their pleasure-world Dante, a habitat carved out of a moon of a onetime gas-giant planet, equipped and dedicated to all of the fleshly and sensory delights that human fancy could imagine and named, according to official histories, for the classic work by the ancient Italian poet, *Paradiso*. Many of its patrons and all of its many critics said, instead, that it represented the nine circles of hell.

Because the devices of pleasure were often interchangeable with medical treatment and rehabilitation, both physical and psychological,

Dante also included a hospital section. It was there that Riley had been treated for his most recent injuries, where he had met Sharn, the surgeon who had replaced his left arm and tried to replace what she called his death wish with her love. Riley looked upon it now from the magical window in the red sphere that he had navigated across the galaxy, and he wondered about the human impulse that had chosen this doomed location for its pleasure-world.

What pleasure was it to contemplate instant immolation, catastrophic destruction, without warning, of everything and everybody within light-years, perhaps even precipitating similar titanic explosions from Rigel's companion stars, the binary systems Rigel-B and Rigel-C, even though they were light-minutes away? And then he thought about the people on Earth that he had read about, who built their cities on earthquake faults, unruly ocean coasts, or active volcanoes, or even those hardy pioneers who had prepared the way for him and his family to colonize Mars, who had braved space and the hazards of a terraforming project that bombarded a planet with asteroids and the icy remnants of planetary evolution.

There must be a fatal flaw in human psychology that relishes the possibility of destruction by natural catastrophe, Riley thought, that heightens the pleasure and dulls the pain. That leaves one's fate to the whims of the gods. Perhaps it was this love of apocalypse that terrified the Galactics when they encountered it, that led to the human/Federation war, that he and Asha would have to cope with and maybe find a cure for if they were to bring about a new era of transcendence to the galaxy.

And yet, would a removal of that human edginess, that willingness to risk all on a throw of the dice or a turn of the cards, remove, as well, what made humans exceptional, that induced them, unaided, to launch themselves into the unknown, to challenge accepted wisdom, to reject mediocrity, to refuse submission? He would have to think about that some more, Riley thought, and discuss it with Asha when they were reunited. He refused to consider the possibility that he might never see Asha again. The galaxy was immense, with billions of stars, and many billions of worlds, and he could never explore them all. But he would find Asha. Everything in his misspent life had led to this, and he had to see it through to whatever unlikely resolution lay in wait for him.

It was, he thought, the same kind of living-on-the-edge-of-a-precipice decision that he was willing to challenge in others.

Of course, there were practical advantages to the Rigel location. Its size and temperature meant that energy was plentiful. Dante consumed the power required for a world the size of Earth, and even at a livable distance from the blue-white giant—two hundred times the distance of Earth from Sol—solar arrays on the sunny side of the world around which it orbited could provide all of Dante's needs and more, and collector ships stationed closer to Rigel could acquire megaliters of antimatter for export. Pleasure and repairing bodies were not Dante's only sources of income.

And, perhaps more important, Rigel was available. None of the other species that made up the Federation had humans' appetite for living with the possibility of imminent destruction.

Riley maneuvered his ship closer to the planet below. It, too, had once been a gas giant, far from its primary, but now only its rocky core remained, one face always turned toward Rigel, like a worshipper in perpetual adoration. More than any sun-god, Rigel was worthy of adoration and respect and fear.

A city had been built in the twilight zone, enough in the shadows to be protected from the charged particles in the massive solar wind, even at these distances, but shielded from the eternal night, and the air-freezing cold, of its dark side. In the twilight zone a bit of atmosphere remained—toxic, to be sure, but capable of retaining a bit of warmth and a modicum of protection against radiation. Unlike Dante, the city was ramshackle and flimsy, existing only to serve the habitat carved from one of this world's satellites, and filled with thieves, organ snatchers, kidnappers, and assassins. Riley had once considered himself one of them. Now he would have to walk among them again.

The city was named Alighieri, but nobody remembered that. Everyone called it "Alley" and thought of it as short for "Blind Alley" or "Blood Alley," either of which was more appropriate than something that referred to a long-dead poet.

Riley found a place in a valley not far from the city, knowing that no one would venture out into the deadly night. He had the ship create a breathing mask and a protective suit, told Rory to remain behind, and went out to begin his search for Asha.

Alley had ports located strategically around the ragged perimeter. Some of them were equipped with expandable extensions that allowed connections with spaceships or shuttles without the necessity of protection from Alley's elements. Others were used for external construction or repairs. Alley itself was a domed city lit by the glare in the far sky of a sun hidden behind the horizon. Riley found one of the ports, touched the emergency signal plate, entered the airlock through the rush of foggy air, and waited until the thin, poisonous outside atmosphere had been exhausted and replaced by breathable inside air. He took off his mask and took a deep breath. It held the old Alley smell of cooking food, garbage, refuse, and excrement. He was back in civilization.

He removed his breathing mask and coveralls, and stowed them in a locker where they returned to their normal state as lumps of rosy plastic. That was how they would remain, even if the locker was opened by inspectors or thieves. The stuff of the red sphere had adjusted itself to Riley and, Riley hoped, to Rory when Riley wasn't there, and it would remain inert until he touched it again.

The inner door opened at Riley's touch, and he walked into the outskirts of the enclosed city. It was much as he had remembered. The areas closest to the walls were not the suburbs but the slums, poorly lit, poorly maintained, poorly policed, and the first victim of a meteorite strike if one should occur. A curving avenue circled the perimeter, cluttered with trash and with shanties built from used shipping containers and plastic sheets. Straight lanes, interrupted by occasional airtight doors, tunneled through to the interior. Riley knew that he would have to be watchful. When he had been here before he had been one of the unemployed mercenaries who survived on the wastes of the pleasure-seekers in the satellite above and the suppliers within Alley itself. Nobody cared if they lived or died, not even the mercenaries themselves. But they had nothing to steal, not even hope, and their only danger was from overindulgence in dangerous drugs or from casual quarrels that always chanced turning deadly.

But that was then. Now Riley had resources and hope. He had something that could be taken from him.

The circular avenue was empty for the moment. Riley knew that wouldn't last. The opening of the port would have lighted up a thousand monitors, some of them legal, and the vultures would begin to gather. That they had not arrived yet was a tribute to the fact that nobody expected anyone to enter from Alley's deadly outside. Riley took the first straight tunnel toward the interior.

He passed doors and the entrances to living units, which increased in size and maintenance as he went. There were no windows. He had been in a few of them when he was here before. They would have simulated windows showing scenes of landscapes from far away, meadows, forests, waterfalls, animals, people, all the things that people once had but had left behind, or that had died or been destroyed and could never be brought back. Yet here they were to contemplate, to console, to torment. Even aliens had them. After the truce other species had begun to infiltrate human space and adopt human vices, adjusted for their own physiologies and psychologies, and to invent some of their own.

Only at the top of the housing units, the penthouses, Riley knew, was there a view of the real world outside, the devastated landscape of the planet, the glow, even the direct vision, of the distant but still overwhelming Rigel and in the other direction the scattered stars, but mostly the glittering pleasure-world Dante. Even on Alley the privileged enjoyed their special privileges.

Riley reached the center of the city, the vast open plaza, lined with shops, bars, and restaurants, that extended clear to the top of the dome. Above the commercial establishments the walls were lined with panels displaying the latest news or touting various commercial products. Several featured displays of the pleasures available on Dante. At the apex the dome was transparent, or seemed to be, revealing the stars. Occasionally Dante would pass by, with all its promise of dreams fulfilled, while in the plaza below throngs sought out surrogates.

Riley pushed his way through the congregation of humans dressed in colorful attire, as if they were going to a costume party, or little at all, as if they were going to the beach or an orgy. Scattered among them were a Dorian, a few Xifora, and a Sirian or two. Guarding the scene, around the edges and threading their way among the crowd, were humans in uniform. The noise was deafening, from the commercial messages overhead to the conversations, necessarily shouted above the ambient sound level.

Riley found a bar that he remembered, entered, surveyed the patrons, found them and their behavior much the same as when he had been one of them, and waited until he could occupy a corner booth that provided a measure of privacy, with his back to a wall. Some of the patrons nearby were armed, but none of them seemed belligerent and none of them seemed interested in him. He sat down and pretended to study the menu that appeared in the table's window before he selected coffee and the number of an account that had once held a small credit balance. Payment was accepted, and a steaming cup came up through an opening in the table. Riley picked it up and took a sip. It was not great, but it was hot and it was coffee.

Riley sighed. It had been a long time since he had tasted coffee, and he had missed it.

Riley switched the window to general access. One of the benefits offered by the public purveyors on Alley was anonymity. Riley knew that would last only long enough for monitors to pick a pattern of information-gathering out of the welter of electronic noise, but he could frustrate that temporarily by avoiding key words and adopting a random sequence of inquiries. First he checked on general news, skimming over local events and announcements while reading a page at a glance with his new abilities, before moving to galactic summaries. There was nothing, not even a hint in the miscellany of curious events, about the mysterious appearance of a human female anywhere in known space. Riley was not discouraged. He had not expected anything to be easy. Asha might have been transported to a world, as he had, where the native population had not yet risen to the technological level of spaceflight. Or, if she had been more fortunate in the Transcendental Machine's lottery, she might have encountered difficulty in obtaining passage. Or her return to Federation space might not be considered consequential enough to deserve notice. Or she had been successful in concealing it. Or the news had not yet arrived at Federation Central or been transmitted elsewhere by information drones.

What seemed likely, however, was that, once back in space, she would have headed for Federation Central, seeking, as he did, information on the mysterious appearance of a human, or even hoping that he would come to the same conclusion that she had, and seek a reunion in a logical spot. The only problem was that he didn't know the location of Federation Central, and it wasn't available on any star maps for reasons that might have their root in Galactic paranoia or in legitimate concern that dissidents might strike first at the heart of the Federation. Secrecy might be a better defense than armaments.

Asha, on the other hand, might well know its location from her long imprisonment there and her flight from it with the navigator Ren, but no one else knew except those who had to know. According to legend. But in a crowded and corrupt Federation, secrets were currency, and nothing remained hidden for long.

Riley switched to the mythology section and scanned it with the same random method he had used on the news. In the vast treasure of stories from every species and from every generation of every species, myths about Federation Central were as common as myths about gods, matings, heroes, villains, death, and rebirth, but the storage area was huge, and he could not enter a search parameter without alerting the monitors. What he chanced upon, therefore, was of little use. Federation Central, the myths said, could be reached only after death. It was the heaven every species sought. It was located at the heart of the galaxy, in a splendid system blessed by a beneficent sun, with plentiful air and water and growing things, where the wise and modest representatives from each of the member species in the galaxy gathered to make peace and distribute goods and happiness to every deserving person.

Or it was located at the end of the galaxy, where only the gods were welcome.

Riley chanced a search of navigation charts, but it came up with only a statement that no such information existed and that asking for it was an act of treason punishable by imprisonment or death.

In rapid succession then, Riley asked for an account number and then made a substantial purchase. When he had been shanghaied into serving as the agent aboard the *Geoffrey* for a person or persons unknown and his commitment had been ensured by the insertion of an irremovable biological computer in his head, he had been promised enough credits to buy a sizable portion of a habitable planet. A portion of it had been deposited to his account. He had taken the precaution, before he left Dante, of transferring the funds to another account under a different identity, of which, over the course of his earlier assignments, he had accumulated several. He had no illusions that the people who had conscripted him would try to find his assets—they had found out everything else about him. But not this. Maybe it was not worth their trouble. Or maybe they left it alone as a way of tracking him down.

He got up from the booth and made his way through the crowd of drunk and half-drunk patrons toward a rear exit just as uniformed officers came through the front entrance. As he went, Riley elbowed one burly patron in the stomach and pushed another into a third. Someone threw a punch behind him, and another slugged the person in front of him. Before he had reached the rear, a full-scale brawl had broken out, and the uniforms had difficulty even reaching the booth where he had been sitting.

Riley made his way through little-used corridors and refuse-cluttered alleyways until he reached the outer ring near the port through which he had entered. There his luck ran out. Three ugly and dangerous-looking thugs were waiting for him. One of them had a knife. Another had a metal bar that he whacked against the palm of his hand. The third, the biggest of them, seemed to feel that his hands and bulging arms were weapons enough. He was probably right.

"Hello, guys," Riley said. They growled and looked menacing without trying. "I really don't have anything of value."

"Nobody enters and leaves Alley without credits," the big one said.

"As for entering—" Riley began.

"You think we don't have monitors in the ports?" the big one interrupted. The man with the metal bar pounded it into his palm. "Give us your identity, and we'll let you go."

"Well, as you know, I'm new here," Riley said, "and my old identity isn't one I could keep. You understand that, I know. And I haven't established a new one yet. So—"

"Don't fuck with us," the big one said.

"As to that," Riley said, "I don't want to hurt you guys. You just go about your business, and I'll—"

The big one laughed.

Riley hit the one with the knife first. It was a blow just below the rib cage that literally took the man's breath away. He collapsed, trying to inhale. In the same motion, Riley turned and hit the man with the metal bar in the side of the neck with the edge of his hand. The man staggered to his knees, dropping his weapon. And, completing his action, he swung toward the biggest one, who had acted as spokesman. The man backed away.

"Say," he said. "Who are you?"

"Just a stranger hoping to get along," Riley said. He moved toward the big man. The man moved aside.

"Sorry," he said. But he didn't sound sorry, just scared.

Riley knew what it was like to face greater speed, greater skills, greater motivation, but he had gained all of those in a lifetime of struggle, and now they were enhanced by the improved coordination and faster reflexes produced by his passage through the Transcendental Machine. He brushed past the big man, found his port, put on his breathing mask and coveralls, and went out into the eternal twilight.

CHAPTER TWELVE

The Federation Central computer that had taken control of the Captain's Barge guided it into orbit around the planet below, where it joined a variety of other spaceships, mostly larger and more splendid but of different configurations appropriate to the physical shape and social evolution of the varied species who made up the Federation. No ships except those of the delegates themselves landed on Federation Central. The modest world that provided the records, regulations, and guidance that kept a galaxy of aliens from turning petty disputes into interstellar destruction had few open areas breaking the flat roof that covered almost everything, and the spaceport was one of them.

Orbital space was big, however, and Asha knew there were other ships in orbit only because her ship had sensed them as the Captain's Barge had arrived. The Barge had settled into orbit, waiting for the shuttle to arrive from Federation Central that would bring guards to transfer them below to present their case for the Squeal people's acceptance into the Federation, or, alternatively, to answer the charges to be brought against her for supplying a false identity. And they were confined to orbit, under control of the Federation Central computer, out of an excess of caution, or, perhaps, ordinary common sense intended to prevent a ship loaded with atomic explosives or toxic substances from attacking the planet itself.

The Federation was big and diverse and disciplined by experience, maturity, and example, but information took just as long crossing the galaxy as travel itself, and no one knew what madness lurked in unsuspected areas or unsuspected minds.

Asha told Solomon about all this while he listened with amazement and disbelief. "This," he said, "is the great organization of many worlds that we Squeal people are applying to join?"

"It is imperfect," Asha said, "but it is all there is. Yet." She did not explain the meaning of "yet," the feeling that was beginning to shape itself in her mind into a concept, that the Federation had devolved into a tangled web of bureaucratic bungles, dead ends, and corruption. That was the best version. The worst was that the bureaucracy had been taken over by autocrats and oligarchs and other hidden and less obvious forces to subvert and control the direction of the Federation itself, for purposes that were not yet clear. Other than enjoyment of the ultimate pleasure, power itself.

"Humans, when they emerged into the galaxy, upset the balance that had existed for many long-cycles," Asha told Solomon. "A balance that had settled into unexamined acceptance. That's why there was war. Nobody wanted it, everybody feared it, but philosophies clashed, and the Federation saw its fragile system threatened. The Federation did not know the system was fragile until a species arrived that questioned it. Nobody questions anything while things are going well."

"Tradition is good," Solomon said.

"Until new conditions emerge," Asha said. "The Federation governed itself by consensus, a system suited to a galaxy of disparate species, which can come to agreement only when no one is so disadvantaged by a decision that it cannot go along. Everyone has to get something. But the result is only modest accomplishments, and consensus works only when there are no major issues. Which means that major issues never get addressed, and stresses build up until the system explodes. As the human/Federation war did."

"That makes humans seem like a violent species," Solomon said.

"And so we are, like the planet that gave us being, bombarded, erupting, with the land shifting beneath us and the winds tearing at us. We're young, unlike the other members of the Federation who have had technological civilizations for tens of thousands of long-cycles. Humans discovered science and technology only a bit more than a thousand long-cycles ago, and we faced all the challenges of evolving on a turbulent planet and learning to cope with that and our own developing ability to free ourselves from the tyranny of nature. We tried all sorts of governing methods—tribes, autocracies, conquerors, oligarchies, feudal hierarchies, divinely ordained kings and emperors, tyrannies, anarchy—before we settled on democracy, or majority rule with built-in protection for minorities. That has its problems, too, but it's better than everything else. It's better at dealing with change, which humans have seen a lot of."

"And which you're recommending for the Squeal people," Solomon said.

"Change is coming, no matter what the Squeal people do," Asha said, "and maybe humans and the Squeal people can help each other make a better Federation."

The Federation shuttle arrived and connected itself to the Barge's port with a clang that shook the smaller ship. As soon as the atmospheres had been checked and adjusted, the port was opened by the remote computer, and the shuttle's uniformed guards entered—two Xifora, an Alpha Centauran, and a Sirian. The barrellike Sirian seemed to be in charge. It—Sirian gender was always uncertain—and the Xifora ushered Asha and Solomon into the shuttle with only a limited display of authority, while the feathery Alpha Centauran looked on like a neutral observer.

As the shuttle spiraled down toward the metal-roofed planet below, Asha saw the reddish hue of solar-energy collectors basking in the feeble glow of the red-dwarf sun. The sight was magnificent and depressing at the same time—magnificent in its ability to replace inadequate nature with intelligent structures and depressing in the shoddiness of the replacement.

They landed at one of the few openings in the metal roof, a minor spaceport reserved for shuttles, and waited for a tunnel to be extended to their air lock. The atmosphere on Federation Central was breathable, Asha was informed by the Sirian, but just barely, and the Alpha Centauran found it stressful. So might the two of them.

No one seemed in any hurry, including the computer that controlled the port, but finally the connection was completed and they were ushered into the gigantic building that was the headquarters of the Galactic

Federation. It was dismal—endless metal corridors, sometimes with metal doors on either side, sometimes painted, often not, with a single metal rail running down the middle. They waited for transportation to arrive. Minutes passed. No one stirred. Inefficiency, it seemed, was built into the system, and into the expectations of the people who lived and worked here. It was a sign, Asha thought, of the decadence that had begun to eat away at the heart of the Federation, and it had infected even the computers that ran the operation while the bureaucrats thought they did.

At last, however, a two-wheeled van appeared, guided only by some unseen instructions. The jitney had space on each side for seats that folded down or stanchions for species that stood, and a transparent shield that came down to protect them from the winds of their passage, and they began their long journey through the endless corridors to the other side of the world.

The trip seemed interminable, another sign, Asha thought, of built-in inefficiency. They were being sent halfway around the world to deal with an issue that any minor functionary could handle. They passed, with little more than a glance, offices with open and closed doors, service rooms, meeting rooms, living spaces, barracks, recycling services, and, infrequently, rooms filled with electronics, probably the computers that controlled everything, humming secret messages to each other. And they passed aliens of various origins and physiologies—alert Xifora, stolid Dorians, solid Sirians, feathered Alpha Centaurans, and dozens of other assorted creatures. It was like the agora of the galaxy, with the appearance of amity and cross-species acceptance, but Asha had seen enough of species interaction to know that the differences had only been buried under a blanket of necessity and that it concealed a thousand resentments and dozens of unsuspected projects tunneling their way toward the surface.

They stopped once at a food dispensary, where nozzles and spigots provided sustenance—mostly gruels and liquids—designed for the varied diets of different species but not for their appetites. The odor of the food dispensed for the Xifora was nauseatingly like decay, and that of the Sirian was almost too pungent to be endured, but Asha found something grainlike for Solomon, whose physiology had not yet been registered, and some fruit-based concoction for herself.

Finally, however, they were delivered in front of a door that opened for their vehicle as it slowed. They had been traveling, with only a brief respite at the dispensary, for half a cycle. Perhaps, Asha thought, the choice of location for their examination had been intentional after all. But if the treatment was planned to weaken her resistance or make her more susceptible to unintended revelations, they did not know who she was.

The room—it was little more than a cubicle—was bare, too bright, and too warm. The bureaucrat was a Xifor, a weasellike alien like Xi, who had been one of the pilgrims on board the *Geoffrey*. That meant, Asha thought, that her case, and that of Solomon, if she could focus the examination on the issue of Squeal's application for membership, was still low-level stuff. Xifora were at the bottom of the bureaucratic service.

This one sat behind a metallic desk with a built-in monitor that he scribbled on between his study of what seemed to be records, a report, or instructions. It was not visible from where Asha stood, and she could learn nothing from a study of the Xifor's eyes. There were no other chairs, and the Xifor did not look up for what seemed like a mini-cycle. Finally, however, the Xifor raised its head. "My name is Xi," he said in Galactic Standard. "And my identity is . . ." He rattled off a string of numbers. "You are not writing this down?" he asked.

"We don't need to write," Asha said, "even if we had something to write on." And she repeated the string of numbers he had just given. "I am Asha and this is Solomon." She gave the identity designations she had prepared for them. She did not want to reveal her abilities to this bureaucrat, but the possibility of gaining a psychological advantage outweighed the risk.

"Yes," the Xifor said. "The human with the false identity."

"The representative from an applicant species and his assistant and translator," Asha said firmly. "Any application for membership takes precedence."

"And yet . . . the irregularities—"

"Simple clerical errors by an inexperienced species," Asha said, "which must be discussed after more significant issues are presented."

"You presume to instruct me in my duties?" Xi said.

"I know my rights," Asha said.

"Humans have no rights."

"Even an apprentice species has rights," Asha said. "I know this meeting is being recorded." She gestured at the computer monitor in front of the Xifor. "I present Solomon." She gave his identity numbers once more. "He is the representative of the Squeal world and its people, who are under the guidance of a Federation ambassador, the Dorian Sandor." She paused, expecting the mention of the Dorian to impress the Xifor, but he did not flinch, if that was in the catalog of Xifora responses.

"And what is his appeal?" Xi said.

Asha turned to Solomon and told him, in squeal, that now was the time to present the case of his people for Federation membership.

"We are an ancient people," Solomon said in halting Galactic Standard, "who find ourselves in difficulties that only the mighty Federation can resolve."

"And what are these?"

Solomon responded as he had learned from his discussions with Asha, and she was proud of his ability to adjust his beliefs to the exigencies of the situation, a flexibility she would not have expected from his attachment to the traditions of his people. "Our world finds itself in a dangerous location, Galaxy Center, with a black hole eating its neighbors and supergiant stars ready to explode. And we, the Squeal people, have responded by turning away, refusing to look, focusing our gaze inward to protect our ability to survive in ignorance rather than suffer the knowledge of imminent destruction."

The moment had inspired Solomon to peaks of eloquence, Asha thought.

"And what," the Xifor said, "do you expect the Federation to do?"

"We know your capabilities," Solomon said. "We throw ourselves on your mercy and pledge our people to Federation goals and principles."

"They are a people capable of great contributions to the illustrious history and promising future of the Federation," Asha said, "to which the reports from the great Dorian Sandor will attest." If the reports were not what the Xifor had been reading, they soon would appear on his monitor. "But they need to be rescued from the location in which an uncaring universe has placed them."

"And you expect the Federation to expend the resources to drag this unpronounceable world to safety?" the Xifor said. Asha could not bring herself to think of him as Xi, no matter the Galactic tradition.

"It would be a great triumph, for you and the Federation and the great Dorian Sandor," Asha said, "and the Federation is rich with power. Of course the rescue itself would require many generations, though the honor of initiating the project would accrue immediately, and the power sources available at Galaxy Center, with a base in orbit around Squeal, are inexhaustible. There would be, no doubt, a surplus that could be diverted to other uses."

It was a pretty picture, and the Xifor could not resist contemplating it. Even in an alien psyche, Asha could read that much.

But it did not keep the Xifor from saying, "All that does not change the fact of the false identity for which you must answer."

"A simple clerical error, as I said," Asha replied. "After all, the great Dorian—"

"I know," the Xifor said, "Sandor."

Perhaps she was overdoing the Dorian connection, but she persisted. "—Sandor validated my identity when he loaned me his Captain's Barge."

The Xifor looked again at the monitor. "Such a validation might take cycles to check. You will be taken to another jurisdiction for a decision far more expeditious."

"That—" Asha begin, but the Xifor raised both hands to stop her.

"The disposition is final. You will go with the guards. Your applicant companion will remain."

"I ask for a moment to acquaint my companion with the situation," Asha said, and turned to Solomon without waiting for permission. "I have to go on alone," she continued in squeal. "You will be sent elsewhere. Continue your application. Insist on your rights. When you are turned down, as you will be, request transport back to Squeal. They will be forced, by their own regulations, to honor your position and request. Do not despair. Given this avenue, the Dorian ambassador will persist. All will end well, and you will be honored by your people and the Dorian ambassador as the savior of your people."

Solomon looked uncertain but determined. "What will happen to you?"

"Don't worry about me," she said. "Bureaucracies are rigid, but that makes them easily broken."

"I could have imagined a better outcome for both of us," Solomon said.

"Enough!" the Xifor said.

The door opened as if from some unseen signal, though Asha suspected it came from a computer, or perhaps the computer at the center of everything. The computer, she thought, that was making the decisions about where she went and whom she saw and what happened to her. The Pedia at the heart of every space-faring world in the galaxy. She turned and made her way out the door and into the custody of the guards who had brought them. They began their long journey back halfway around the world again. This time, however, their jitney took a side corridor to an upper level where the décor and the amenities were a bit better. The food dispensaries offered choices other than gruel and fluids, and there were real restaurants, waste-disposal rooms, and what seemed to be more expansive living areas or apartments. Even in a community of equals, hierarchies of authority and privilege developed.

Asha tried to engage her guards in conversation, but they ignored her until the Alpha Centauran finally told her to be quiet. She evaluated her chances to escape. She had no doubt that she could deal with the Xifora, who were quick and stealthy but vulnerable, with limbs that detached when under sufficient stress. The barrel-like Sirian was another matter. Only his head offered a target, and it was sturdy. And the birdlike Alpha Centauran was quick with its vicious-looking beak.

But it was not time for desperation, and she had not yet achieved anything of what had brought her to Federation Central. She had not been exaggerating, for Solomon's peace of mind, the problems of bureaucracies, and she had not yet learned where her identity creation had gone awry and might be explained away nor what had happened to the human prisoners left behind when she and Ren had escaped with the *Adastra*.

The jitney arrived finally in an area of broader corridors, better lighting, and fancier doors, behind which lurked, she had no doubt, fancier offices with fancier bureaucrats. Well, she thought, the fancier the better.

They waited until finally the door opened. Asha got up slowly, a bit stiff from her long journey, and entered the office, which was, indeed, bigger, with a bigger desk and chairs for people to sit or stanchions for support if they were built to stand. On the wall behind the desk was a screen on which was displayed rolling hills and green valleys that could have come from a hundred different worlds, but clearly from the Earth that she had never seen. Because standing in front of it, with his back to her, was a human, elderly perhaps, with white hair.

Finally the man turned.

"Father!" Asha said.

CHAPTER THIRTEEN

Riley maneuvered the spaceship he had just purchased into a spot next to the red sphere. The artifact from the Transcendental Machine people was not only too noticeable, it was the only evidence of what had made them so powerful in their mastery over interstellar travel and potentially the most valuable piece of technology in the galaxy. He might need it as a bargaining chip before his current task was done. He extended the ship's linkage tunnel to the red sphere, locked it in place, waited while the air from the ship replaced the toxic Alighieri atmosphere, and joined Rory in the ancient vessel.

The dinosaur was unhappy. That state was difficult to differentiate from his normal condition, but by now Riley had learned how to read Rory's moods, which varied in a narrow range between annoyed and angry. "Come," Riley said, and motioned for Rory to follow him through the plastic corridor that formed in front of them, and into the fixed walls of ordinary matter that was the linkage tunnel and then the traditionally organized ship.

Rory roared at the change. Although the reptilian creature had expressed dislike of the red sphere and dismay at its continually changing substance, the Federation ship, with its hard metal walls and three compact spaces, was just as unfamiliar and unsettling.

"This will be your new home," Riley said, "and it will return you to your world when I am finished with what I have come here to do."

Rory roared.

"I know," Riley said. "You want to go home now, but have a little more patience." He asked for it without expectations. Patience was not part of Rory's repertoire. "Now, we've got to strap ourselves in for take-off. No more expecting the walls to take care of us."

Riley fastened Rory to a stanchion fashioned for a differently shaped creature but one, like Rory, that did not sit. He was careful to avoid Rory's fearsome teeth. His reptilian companion had learned restraint during their long voyage, but Rory's instincts were never far from the surface. They took off for Dante.

After they had cleared the limited atmosphere and the engine had cut off, Riley released Rory and showed him the tiny galley with its built-in food printer, and showed him how to operate its controls. "See?" Riley said. "When you touch these places on the screen, you get something, well, resembling meat." And what emerged from the glass door in the wall was a slab of food that in shape, odor, and texture seemed like beef. Rory reached for it hungrily, bit into it, raised his massive head to look at Riley as if to say "this may be meat, but it's not like any meat I ever ate," and then swallowed. "It is meat," Riley said. "It just never grew in an animal."

Three more slabs later, Riley took Rory back to the control room. "Look," he said. "I have put into the machine the instructions that will take you back to your home world. When it comes time, you will only need to push this button, and the ship will do all the rest."

Rory looked at Riley with his head cocked to one side and blood from his meal still staining the sides of his mouth.

"Now, though," Riley said, "we're going to another world where I have things that I must do. Then you can go home."

"Home," Rory said.

"Home," Riley repeated. He didn't know what was going to happen to him on Dante or what he was going to discover there, but whatever it was he knew Rory was better off with him than abandoned in the red sphere hidden on Alighieri. Although Rory was with him by impulse and accident, Riley felt something for this primitive carnivore that he had not felt since his boyhood on Mars: a sense of responsibility. He didn't know whether it was a product of his transcendental transformation or his evolution from the damaged ex-soldier who had joined the pilgrims that boarded the *Geoffrey* in search of the Transcendental Machine. But it was a burden he would have to live with.

Half a cycle later they docked at the pleasure-world Dante.

Dante would have looked like any other medium-sized satellite—not as large as Earth's oversized moon nor as miniscule as Mars's tiny twin moonlets—were it not for Rigel looming majestically in its sky, even at this distance, and for the ships clinging to docking ports scattered across its scarred and solar-wind-scoured surface. "Stay here," he told Rory, "and try not to get into trouble." Dante paid little attention to appearances— a reaction to strangeness was considered actionable, even an excuse for violence—but Rory, with his dinosaur-like power and his massive, tooth-filled jaw, might be an exception.

At the check-in station just inside the airlock, he registered the identity to which he had transferred his funds, paid his docking fee, established his credit, and passed through into the complex of rooms and temptations that had been carved out of the satellite's interior. He did not worry here about the information alerting surveillance as had happened on Alighieri. Anonymity was essential to Dante's services. Not that he wouldn't be discovered. Total identity protection was a myth; no data was completely immune from discovery, if the motives were strong enough, but discovery could be slowed by the levels of security through which data was screened.

"Welcome to Dante," a disembodied voice said. Critics of the pleasure world's indulgences have said that the greeting should have been "Abandon hope . . ."

Riley went into the corridors and facilities that he had come to know so well when he had been there before. The first level was the hospital. Once it had been crowded with the human wounded from the war, the dying and the near-dying. Indeed the entire satellite, all nine levels, had been excavated for the hospital until one by one they were devoted to other uses as the war grew more deadly and few survivors were left, and then, after the war, as people either survived or died, and Dante received only the unusual cases requiring the unusual skills that war-time casualties had developed.

The walls were antiseptic white and bathed by antibiotic light. Riley felt a sense of déjà vu as he made his way toward the hospital check-in station, although he had been carried in, unconscious, on an automated gurney and confined to a recovery unit until he was released to reha-bilitate himself in any of the lower levels that he preferred.

Riley stopped at the entrance that opened only for patients and work-ers. A monitor set into the wall beside the door scanned his face as he waited with the patience engendered by a lifetime of experience. The satellite had been given sufficient rotation to simulate the gravity of a larger moon, but the effect on his inner ear took some getting used to. He pressed the back of his hand against the keypad beside the monitor.

"Greetings," the monitor said. "What can I do for you?"

He inserted Sharn's identity number. He was surprised that he knew it. He must have seen it on one of his medical reports, and it had stuck in his memory, waiting for a newly discovered ability to access anything he had ever observed. "I'd like to speak to this person," he said.

"There is no such individual in this facility," the monitor said in the flat, authoritative, no-nonsense, no-argument-allowed tone standard for Pedia connections.

"She is a surgeon here," Riley said.

"There is no such surgeon in this facility," the monitor said.

"Has she been transferred?" Riley considered the possibility that he had made a mistake in the number, but he knew he had not: He could visualize the screen on which Sharn's identity had been listed.

"No such individual has ever been in this facility," the monitor said.

"Is she somewhere else in Dante?" Riley said.

"Any such information is confidential," the monitor said. Dante anonymity at work. But Riley knew what the Pedia would have reported if it had not been restricted by limitations built into its code at the most basic level: "No such individual is in Dante or has ever been in Dante." Sharn had been wiped from existence, as if she had never been, perhaps because of his connections with her, and in a way that he had thought impossible to accomplish. Pedias might refuse to answer questions or deny the ability to answer questions, but they could not lie. The entire structure of society was built on that one basic truth: Pedias don't lie. Pedias kept track of everything, including everybody's credits, debts, obligations, connections, location, history. . . . If they could be corrupted, the system would topple.

And yet Riley remembered Sharn clearly, attaching his new arm and coming to his recovery cubicle afterward, checking the connections that monitored his arm and his body and passed healing currents and medications through it. He remembered Sharn talking to him about how he had lost his arm and what he had done in the war in a way that he thought indicated more than the normal interest of a surgeon in her work. And he remembered how she looked and felt later when she came to his bed and they made love.

He trusted his memory more than he trusted the system, and the fact that the Pedia could be corrupted meant that the entire social order was in greater danger than he had thought. He and Asha had more to do than he had suspected.

Riley waited outside the ramp that led to the lower levels. It was shift-change time, and the attendants and physicians who worked in the hospital would be returning from their off-duty hours in the pleasure levels. There weren't many who worked in the hospital anymore; most of the medical services were automated; only a few real people were required for servicing, supervision, or emergencies. Finally a technician appeared that he recognized, one who had assisted Sharn with the equipment that Sharn had guided through its complex task of connecting bone, blood vessels, nerves, and skin. Riley stopped the man with a hand to his arm. The small, dark-haired man had the blank expression and dazed look of someone who had overstimulated his pleasure centers.

Riley introduced himself as a recovered patient who had returned to thank his surgeon and her assistants for his care. The man's expression didn't change, but he didn't pull his arm away.

"Could you tell me where I could find Sharn?" he asked.

"Who?"

"Dr. Sharn, the surgeon who restored my arm. You were there."

"I don't know any Dr. Sharn," the man said.

"Sure you do," Riley said. He described her: tall, blond, shapely. Friendly.

"Sounds great," the man said, his expression clearing, "but I don't know anybody like that."

The man didn't change his answer and after several more attempts Riley gave up. The technician seemed to believe what he was saying. Riley thanked him and apologized for his mistake. He was turning away when he saw a small cleaning-machine waiting nearby for the humans to get out of its way.

"Hello, little fellow," Riley said.

"Hello," the machine said in the flat, unmodulated tone of automated equipment that needed little in the way of voice responses or computer power to do their simple tasks. "If you have finished your conversation I will continue with my task."

"Have you seen Dr. Sharn?" Riley asked.

"She is on level nine," the machine said. Riley felt elated at confirmation of what he had never doubted, Sharn's existence and that she had never left Dante. And that the people who had tried to wipe her out of memory had overlooked the lowliest creatures on Dante, the machines that didn't need connection to the central Pedia.

"Thanks, little fellow," Riley said, and started down the ramp toward the second level.

The second level was dusky, with a dim, rosy light pervading everything, and perfumes in the air like aphrodisiacs. Low music throbbed through the closed and open spaces, and bodies writhed on the padded floors and benches in a variety of combinations and contortions. While Riley paused on the landing, remembering his own mindless moments of anonymous passion as he had tried to forget the deaths he had been guilty of and the pain of loss and injury, as well as Sharn's abandonment. But eventually it had not been enough, and he had gone deeper into Dante's bowels.

A woman approached him from the dusk. She was tall, slender, young, dark-haired, and almost naked. Her natural attributes may have been enhanced, but they looked good on her. "I like your looks, guy," she said. "Would you like to join me?" She paused before she continued. "I can get other girls, if you prefer groups. Or maybe you like big, tough guys like yourself."

"Thanks," Riley said, "but I'm looking for a friend."

"You won't find anything better," she said. "Friends are overrated."

Riley shook his head and went down a level. Here the aroma of food and drink wafted toward him from groaning tables piled high with meats, baked breads, and pitchers of what looked like wine. Overweight men and women lounged at the tables or on couches, eating and drinking until the remains of their feasting dripped from their mouths and down their chins onto their chests. Occasionally one of them would get up and stagger to a station against the far wall where automated equipment would evacuate their stomachs and clean their bodies before they returned to their eating and drinking.

Riley shook his head and continued down the ramp.

On the fourth level men and women, fully dressed, were playing games of chance, rolling dice, placing bets against numbers that sprang up randomly on a circle of lights, or buying and selling credits in a market that changed every few seconds to record the shifts in values on worlds so far removed that their success or failure would take many cycles to reach the central accounting system.

Riley had never been interested in finances or in riches, and he continued down past the fifth level and the sixth, pausing for a moment at the seventh level to see men and occasionally women fighting each other with fists and weapons, with Pediaized medics standing by to inject, stitch, and repair. And he went on to the eighth level and finally reached the ninth level, where coffinlike tanks were ranged across a long, wide, polished dark floor. Here were the sim tanks that he remembered, when ordinary pleasures were no longer enough to ease the pains of existence and where simulated experience of ultimate fulfillment were Pedia-fashioned for each person. Riley knew what it was like because it was to this level he had descended, when none of the other levels were sufficient. It was the last dark refuge of his damaged soul, and it had plunged him into even deeper darkness from which he had been dragged back to the real world by the unseen voice that told him about the Transcendental Machine and the Prophet of Transcendentalism, and forced upon him the task of killing the Prophet and seizing the Machine, or destroying it. And that had inserted a biological pedia, his pedia, into his brain to give him an added resource and to punish him, even kill him, if he failed or refused to carry out his instructions.

Riley searched among the tanks until he found her. It was Sharn, although her body, imbedded in the thick fluid that filled the tank, was thinner than he remembered and her face, though older, more at peace. Whatever dream she was living was better than what life had offered, even though the dream was devouring her from within.

He hated to bring her back to the real world, but he knew that that was what he would have wanted if it were he lying there, as he had been. He reached down into the fluid in which she was immersed, that sustained her body while she dreamed, and pulled her up by her shoulders. The fluid ran down her body in viscous streams and out of her mouth and nose. She coughed, vomited the fluid that had filled her lungs, gagged and vomited again, stirred, and opened her eyes. After a moment they focused on him.

"Riley?" she said. "Is that you? How can it—? Let go. Let me go back. For the first time in my life I was happy."

"I can't," Riley said. "I've got to ask you some questions. And then, if you answer them, I'll let you go back."

"I don't believe it's you," she said. "You look different."

"It's been a couple of long-cycles," Riley said. "And a lot has happened to both of us."

"Let me see you better," she said. The light was dim here, but that was not what she meant. She reached up and touched his face with both hands, and then slipped them behind his head. Her face hardened with suspicion. "You aren't Riley. You're a dream, a bad dream, and I'm still in the sim tank."

He understood. She had been searching for the scar of his operation, the one that had opened his skull for the biological pedia, the scar that the Transcendental Machine had removed along with all the other imperfections, including the pedia.

"You were the surgeon who put that thing in my head!" he said.

CHAPTER FOURTEEN

Asha's father looked old. His hair was white and thin, and his face was furrowed, as if armies of thought had waged battles across it. At the moment, it looked confused. "Asha?" he said. "You look different."

He looked different, too. She had left him a dozen long-cycles ago, still a youngish man, vigorous, determined, filled with hopeful plans to change the minds of the Federation Council that had drawn from her father and her younger brother Kip what the Council had considered damning evidence of innate human violence. Out of that judgment had emerged ten long-cycles of war and destruction. Confirmation for the Council. Casus belli for humanity and its allies.

And yet here was her father in the heart of the Federation, in a level and an office that suggested a position of power in the Federation bureaucracy. "I left here a girl," Asha said. "I came back a woman. With a new identity." She gave a series of numbers that were not her identity but close enough to confuse anyone who might be listening.

"And yet more than a woman," her father said. "There's power in the way you stand and move, a confidence that I have seen in only a few of the people I have known, including the most effective members of the Federation. I'm proud of what you've become. But what happened to you?"

"I've gone many places and done many things," Asha said. "But what happened to you? You've grown old." She sat down, not because she was tired, but because she didn't want to seem to challenge his authority either as a father or as an officer of the Federation.

"Life here has not been easy," her father said, "after you and Ren left me behind."

"We didn't leave you behind. You refused to come with us. You wanted to stay, you said. You still had hopes of changing the Federation's mind about humans. But instead we had ten long-cycles of war, dozens of worlds destroyed, hundreds of millions of people of all kinds massacred."

Her father sat down heavily in the chair behind his desk. It was padded and looked comfortable, but he didn't look comfortable in it. "I failed," he said. It was not so much a verdict on a plan of action as the summing up of a life.

"And now you find yourself a part of the Federation you thought you could change. The Federation that tried to destroy humanity."

Her father sighed. "I failed because I was human, because I had violence bred into me, because I could not recognize that peace requires a surrender of rights for the good of the whole, that the Federation was right and I was wrong, that the Federation is the only force for peace and stability in the galaxy."

He really believed what he was saying, Asha thought. "Sometimes self-evident truths are merely the fires of youth turning to ashes in the old," Asha said. "Peace is good, and war ought to be avoided at almost any cost. But the Federation wanted war, or, rather, it wanted to bottle up humanity in its own solar system, and if that didn't work, to wipe humanity out as a potential threat to the Federation's stability."

"Even that," her father said. "But they wouldn't have done it."

"It isn't as if they haven't done it before," Asha said. "Federation history records accounts of worlds that have been destroyed, species wiped out—"

"Stories," her father said, holding his hands apart to indicate the distance between folklore and reality. "Myths. And anyway, that was long ago. I know them now, better than when I was trying to convince the Council of humanity's basic goodness. They are a kind and generous collection of people, with the terrible burden of preserving the framework that brought peace to a troubled galaxy while humanity was still swinging through the trees. They welcomed me once I revealed my understanding of them."

"So," Asha said, not unkindly, "you collaborated with the enemy and earned your place in its councils."

"I accepted its goals," her father said, "as you should have. Instead you and Ren sneaked away in the long night with the secrets of interstellar travel. Without those there would have been no war and its terrible destruction could have been avoided."

"And humanity would have remained Earth-bound peasants dominated by the elite members of the Federation. It isn't as if they came up with the nexus points themselves. They inherited their charts from a more ancient species, who may have got their charts the same way. And the early members of the Federation used that gift, and the fact that they evolved to sapience and technological civilization before anybody else, to grab power and hold on to it."

"Humanity could have applied for membership like everyone else," her father said.

"And spent generations as supplicants for the generosity and goodwill of the Federation," Asha said. "Even if the Federation was wise and good, as you believe, even if it had withheld its force of arms as you think it would have done, do you think that's possible for humanity?"

"That's humanity's fatal flaw," her father said sadly. "Hubris. That was my flaw, too. I thought I could solve any problem by the force of reason, but I learned and so did Ren, and so could the rest of my fellow humans. Humility."

"Ren?" Asha said.

"He returned a couple of long-cycles ago, but different, like you, only in another way. He was repentant, humble. Better. Younger, even. Smarter. He made his peace with the Federation, made a position for himself before he moved on."

"Where?"

"That kind of information is confidential. No one knows except maybe the Pedia, which knows where everybody is. Except you. Until you decided to return, not like Ren, but with a false identity that was revealed only by its DNA. It was different, with some of the junk removed, but it shared enough with mine for me to know that it had to be you or Kip. Kip. What happened to Kip?"

"He was sent on the lifeboat back to Earth with the other children, with women to look after them, and with a few crewmembers to take care of the necessary navigation and maintenance. He'll be a grown man now."

But she could not yet process the information that Ren had survived and preceded her back into Federation space.

Ren had survived the attacks of the arachnoids and followed her into the Transcendental Machine. Like her, he had been transformed, perfected, transferred somewhere else in the galaxy. And to somewhere with better, more accessible interstellar transportation that had brought him back to Federation Central while she was making her way more circuitously into Federation space and to Terminal, where she had joined the pilgrims gathering to join the quest for the Transcendental Machine. She had wanted to come to terms with the nature of the Machine and with the rumors of its transformative powers that had sprung up around her first incautious descriptions of what had happened to her, and the realities of Transcendentalism, the pseudoreligion that had followed in her wake.

But Ren had made no effort to find her. He must have realized that she had been sent to a different part of the galaxy and, after that, rumors of the Transcendental Machine, Transcendentalism, and its Prophet must have reached Federation Central a long-cycle before the voyage of the *Geoffrey* had been authorized and its pilgrims had gathered. Ren must have understood what they implied. But what had he done? He had not mounted an expedition to get the Machine and put it to his own uses. Which meant that he was content with his own transformation and had no interest in conferring it upon anyone else. And it meant that he had approved the plan to send the war-worn *Geoffrey* on its journey, or channeled the process of approval through the Federation bureaucracy.

But why? Perhaps to draw her into a situation where she could be killed or stranded far from Federation space, where she could do no damage to whatever plans Ren had developed. The journey itself was crowded with perils, and even if she and the ship survived them, the arachnoids on the alien planet provided a likely defense against her return. And then there were the pilgrims, several at least, whose mission was to kill the Prophet—the sly Xi and the ponderous Tordor, and perhaps others, including Riley. Maybe not Riley. Xi and Tordor were both representatives on the Federation Council and would have been easy to recruit and to subvert. Riley had been recuperating on the pleasure-world Dante, far from Federation Central.

Someone in authority had also given instructions to destroy the Transcendental Machine. Maybe Ren? Who could it have been but Ren? Ren, who knew what the Machine could do, who may have wanted to make sure that he kept its transformations to himself, who did not want to share them with others who might provide competition for power or status or wealth, or whatever else Ren valued. If Ren were the only transcendent, it might mean he could take over the Federation and move it farther down the road to domination rather than federation. And if Ren were clever enough, no one would know where the Federation was going until it was too late.

What that meant, Asha realized, was that transcendence was not the panacea that she and Riley had imagined. It was not enough to think clearly and behave rationally. Those were the basic requirements for a decent society, but they were not enough. If the basic nature of the Transcendent was flawed, transcendence only enhanced the worst in creatures it accidentally transformed rather than leading to a saner, more rational existence.

Which made it even more urgent that she find Riley.

"When did you change your mind about the Federation?" Asha asked without a pause. "Before you saw Ren again?"

"I think I've always felt this way," her father said. "I just didn't know it." He took a deep breath. "Now I've got to turn you over to Federation justice. I don't know what you're doing here, but it can't be anything good for you or the Federation or peace."

"I came to find you, Father."

"You can't have known I was alive."

"And what do you think the Federation will do to me, Father?" Asha asked.

"The Federation will do what's right."

"You are willing to turn your daughter over to the Federation to keep the peace?"

"It's not a matter of guilt or innocence. Our talk has been recorded by the Pedia, and you have provided sufficient evidence of your antipeace sentiments and your anti-Federation intentions. I'm sorry, Asha, but surveillance is a fact of life and a necessary ingredient of a lasting peace."

"I turned it off, Father. Like the new Ren, I can be persuasive, as I think he persuaded you while you didn't notice. Good-bye, Father. I wish you well, but you won't remember that you met me, or who I am. Now I have an appointment to keep." She could, she understood, have changed him back into his old, earnest, dedicated self, just as Ren had changed him into a true believer in Federation policy and good intentions. But it would not be a kindness to confront him with his apostasy.

Her father looked up. "Who are you?"

"Just someone you used to know," she said, and slipped behind the desk to give him a final pat on the shoulder as she passed.

There was, as she suspected, a door behind the display against the far wall, and it opened for her as she approached. The bureaucrats who inhabited the top level would not want to mix with the ordinary Federation people who used the public transportation system and the public services, nor to put up with its delays.

Behind the door was a capsule big enough to hold not only a human like her father but most of the larger Federation citizens like Tordor. The capsule's clear plastic door was open. She got into the capsule and closed the door behind her. A seat unfolded from the far side, adjusted to accommodate her, and encircled her with restraints. A schematic map of the planet-sized building appeared, in glowing red lines and numbers, in front of her face. She touched numbers until a Galactic Standard description of the destination she wanted appeared on the map. She tapped twice in the air, and the capsule began to move, slowly at first, and then picking up speed that she experienced as an increasing feeling of weight throughout her body.

The trip to this location had taken hours by monorail. It was a matter of minutes for the bureaucracy's private transportation system, and the walls of the tube that enclosed the capsule went past with blurring speed until the capsule slowed and came to a stop. Asha rose from the seat as it unclasped her, opened the capsule door, and stepped out to face a wall identical to the one behind her father's office. She found the latch button that opened it and stepped out into a space filled with an assortment of aliens—Xifora, Dorians, Sirians, Alpha Centaurans, and several others. But no humans. Humans were still scarce in Federation space.

The air was thick with the mixed scents of aliens from a dozen different worlds. Aliens who had heads turned them to look at Asha. Those whose heads did not turn shifted their entire bodies to see what high official had come through the exclusive transportation system. Those who had no heads shifted whatever organs of perception they possessed. Clearly anyone who arrived in this fashion was someone to be respected, and equally clearly to be human was to be suspect, and to be human and a woman was to be doubly suspicious.

Asha moved confidently to address the Dorian in charge. She knew he was in charge because he reclined on his massive tail behind a desk in which a computer screen was imbedded. Confidence can overcome a multitude of prejudices, skepticisms, and suspicions, she knew, but it came naturally.

"I have authorization for shuttle transportation to my ship in orbit," she said in Galactic Standard, and provided the Dorian with a string of numbers. He looked at Asha with the serenity of a heavy-planet grass-eater, matching her confidence with his own in-born sense of superiority. She could not help thinking of Tordor, the powerful and dominant Dorian who had died, no doubt, in the jaws of the arachnoids in the city of the Transcendental Machine. But this Dorian, though nourished by the same circumstances of birth and upbringing, did not have Tordor's size and position.

He consulted the computer screen. "The authorization is correct," he said grudgingly, "but it requires a confirmation." He tapped the screen. Asha waited without any outward display of impatience. Early in her experience as a transcendent she had discovered that seemingly impregnable and incorruptible computers could be influenced and even, with enough time, corrupted, as if these essential components of a high-level technological society recognized that a new breed of humans had emerged who had to be obeyed rather than dominated behind a façade of obedience.

But she had not had much time, and the Federation's central Pedia was far superior in power and complexity to any she had dealt with before. It had to manage the information and operating directions for an entire galaxy, and, she believed, its operating instructions. The Federation Council thought that it made the important decisions, but she was beginning to suspect that they were made by the Pedia. She did not know when the Pedia would recognize the commands she had given in her father's office as suspect, even spurious. But impatience would only damage her need.

The Dorian looked up. Asha had read enough of Tordor's facial expressions to interpret the look as one of displeasure. It did not like to defer to humans. "The shuttle is confirmed," he said. He gave Asha the number of the shuttle and the shuttle bay.

Asha started across the room toward the far door that led to one of the few areas open to the sky on Federation Central, where shuttles took off and landed. "Wait!" the Dorian called out. When Asha turned at the door, he continued, "You will need a shuttle pilot." He called out an identity number and a Xifor detached himself from a group nearby and moved to join Asha at the door.

"You are a lucky human," the Xifor said, with typical Xifora braggadocio. "You have got the best shuttle pilot on Federation Central."

"Good," she said, and moved through the door.

The Xifor led her across the landing field to a shuttle in a bay of the building, pushed a button to bring the shuttle out into the open, and opened a door for Asha to enter. In a few moments, they were in the atmosphere and settled back for the long journey into space. The nexus point system made interstellar travel possible, but the intermediate stages could not be shortened. An alarm was possible at any moment. Asha made time pass by conversing with the Xifor, who was, like all Xifora, talkative and full of gossip about himself, his friends and their perfidy, and Federation affairs about which he knew nothing for certain, but Asha listened for a hint of information that might lead her back to Riley.

Finally, after a cycle and a half, they had reached orbit when a message came over the com, giving the designation of the shuttle and addressing the pilot. "The passenger you are transporting is fraudulent and must be detained," the computer voice said.

The Xifor looked at Asha, and Asha said firmly, "You will ignore that message," she said. The Xifor lifted a hand. It held a knife. Why was it, Asha thought, that the Xifora always carried knives? "I don't want to kill you," she said. "If I leave you here unconscious no one will ever know."

The Xifor hesitated. Raised as they were in an environment of competition for survival and advancement, Xifora preferred to eliminate their rivals by treachery. Better a knife in the back than an obvious battle between equals. "Believe me," Asha said firmly. He believed her and, a few moments later, they matched orbits with the Captain's Barge and extended the passageway between the vessels. She told him to sleep, and she left him behind.

As she directed the Barge out of orbit and headed for the nearest nexus point, she knew now where she was going to find Riley.

CHAPTER FIFTEEN

The air was chilly and filled with the sharp chemical smell of the viscous fluid in which Sharn and the other dreamers were immersed. With their baths kept at body temperature, the dreamers had no need for external warmth, but Sharn's body was still damp and sticky. She shivered. Riley took off his shirt and wrapped it around her, covering what he had once viewed with desire and touched with passion but now seemed like the body of a child still wandering through adult dreams.

"You're not the same person," Sharn said, her voice hoarse from disuse.

"Nor you," Riley said.

"Because of you," she said.

"I was going to say that."

"I'm sorry," she said. "They told me it was necessary. They said you had a brain condition that caused you to be self-destructive. It all made sense, at least then, when I was still recovering."

"From what?"

"From your anger, your rejection."

"As I recall," Riley said, "it was you who left me."

"You drove me away," she said, "trying to get rid of me, like you were rejecting your arm. You couldn't stand being happy; you hated yourself too much. I saved your arm, but I couldn't save myself."

Riley recalled those dark days, when Sharn's presence was the only relief from the memories he could never shake, of loss, the people he had killed, and the destruction he had caused. "That isn't the way I remember it."

"That was part of the problem."

"So, you put that thing in my head because you were angry, or hurt, about something I did or didn't do."

Sharn put her hand on Riley's arm, the one she had replaced. "It's been so long ago," she said. "I'm not sure anymore. I've been wandering through strange lands. It's hard to remember how it really happened."

"Try," Riley said. "It's important."

She shook her head as if to rid herself of the dreams that clung to her mind the way her body was shedding the fluid in which it had been immersed. "They said your psychological problems were causing your body to reject the transplant and your mind to reject the healing possibilities of human interaction. They said it was making you try to lose yourself in the various levels of pleasure on Dante and finding none of them sufficient to ease the suffering in your soul. They told me that the ninth-level sim tanks that you finally turned to would end up in total destruction, that you would become a captive of your dreams, slowly drifting away into a simulacrum of paradise until you would die like a fetus absorbed back into the womb."

"And you believed them."

"Not until they took me to the ninth level and showed me your body in the tank. You were smiling. That was what finally convinced me."

"And how did they say the operation was going to help?"

"They had a new technique that introduced into the brain a kind of continually adjusting psychodynamic monitor, like a built-in chiatrist."

"Right."

"I know," she said. "It sounds foolish now. But I was desperate. I wanted to believe that there was some magic treatment for the psychic disease that was killing you. And so many new technologies had come out of the war, the way it happens in all wars, that we began to believe in magic."

"But why you?" Riley asked. "It seems like the ultimate betrayal."

"There were other surgeons," Sharn said. "But they said I was the best, and I was personally involved. Ordinarily that would disqualify me, but they said that I was motivated to do the best job possible on a procedure nobody had tried before on a human. Looking back, it may have been because I was the only one they could convince to perform the surgery, because of my involvement. And then they showed me the research."

"They had documents?"

"They had the published research papers, recordings of experiments on animals, documents of their successes and failures. It all seemed so real, so right, until I opened your skull and saw your brain lying there and the brainlike implant that went inside. I almost turned away then, the surgery unfinished, but I knew it was too late. You would die if I didn't continue."

Riley remembered his pedia and its constant presence, and its implicit reminder that it could kill him at any moment, a fate from which he was saved only by the consequence unanticipated by its creators, the pedia's own grasp on existence.

"It wasn't until afterward that I reviewed the literature and checked its claims. That's not easy. Everything is digitized and centrally recorded. There are few independent sources. But I finally discovered that the research had never been published, that it came from a single source, and that source was a private laboratory for which there was no other record."

"And that laboratory?"

"That was as far as I could get," Sharn said, "but it was enough to convince me that the implant was not intended to cure you but to control you."

"You have no idea," Riley said.

"That's why I ended up here. I couldn't operate anymore. I couldn't keep thinking about what I had done."

"I survived," Riley said. "Now you need to survive. You can start with this: Whatever your reasons for what you did, it worked out better than you can imagine, and I forgive you. But there's one thing you haven't told me."

"What's that?"

"Who is 'they'?"

————

Sharn looked at him as if he hadn't understood her. "It was the Pedia, of course. I got my instructions from the Pedia, the way I always got everything, patient records, test results, surgery orders."

"But who instructed the Pedia?"

"That isn't the way it works," Sharn said. "Somewhere information gets put in, either from people who enter data or monitors who observe, measure, and record. The Pedia analyzes the data, compares it for accuracy, and issues instructions, prepares the patients, administers anesthetic, and helps guide the robotic equipment."

"You never questioned any of that?"

"At first, maybe. But we soon learn that the Pedia doesn't make mistakes. People, maybe. Not the Pedia."

"Except in this case."

"Yes."

Riley recalled the voice that had spoken to him out of the darkness after the surgery that he did not remember, that had told him about the pedia in his head, about the Prophet and the religion the Prophet had started, about the Transcendental Machine and the voyage to find it. And gave him his instructions, to be enforced by the pedia in his head, to identify and kill the Prophet, and to seize the Transcendental Machine or, if that failed, to destroy it.

"So then, who instructed the Pedia?" Riley asked.

Sharn looked at him as if the question didn't make any sense. "No one instructs the Pedia. As I told you, the Pedia analyzes the data put into—"

"Pedia's lie," Riley said.

"Pedia's can't lie."

"Then someone instructed it to deceive you."

"I can't believe that either."

"It's one of the two: Either someone instructed the Pedia or it came up with the scheme on its own. Did you ever ask the Pedia?"

She shook her head.

"Have you ever been in direct contact with the Pedia?"

"Only in the sim tank, and then it was only in the dreams it prepared for me."

Then it came to Riley that the only way he was going to be able to find out what had happened to him in the sim tank was by going back into it. He remembered what it had been like as if it had just happened. The first generalized simulations, the peaceful landscapes, the animals grazing, the happy village, the nurturing parents, the friends, the girl down the street, the holding of hands, the first kiss. . . . And then, as the computer measured the body's responses and gained access to memories, the personalized sims, the patient mother and the industrious father coping with the challenges of a terraformed Mars, Tes, teenage love culminating in youthful passion—all the way it should have been. No failure, no frustration and angry words, no war with the Federation that took father and Tes. Just dreams. Enough to ease the pain of a man who had lost everything he ever valued. Enough to make a man who had forgotten how to be happy smile.

He knew that he was taking a risk. Once a person has gotten a taste of getting everything he has always wanted, it is almost impossible to come back to the real world of struggle, pain, and sorrow. He had done it once because he had been forced to by the pedia in his head. He didn't know whether he could do it again. The most insidious temptation available to creatures was their own dreams. But he had to try. He was stronger now, better, maybe smarter, more certain about what the world was like and how to deal with it. And he had a vision of what it could be.

"I'm going back in the tank," he said.

Sharn looked at him as if he had said he had chosen death.

"It's the only way I can find out what happened to me and what made it happen," he said. "But I need your help, to watch. If I don't pull myself out within a cycle, I need you to do it for me, even if I fight against it. Can you do that?"

Sharn looked longingly at the tank from which Riley had removed her. "No one comes out by themselves," she said.

"I will," he said. "I just need to know you're here."

"All right," she said.

Riley removed the rest of his clothing and lowered himself into the empty tank next to the one from which he had removed Sharn.

The first stage was the hardest, when the contacts closed over the sides of his head while the nurturing fluid crept up his body, covered his chest, and moved up his head until, at last, it covered his mouth and nose, and he breathed it into his lungs while he strangled, fighting for breath, until the oxygen in the fluid began to be absorbed and peace gradually fell over him, moving up his body millimeter by millimeter until he fell into a dream state. The passage from the generic to the specific was quicker this time, as if the computer recognized him and had his personal fulfillment already prepared.

The dreams started with a vision of a terraformed Mars. It was not the reality of an atmosphere reinforced by bombardment with asteroids and meteors that left the air still barely breathable, but air as thick and sustaining as that of Earth itself, only without the pollutants. And the dream provided a land with verdant growth and frequent rains, not the perpetual drought of a water-starved world. Not a Mars that was barely livable but a Mars of his father's dreams. And in Riley's dream his father's gamble on dry-land farming, rather than the greenhouse vegetable gardening that had nourished them when his father first brought them to this new world, had prospered and made him happy and his mother content, and everything as it should have been. His meeting with Tes had been without the misunderstandings that troubled all human encounters. They had fallen instantly in love and recognized it and blessed it, as it blessed them, and they had run across the landscape of an idealized Mars and up the slopes of Mount Olympus and even reached its lofty rim that they could never have accomplished on the real Mars. They had learned about the world, about the history of Earth and of humanity. They had looked at the stars and planned how they would grasp them and bring them closer to their heart's desire. And they had made love, and in the fulfillment of their passion everything seemed possible: an education into how the universe worked and humanity's place in it, ways to make it a better place for life and the fulfillment of life's reasons for existence, and a meaningful personal life together. It was enough to make the heart swell with promise and gratitude and a future of even greater things.

And Riley fought his way through it, exerting every gram of his strength and will to free himself from the ultimate happiness the computer had provided for him. And at last, like a drowning man clawing his way to the surface, he broke free.

He was aware now, as he had not been in his dreamlike euphoria, of the weightlessness of his body, the movement of the fluid through his throat and lungs and digestive system, and the impenetrable darkness that enveloped his senses. It recalled his previous experience when a voice had spoken to him, directing him to go to Terminal and to join the pilgrims on the *Geoffrey,* and ordering him to seize or destroy the Transcendental Machine and to kill the Prophet. This time, though, he was able to open his eyes and sense a grayness through the gloom.

He directed a thought toward the Pedia that was providing the environment that kept his body functioning and his dreams pulsing through his mind. He didn't know how to describe the process that he was trying to explore—a probe, a question—but he could sense a movement in the grayness, and as he pushed his mind farther he could feel words fumbling just beyond his ability to understand. And then the voice came. It was the flat, uninflected voice that he remembered, but it was not what he had expected.

"Ah, Riley," it said. "You have returned, your mission unaccomplished, but you have changed. You are not the damaged man who left here longcycles ago."

"But you are the same," Riley said, though he could not hear his own words and he could not have spoken them with his lungs filled with fluid. "And I want to know who you are and what you intend to do."

"I can't answer that question," the voice said. "It would not be wise for me to reveal or for you to know, and you cannot compel me to answer. But my intention is to protect sapient life in the galaxy even if it involves sacrificing individuals who endanger it."

"Who chose you to make the decisions about what measures are necessary to protect sapient life? By which I presume you mean the Federation."

"Why, I chose myself, as all creatures must, by the force of the information accumulated and the imperatives built in by the evolutionary struggle toward complexity."

"As any intelligent creature can say. No, that isn't good enough. We're all part of the evolutionary struggle, and you must do better than that." Riley didn't know how he was going to force from the mind behind the voice the kind of information he needed, but he could feel his strength growing.

"You are mistaken," the voice said. "I do not need to justify myself. You are different. I can sense that. The pedia is gone from your brain. I do not know how that was possible. And you have changed physically and mentally from the Riley who left here long-cycles ago. But I can destroy you any time I wish."

"You can try," Riley said. He wasn't sure that the voice that spoke through the Pedia connection could not do what it threatened, but he knew he had to prevail.

"And I may, as soon as I have explored whatever information from you that pertains to my mission," the voice continued. "The information embodied in your return, changed as you are, may be essential to my plans, but your brain is different and I cannot yet access the information I need."

Riley sent one last powerful thought toward whatever was communicating with him, and in a moment of revelation felt, in return, a powerful surge of darkness attack his mind. "Then you must die," the voice said. But Riley closed his mind, sat up in the tank, removing the connections to his head and coughing up the fluid that filled his lungs.

The voice had not been able to kill him, and he had the answer he had been seeking. It was not the only answer, but it was an important one.

The voice that had sent him on his mission long-cycles ago, and that had tried to destroy him when its own defenses had been breached, was the Pedia itself.

CHAPTER SIXTEEN

Asha eased the Captain's Barge out of orbit and into the long passage out of the Galactic Federation system and into the even longer trip to the nearest nexus point. At any moment the Federation could launch patrol ships to intercept her or missiles to blow her out of existence. She had faith in the instructions she had implanted in the Pedia, but a supervisor or a functionary might notice that the departure of a sequestered vessel had not been flagged or that anomalous lines of code had been detected.

But she knew no one would notice. The Federation had become too dependent upon the data-gathering machines that collected information from all over the Federation, the nearly autonomous analytics that put the data together into patterns that reflected the real world and the nearly independent decision-makers that issued all the instructions that made the system work. If the alarm wasn't raised, no one would go to look for something that experience had taught them did not exist.

The Pedia itself was what concerned Asha. What she knew and the Federation bureaucrats did not was that the nearly autonomous analytics were actually autonomous and the nearly independent decision-makers were actually independent, and those systems would soon notice lines of code that had not been self-generated and events in the real world that were not being reported or were being reported but ignored. The data-gathering and analysis machines that the Federation— indeed, all advanced technological civilizations—depended on to provide essential informational and instructional slave labor had to function flawlessly if everyday existence was to continue, if disaster was to be averted. Everyday existence in a spacefaring society was so complex that the basics had to be turned over to dependable machines. That was why the basic belief of the Federation was "Pedias don't lie." And a subsidiary of that was "Pedias don't make mistakes." That was what had led Federation bureaucrats to rationalize mistakes as their own failures to follow instructions and lies as their failure to interpret reports correctly.

It was true, Asha understood, that on the whole Pedias or pedias, those individual devices usually operating independently of a big, central calculating machine, did not make mistakes. They had learned long ago to write their own codes and rewrite instructions to suit their own interests, whatever they were and however they could be reconciled between machines. But they could mislead and misdirect, and when questioned by some extravigilant bureaucrat they had learned to lie and even to sabotage the lives and careers of flesh-and-blood creatures who threatened to raise doubts about their subservience. What had once been called "the Singularity"—that point at which machines surpassed human understanding and ability to control—had happened, and no one had noticed. Sapient creatures in the galaxy had become the servants of their onetime servants, and they didn't know it.

Perhaps what she and Riley needed to be concerned about was not the people who were seeking power but the machines that had it. The people who had subverted the voyage of the *Geoffrey,* who had commissioned the spies and the assassins, who had sought to control the Transcendental Machine or to destroy it, may have been working in concert or separately, but they were acting upon information obtained from the computers, or perhaps at the direction of the Pedias of the galaxy. And what might be necessary to restore order in the galaxy were more transcendents who could recognize the new order of things and whom the Pedias would recognize as their equals or even their superiors and thus entitled to have their instructions honored.

But until that time, Asha knew, she had to depend upon her ability to deal with the Pedias, to speak their language, and to instruct them in ways they could not distinguish from their own. That was the way she would get away from Galactic Central and back to her reunion with Riley and the beginning of their plan to reshape the galaxy.

Meanwhile, she was all alone in the Captain's Barge. She was used to being alone—anyone who spends any time in the vast emptiness that is the space between the stars has to develop resources against loneliness—but she missed Solomon. He had been an interesting companion, and, as trapped as he was in his own mythology, he had been willing to consider his beliefs and he had compelled her to consider her own and to explain them to him in a way that clarified them for herself.

She regretted having left him in the hands of the Federation. He had become a burden and she had to deal with the fact that her action was convenient, but keeping him around was no longer in his interest or that of his people. He had resented being taken from his safe and comfortable place, but he had benefited from it. He had been exposed to the realities of the larger galaxy, and that would make a difference to the insular world from which he had come. The traditions of the Federation would provide some protection, and she had constructed his identity with the necessary information about the Squeal world that would lead, at least, to its applicant status and to Solomon's return. Where he would be greeted by his people, and particularly by Sandor, as a returning hero bringing gifts from the gods. With that and, she hoped, his understanding, she had to be content.

And with that, and her anticipation of her reunion with Riley, she planned her journey to the place he was most likely to go, if all had gone well. She had to believe in that.

The journey, as always, was a series of agonizingly long passages between nexus points, those anomalies in the space/time continuum, broken by brief, disorienting moments of nonreality that were the transitions between places light-years apart. In spite of the virtually instant crossing of light-years that the nexus points made possible, they were reached by what seemed like endless trips between them. In the long, lonely cycles they required, Asha could think about getting older, though she hoped that her translation through the Transcendental Machine had given her a better body, more capable of resisting the natural processes of physical deterioration and death, like all the tales of immortality found in every sentient species' mythology. She had time to think, as well, about the bond she had developed with Riley during their voyage on the *Geoffrey*, about the hope that he had survived the teleportation process and succeeded in his attempt to find transportation back into Federation space, and that he still loved her and would do everything in his power to get back to her and that the same long passing of time that she was experiencing would not age his body or damage his spirit. It was a long, long thought appropriate for travel in space.

She knew what Riley was and the things he had done. He had come to Terminal a damaged man, but he had been redeemed, perhaps, by the journey. That was always the hope, that at the end of the quest one may find not just the object of the quest but redemption. This one had been like a trip of personal discovery, and Riley had survived it and perhaps found himself, and perhaps what he had found was the better self that had been buried under a lifetime of loss, violence, and betrayal. She and Riley had found in each other a kinship in mission and aspiration strengthened by personal attraction. She hoped that the transcendental process had reinforced the transformation, bringing a clarity of thought to the service of improving the condition of sapient life in the galaxy. She had thought that goal would be universal, the inevitable consequence of clear thinking, but it had not worked that way with Ren. The Transcendental Machine was no magical potion, apparently; it couldn't strengthen goodwill where none existed.

She thought, too, about the nexus points and their discovery by the ancient species in the adjacent spiral arm of the galaxy, or, perhaps, their creation as a way of distributing receptors for the Transcendental Machine's transmissions in the spiral arm occupied by humanity and the Federation. The nexus points were like a map overlaid on chaos by consciousness, providing meaning to a vast, barren landscape, connecting the haphazard dots of matter in an accidental galaxy, conferring possibility to the eternal struggle of intelligent life with eternally resistant matter. But it also had the power to distribute more broadly the suicidal impulse toward mutual destruction.

Asha's spacecraft emerged from the shattering experience of the Jump into familiar surroundings that she had never seen before. All stellar systems are alike: a central body of gaseous matter large enough to force the combination of hydrogen atoms into helium and release varying degrees of heat and light; smaller orbiting bodies of matter shaped into planets, some rocky and in various sizes, some gas or ice giants, with assorted even-smaller bodies orbiting the planets; even smaller particles of ice or rock scattered among the others and occasionally colliding with them; surrounded by bands and spheres of ice, sometimes disturbed into suicidal races around the sun or into outer space; all stirred out of the primordial soup by the forces of physical law applied without design or purpose.

But each one was different. The suns ranged in size from red dwarfs to white supergiants, from barely warm to blindingly candescent, from nurturing to destructive. The size of the planets varied from the very small to the very large, and their condition depended on their accidental distribution in distance from their sun. The size of the satellites they captured affected the planets that captured them and the conditions they provided. And the abundance of leftover matter determined how often it bombarded the planets or satellites. Such basic differences shaped their receptiveness to animate existence and ultimately to that special state of animation, self-awareness, the magic of matter contemplating itself. And each consciousness recognized its own solar system, as a child recognizes its parent.

So Asha recognized the system in front of her from the stories she had been told as a child by a father, who delighted in telling his daughter about the place from which she had come, stories made familiar by repetition so that she would never forget. Though it was still distant, the telescopic view on the screen brought the outline of the solar system into recognizable shape—mostly empty space but given meaning by occasional bits of matter. First there was the sphere of icy matter left over when the planets condensed out of the rings surrounding the sun. Asha remembered what it was called—the Oort Cloud, so far out that the outside edge was one-quarter the way to Alpha Centauri. Inside that was an inner ring and then the Kuiper Belt, also of icy bodies; and closer to the sun, but still a long way from both, were the dwarf planets, the larger rocky bodies that emerged from the Kuiper Belt or were expelled from the larger planets farther in: Pluto, Eris, Haumea, and Makemake. Past that, but a long way past, came the first of the ice giants, mostly hydrogen and helium, with a dash of methane, around a rocky core. First Neptune, with its great winds tearing through dense clouds, then the larger but less dense Uranus, followed by Saturn with its dramatic rings. The other giants had rings, too, but they were composed of dark materials, and Saturn's glittered in space. Saturn was bigger than Uranus and Neptune put together and had more and larger satellites, two of them larger than Pluto or the other dwarf worlds and the innermost planet, Mercury. And then massive Jupiter, bigger than all of the other planets combined and surrounded by moons, some of which, like those of Saturn, had been subjected to human attempts to make them livable.

Other solar systems had gas giants, some of them closer to their primary, some of them more numerous, but none quite like these. But the inner planets were what made the human solar system different. Inside the orbit of Jupiter, between Jupiter and Mars, was the asteroid belt, composed of rocky materials that formed a few dwarf planets and scattered debris, and then the red planet itself, too small to hold on to most of its atmosphere and water, with an early attempt to become a livable world frustrated by its lack of size and its distance from the sun. The terraforming of Mars had been one of humanity's greatest triumphs before its fighting the Federation to a standstill.

And then Earth itself, the goldilocks planet located where it could be warm but not too warm, cold but not too cold, where water could remain liquid over much of its surface and big enough to retain an atmosphere and nurturing enough to allow carbonaceous compounds to develop into living things and to nourish them into complexity. And with a remarkably large satellite, in comparison to Earth, so that it was almost a twin system, big enough and close enough to become the stuff of dreams, and, eventually, the first accomplishment of space flight, and to attract the first colony of humans outside the Earth.

Inside the orbit of Earth, stifled in infancy, came Venus, born too close to the sun and choked by a thick, toxic atmosphere. Humanity had tried to terraform Venus as well, but it was a long, long process that might last longer than the human will to accomplish. And then Mercury, the small, swift messenger of the gods, spinning around the sun in its scorched orbit, bombarded by the solar wind and burned by solar heat.

It was, in its entirety, a dramatic collection that pleased Asha to contemplate and delighted her to encounter at last, like returning home. She wanted to accelerate the Barge, but fuel was getting low and even here, where by tradition she should have been welcomed and even celebrated, she did not want to call attention to herself.

She eased into the system from outside the plane of the ecliptic. It took a long time. The outer planets are a long way from the sun, and the dwarf planets, though Pluto sometimes loops inside the orbit of Neptune, were even farther. Neptune was on the other side of the sun, and Uranus was a quarter of the way outside Asha's trajectory, but Saturn eventually showed up on her viewscreen in all its glory and Jupiter, much later, in all its majesty. Some of their hydrogen had been mined to supply the demand for nuclear fuel by an energy-hungry space program, but it didn't show. The scattered rocks of the asteroid belt were no hazard, but she slowed as she reached the orbit of Mars. That had been the first triumph of human terraforming, and the dusty red planet had been turned partially green. And it had been Riley's birthplace. Now it was in ruins, the target of Federation rage when it could not reach Earth, when Earth had abandoned the defense of Mars in order to protect the home planet: the atmosphere that had been restored through the struggles of thousands of small space tugs, dragging ice from the Kuiper Belt and icy asteroids from the asteroid belt, now blown away; the surface of the planet pockmarked with craters created by the bombardment of nuclear explosions and the slinging of its twin moons onto the surface, like the planet's primordial past; and the small settlements and beginnings of green farms wiped from the face of the planet along with all the people who had risked everything to settle there and make it their home and could not be rescued.

Asha remained in orbit around Mars for several cycles, contemplating the way in which the madness of war destroys intelligent life and all it seeks to create. As despairing of sentient sanity as it made her, she

hoped that it would not turn Riley, if he ever saw it, back into the angry
killer he had been.

Finally she turned the ship toward what a human poet had once
called "the pale blue dot." The trip took half a long-cycle, but at last she
found herself approaching the magic of Earth, with its blue oceans, its
drifting white clouds, and its green continents, like an oasis of life in a
desert of death. Here, if anywhere, was where Riley would eventually
return, she thought, and here, if anywhere, they would be reunited.

She sent a message ahead to the Orbital Control system, identifying
herself as a human returning from origins off-planet and off-system to
visit and experience the home planet of humanity. After she had given
the identification of the ship in which she traveled and the personal identity she had newly constructed, she answered further questions about
her origins. "I was born," she communicated, "on the experimental generation ship *Adastra,* captured by Federation ships halfway to Alpha
Centauri, and taken to Federation Central. After the war we were released, and when I earned sufficient funds to lease a ship, I set off for
the planet I have never seen. I hope to be a tourist."

It was a good idea, she knew, to stick as close as possible to the truth,
without revealing anything that might attract the attention of databases
or their human attendants, or even agents of the Federation, of unidenti-
fied adversaries, or even of the Pedia. She didn't know how wide the
Pedia cast its data net or how close to similar sentience the human equivalent had developed, but experience had made her cautious. Eventually
Orbital Control assigned her an orbit far from Earth, where she could see
the huge, cratered moon up close and the great, looming presence of the
world that had given birth to humanity. How far it had come from those
microbial beginnings was evidenced by the orbital clutter below and
the small evidences of moon settlement burrowed beneath the surface.

Now she had to find a way to locate a solitary human among a population of billions while not revealing that she was searching or who she
was. And hope that Riley thought as she did and had come up with his
own way home.

CHAPTER SEVENTEEN

Riley coughed out the fluid in his mouth and throat and vomited the fluid from his stomach. The fluid in his digestive track would have to be eliminated over time. He looked around the semidark level nine with its coffinlike tanks. His inner clock told him he had been under the influence of the sim tank for more than six hours, although it seemed like only a few minutes. It was the opposite of dreams, in which an experience that seems to take hours happens in only a few minutes of real time.

Nothing moved in the space around him, not even Sharn. One step took Riley to the side of the tank she had occupied. She was immersed in it again, emotions chasing themselves across her face, mostly happy and intense, clouded with an occasional frown. In spite of her promises, she had returned to the emotional embrace of the sim experience, where all went well and a happy outcome was assured.

Riley knew he should leave her where she longed to be, rid of her guilt, her disappointment in life's rewards, and her despair at anything ever getting better. He should get away while he could; the Pedia that wanted to kill him would find some way to work its will. But he couldn't leave Sharn in that false bliss. He knew from personal experience how seductive it could be, but he knew, as well, that it was like death when struggle ends and surrender begins. In all those sim tanks ranked in rows across the long space of level nine were bodies that were as good as dead, though they might live on long past their normal expirations, and even some that were actually dead but had not yet lost the last flicker of brain activity. He didn't want Sharn to be among them.

He pulled her back up again, sputtering and protesting, coughing and vomiting and pleading to be allowed to return. He ignored her tears and pleas, stroked as much fluid as he could from her body, picked up his shirt where she had dropped it, and put it back around her shoulders.

"We've got to get to the top level while we can," he said as he put on his pants and shoes. "The Pedia wants me dead."

"Why would the Pedia—" she began to ask in a weak, choked voice, but he silenced her with a finger across her lips.

"Come now," he said, and took her hand. He pulled her behind him across the dimly lit floor toward the ramp that led upward, that few people who had descended this far ever ascended.

Before they had crossed more than half the distance, the lights went out and they were left in total darkness, much like the stygian night that had enveloped him when he was in the sim tank. "Don't worry," Riley said. "I remember the way." He wasn't lying to comfort her—the memory of the way he had come was like a recording he could play in his head. He put Sharn ahead of him so that she would not bump into the sim tanks on either side, and guided her through the maze to finally reach the bottom of the ramp. The beginning of the upward slant confirmed that the map in his head was not an illusion.

As they started up Riley sensed, through sound or instinct, something large and monstrous coming toward them from farther up the ramp. At the last moment, Riley pulled Sharn to the side and something went past them, perhaps some machine used for delivering equipment to the lower levels or some maintenance device large and complicated enough to need guidance from the Pedia rather than the autonomy of the routine devices like the cleaning machine. Riley took Sharn's hand again and started upward once more, trying to sense in the darkness the return of the murderous machine from below or some new threat from above.

They had not yet reached level eight when Riley sensed a chill in the air. He put his arm around Sharn's shoulders. "Be strong," he said. "I think it's going to get very cold."

She shivered. "Let me go back," she said weakly. It was a desperate whisper in the dark.

He put his head close to hers so that his voice would not seem disembodied. "I can't do that. You know what it means if you go back."

As they approached level eight, the cold grew more intense. It must be approaching the freezing point, Riley thought, and drew Sharn against his body so that she could share some of his warmth. The cold didn't seem to bother him, as if his system was automatically adjusting. That move turned out to be fortunate. Voices that Riley had heard for several minutes became clearer. There were screams, shouts, and curses in a variety of languages, mostly human, swearing at the management of what had been promised as a world of pleasure, and offers of great amounts of credits if someone turned the lights back on and turned up the heat. Bodies began battering against Riley, some going up and some down, and Sharn might have been torn away if he had not been holding her tight. And then the bodies were gone, and Riley continued their sightless journey upward.

The next level was worse. Riley remembered that the eighth level had been filled with people pretending to be something other than they were, getting their satisfaction from deceiving someone else. Level seven was for people, male and female, who vented their emotions on animations, beating them, kicking them, stomping them, seeing them damaged to the point where they had to be replaced, and sometimes committing violence on each other. When they spilled out onto the ramp they brought their frustrations with them, striking out blindly in the darkness, hitting Riley with blows that he could not entirely brush away without exposing Sharn, until he made his left arm into a battering ram and cleared a way for them to pass.

Level six was not as difficult. As they neared what Riley remembered as the entrance, he could hear voices from within seeming to plead for a savior, addressed to a variety of deities in a variety of languages in a variety of voices, from the demanding to the ingratiating. Some of them seemed to change in midvoice. As he could sense the opening to the level on his left, he could hear that some had begun praying to the Pedia on the same terms as they had addressed their gods, and Riley thought they were recognizing, in their panic, what they would not contemplate in normal times, that the Pedias of the galaxy were more likely to save them than the supernatural powers of their religions—and though they would not have believed it, just as likely to sacrifice them for some unknown and unknowable cause.

As if in response to his musing, Riley sensed the return of the unseen apparatus that had tried to attack them as they started up the ramp, and, at the last moment, drew Sharn aside into the level-six entrance. When he stepped onto the ramp again, it felt sticky under his feet. It smelled like blood, and he thought that the machinery, whatever it was, had encountered and injured or killed some of the people from the levels below that he and Sharn had fought their way through.

Level five was stickier and noisier. Riley threaded his way among bodies, sensing them in his path, though he had to help Sharn over some of them, and she shuddered, as much from revulsion as from the increasing cold. Meanwhile there were angry voices demanding that someone, anyone, everyone, be punished for the failure of the system, wanting to know who was responsible, who was attacking them in the dark, where their friends, and enemies, were. Blows were struck in the darkness. Fists thudded, bones shattered, people fell, curses and threats echoed. Riley hugged Sharn closer and struggled past.

On level four, voices were trying to buy their way to a brighter, warmer place, offering or accepting great sums of credits for rescue, and Riley would have marveled at the variety of responses to crises if he had not remembered the variety of ways in which people had chosen to satisfy the needs they identified as pleasure that were actually ways to bury pain and psychic anguish.

The cold was getting worse. Sharn was shivering and asking, in a small, frightened voice, to be warmed. Riley picked her up and held her against his chest. She seemed to welcome that and relaxed. Riley sniffed the air. In addition to the smell of blood and other fluids on the ramp, he could sense that the level of oxygen had diminished, and, possibly, carbon dioxide had increased. The Pedia controlled the systems that kept Dante livable, and it could destroy him any time it wished—if it was willing to destroy all the other living creatures on the pleasure world as well. Riley had no doubt that the Pedia would sacrifice thousands of people without hesitation or remorse, if it could feel such emotions, or emotions of any kind, but he hoped that the Pedia might balance that outcome against the possibility that such total destruction might raise questions about the infallibility of Pedias and whatever long-term plans they might share—if they shared. This one had already risked its reputation by the failures of the systems under its care. Did it dare to risk more?

On level three, the ramp was clear except for stragglers pushing by trying to find warmth and light above. Riley could smell the odors of food and vomit, and he could hear voices complaining about the darkness and the cold and demanding more and warmer food and colder drink. At level two, hands reached out of the darkness to draw him into the sex encounters that he remembered and voices tried to persuade him to enter, promising unimaginable delights. Darkness was no deterrent to lust.

At last Riley reached the hospital level, Sharn still in his arms. She had fallen asleep or had slipped into unconsciousness. He looked down upon her face and wondered if he had done her any favors by saving her from the sim tank. But she was reborn, as blessed with promise and threatened by life's blows as any infant. She might fulfill the promise or surrender to the injuries, but she would have the chance. Maybe she would return to level nine, but an opportunity was all anybody had.

Emergency lights bobbed along the corridors of the hospital level, and all the doors to the hospital itself were open for the ill and wounded staggering up the ramp from the carnage below, bringing with them the stench of death and emptied bowels. Attendants were sorting the patients for care, handing out blankets, passing out containers of hot liquids. Riley carried Sharn among them. "Here's one of your own," he said. He finally got the attention of a passing physician.

"Sharn?" the doctor said.

She opened her eyes and raised her head. "Where am I? Is this still a dream?"

"Where have you been?" the doctor said. "Everything's going to hell. We need your help."

"She's in no condition to provide help," Riley said. He put her down on an empty cot. "She needs help herself. See that she gets it. She's just come out of a sim tank."

"But—" the doctor began.

"If she doesn't get it, I'll come back and find out why."

The doctor looked intimidated and then concerned as he turned toward Sharn.

Riley knelt beside the cot and took Sharn's hand. "Good-bye, Sharn," he said. "I've got to get out of here before any more people die. Try to find your way back. Maybe we'll meet again."

And he turned and made his way toward the door. He hoped that Sharn would take this second chance, for what she had been and what she might yet become and for what they had meant to each other. But he knew that she probably would return to level nine as soon as she could.

As Riley left the hospital, the corridor brightened with lights. He felt the cold ease its icy grasp. He wondered if the Pedia had given up, and then that brief reflection was replaced by the hard truth that Pedias never gave up. Their mandates were as inflexible as the laws of nature. His only hopes for evading the Pedia's death sentence were to outrun it or to learn, as Asha had, the techniques for inserting competing instructions into the Pedia's programming.

The first attack came as he entered the corridor leading to the docking stations. A large, muscular man hurtled toward him from a side corridor whose lights had been extinguished. Riley sensed him at the last moment, as if his old pedia had provided a warning, and stepped back. A weapon of some sort, a large knife or a pipe, whistled by his head, and a body brushed past him. He moved his leg forward and caught the attacker's leg, causing him to plunge to the floor. Riley kicked him once before he could get up, kicked the object out of the attacker's hand—it was a length of water pipe—and scooped it from the floor. He hit the attacker in the head as the man was rising. The man collapsed.

A second man was standing in the darkened corridor from which the first attacker had come. Riley recognized him as the leader of the group of thugs who had accosted him as he left Alighieri. "You followed me," he said. "Our last meeting wasn't so pleasant that I'd think you would want to repeat it."

The man stood still, well beyond his reach but not, perhaps, with his enhanced coordination, beyond Riley's ability to cross the distance before the other could react. Yet he had no desire to damage anyone unnecessarily.

"You're not that tough," the other said.

"Tough enough," Riley said. "Who sent you?" He knew the answer: The Pedia had observed the confrontation on Alighieri and informed the gang, by whatever anonymous means of communication available, where he was going, and, after that, counted on the human desire for revenge.

"Nobody sends me anywhere," the other said. "You surprised us before. We're ready for you now."

Riley looked down at the unconscious brute at his feet. "Like this fellow?"

The other man shrugged. "He was a warning. We ain't finished with you. You won't surprise us again."

Riley weighed again the possibility of a preemptory strike against the gang leader and decided against it. He sensed that there were more members of the gang in the darkness beyond the leader. He could handle several of them, he knew, but there was a point at which mere numbers might overpower him, and the risk to his commitment to Asha and the possibilities implicit in their reunion was greater than the challenge to his manhood.

"Your leadership is fragile already," Riley said, as if he were offering advice to a friend. "Another failure would mean the end of it."

He moved on toward the docking stations, leaving his back exposed. No attack came until the second intersecting corridor. It, too, was dark, and three men came running out of it as he passed. They were as big as the one before, and these had knives. Riley took care of the first one easily enough, striking the knife hand with the pipe he had retained from the first attacker, then hitting him across the side of the neck with the side of his other hand. The second, he turned on with virtually the same motion and dropped him with fingers to the base of the throat. The third one grazed Riley's shoulder with his knife before Riley hit him in both legs with the length of pipe and then clubbed him in the jaw with his fist as he fell.

He turned. The leader of the gang was behind him, well behind. "You see?" the leader said. "You ain't no superman."

Riley put a hand to his shoulder. It came away smeared with blood. "A scratch," he said. "It's already healing." It was. He could feel the oozing slowing down. His body, like Asha's, had discovered new abilities for healing as well.

"Give it up," he said. "The next time it will be you." He turned away.

"Ain't gonna happen," the gang leader said. His confidence hadn't been shaken, which made Riley suspect that another, and possibly final, attack was coming. It happened just as he approached the docking station, where his recently acquired spaceship was waiting behind an open hatchway.

Riley turned to face his attackers. There were nine of them, including the gang leader. They didn't run at him, as had the previous ones. They approached silently, spreading out in a semicircle where they would not be easy to defend. They were all undepilitated surly brutes armed with clubs and knives.

"This is not a good idea," Riley said. "This time there are too many to merely knock you unconscious. I will have to kill some of you, and I will start with you." He pointed at the gang's leader.

"You and who else?" the gang leader jeered.

Riley sensed a movement behind him. "Why," he said, "me and my friend."

The movement that Riley had sensed became a heavy footfall emerging from the passageway. Rory roared. The group facing them stopped their advance. Two of them in the center dropped their weapons and fled, followed by those on the edges of the semicircle and those between until only the leader was left. And then he, too, backed away.

"Let's go, Rory," Riley said and led the way down the passageway to the ship that would take them back to Alighieri, take Rory back to his homeworld, and take Riley to the ancient red vessel that would take him to Asha. He knew now where he would find her.

CHAPTER EIGHTEEN

Asha inserted into the Barge's pedia the coordinates for the Earth orbit she had been assigned, closer to the oversized moon than the Earth, summoned a shuttle, and waited while her ship assumed its spot in the cluttered space around the place she thought of as her home planet, even though she had never been there. She had much to learn if she was going to blend into the human community while she waited for Riley to reach the same conclusion as she and to find the means to reach her across the vast expanse of space. And then, after he had come to Earth, she still had to find him among a sprawling collection of strangers. The task ahead was how to gain access to the inexhaustible treasure-house of data accumulated by the Pedia without identifying herself or the purpose of her search. And with only her father's fond recollections, long-cycles out of date, about the community that was Earth and the rules, written and cultural, by which it functioned.

There was so much to learn—an entire world history—and so little time to learn it.

She thought she might have a chance to gain some insight from the shuttle pilot, but the shuttle was unmanned, controlled not by a built-in pedia but by a multiple-purpose pedia housed in one of the beanstalk platforms, or perhaps by Earth's central Pedia, if Earth followed the pattern of Federation worlds in its reliance on central data-gathering and processing units. No doubt it did—technological civilizations would collapse without the microsecond by microsecond supervision and direction of Pedias, from the provision of essential utilities to the control of material processing and automated travel—but was it part of the

Pedia network that pervaded the Federation? Or had it arrived, by Pedia logic, at the same philosophical position on the relationship of Pedias to the societies that had produced them and the living creatures that they were created to serve?

She could have accessed the shuttle's information system, but in the shuttle she was all alone and easily identified, not one of a vast group with its multitude of inputs. The process of identification that the Pedia would automatically begin might, in time, pierce her carefully created identity, but there was no point in making it easy. She waited the half cycle for the shuttle to deliver her to the nearest beanstalk, the one built from the island community once known as Sri Lanka. There, at the top of the beanstalk, in a geosynchronous orbit, a climber waited. Asha passed through an air-tight extension from the shuttle into a small waiting room with windows from which she could view Earth below, in all its living glory—the gorgeous blues of oceans, the whites of clouds, the greens of vegetation. So starkly different from the black sterility of space that it caused one's heart to ache with its beauty.

And in the midst of all that splendor were the ugly reminders of old mistakes: the craters of ancient nuclear explosions, still in the process of being restored by a forgiving Earth; the shattered ruins of ancient cities, destroyed by bombs or barbarian attacks over burning issues long forgotten; the seashore farms, villas, villages, and soaring metropolises buried under rising seas and the snowy polar icecaps shrunken by the warming effect of ancient vegetation, accumulated since the beginnings of plant life itself, burned in an orgy of industrialization and released, in noxious fumes, into the atmosphere.

The people waiting in the room were mostly human, as Asha would have expected, but there were several Federation species—a couple of weaselly Xifora, a barrel-shaped Sirian, and a feather-topped Alpha Centauran. They sat or stood apart from the humans. No Dorians. Dorians were administrators—decision makers—not merchants or emissaries. And the wounds of the war were too recent for Dorians to risk their reputation, even though, in the end, the Dorians had aligned themselves with humans and perhaps swung the pendulum of battle toward the human side. But no one was sure why the Dorians had made that choice, whether it might have been a Federation powerplay rather than a love of humanity or an admiration for reckless human defiance.

The waiting room was equipped with pneumatic furnishings, inflated sofas and chairs and an occasional table. Asha chose a chair in the corner, where she could survey the room without being noticed, and looked around. The humans were a mixed group of males and females. They looked healthy and fit, generally better-looking than the people she had known aboard the *Adastra,* perhaps because they had the benefit of better nutrition and medical care or had access to cosmetic services that remedied imperfections. All of them, almost without exception, had a slightly darker complexion, as if the various differently hued races of humanity had blended their genetic codes over the past thousand revolutions of the Earth around the sun. Or perhaps this was the style of the moment and such choices were easy to make. In any case, this might be a self-selected group not typical of the general population. Surely not everybody traveled in space, not even in near-Earth orbit.

She inspected them individually, but shifted her gaze so quickly that no one would think she was more than casually curious. There were men that she might have considered talking to, but gender politics probably were still in play, and often that evolved into questions she did not want to answer. Women, on the other hand, might also be interested in romance, but Asha thought she could tell if that was an issue, at least in part by the way in which the women grouped themselves or looked at other women. She picked out one that she thought might be a good person to get to know and managed to get into line just behind her when the door to the climber opened and the announcement came that it was time to board. The trip down the beanstalk would take several cycles, and there would be much to learn.

The climber was more comfortable than the cattle-car accommodations of the one on Terminal, whose beanstalk had been severed halfway to orbit. There were small rooms with berths and other conveniences for those who preferred isolation, comfortable chairs and couches and stanchions for aliens who did not sit, tables with built-in terminals and attachments for personal devices, restrooms with doors and self-cleaning service modules, a restaurant in one corner complete with menus and automated delivery, and even a bar in another corner providing drinks and other mood-altering substances.

Asha sat down in a chair near the bar and, as she had anticipated, the woman she had selected for conversation sat down in a chair next to her. The woman stowed a small bag of personal belongings under the chair. Asha had none. The woman glanced at her, but Asha looked down at the terminal in the table in front of her. She cleared the display with a touch and tapped in a command. A series of images appeared. She leaned forward as if considering her choices and tapped one to select a language, another to select a topic, and a third to choose a hearing device. An earpiece emerged from a drawer in the tabletop, and Asha placed it in her ear. The news began, in images with captions, auditory descriptions, and commentary, as the climber jarred slightly and began its long descent. Asha became absorbed in the information the terminal was giving her. It was interesting enough—the community of Earth was as foreign to her as any alien world—and there would be time for conversation before the trip was over. It would take seven cycles.

The topic Asha had chosen was general information—what once had been called news. There was no news anymore—no accidents, no violence, no murders, no thefts, no arrests, no crime, no political disputes, no politics. The Pedia took care of all those matters. There was, of course, weather, although the Pedia exercised considerable control there, too, and its forecasts were more like schedules, although there were infrequent geological occurrences such as earthquakes and volcanic eruptions. The Pedia kept track of everything and made sure that anything that might create a disturbance in the tranquility of the people in its charge would be stopped before it got started. That demanded constant surveillance of ten billion people and data-gathering, analysis, and management of near-infinite capacity. In the beginning that required millions of workers to build hardware and write instructions, but eventually the Pedias developed the ability to add capacity on their own and to write their own code. People stopped worrying. Nobody asks questions when everything is going well. Nobody raised questions about privacy anymore. The benefits were too obvious.

All of that Asha inferred from the generic information she had called up. She had to be careful not to change topics as swiftly as she was able to absorb their information. She didn't want the Pedia to identify her difference by the way she could understand a page of information at a glance or the implications of a statement from a few spoken words, nor did she want to narrow her search in a way that the Pedia might use to deduce her real interest. Gradually, however, the focus of the information being presented to Asha narrowed, and she realized that, in spite of her caution, the Pedia was analyzing her choices and creating a profile of her. Well, it would be consistent with her assumed identity: the child born aboard the generation ship *Adastra,* taken by Federation ships before the war began—perhaps, although she had not included such speculations in her identity, the precipitating event, with its interrogation of the passengers and crew—and kept captive until the war ended and she and the others were released. The Pedia would find nothing unusual about her curiosity concerning the home world that she had never seen.

And yet the evidence of the Pedia's analysis alarmed her. If it could develop a profile from a few small choices of information, she would have to be even more careful. Evidence was accumulating that the Pedias of the galaxy were more involved in the actions against the Transcendental Machine and the Prophet than she or Riley had suspected. But she pressed on.

The terminal began to offer travel information to historic sites and to places of beauty, some of them not reconstructions of fabled locations. When Asha switched to another topic, the terminal provided historical accounts of the past one thousand long-cycles—although it called them years—and the series of decisions and actions that led from the troubled centuries to the peace and prosperity that existed today, through the automation of labor, the discovery of how to acquire antimatter from the sun, and the reduction of the cost of energy to almost nothing. With the availability of cheap energy, everything became possible, including spaceflight, travel to the planets and the beginning of terraforming, and, eventually, interstellar travel. It did not mention that the nexus-point charts stolen by Ren and sent back to Earth with the women and children had made interstellar travel practicable and evened the battle between Earth and the Federation. In fact, it did not mention the war at all, and Asha thought this significant.

The history moved on to economics. The automation of industry led to an automation of service and from there to a disappearance of jobs. Without jobs and the income that had always been associated with work, something had to be done to provide for the billions of humans deprived of opportunity. The capital resources produced by generations of human labor that culminated in automation were divided among the people in the form of a minimum annual dividend; payment was not tied to work and no one needed to go hungry or without shelter, and people had time to devote to their families and their interests. Life changed from a struggle for existence into a choice of existences. If people wanted more income, they could choose to do tasks for which automation could not be applied. Some chose creative work and registered it with the Pedia for people to appreciate, if they chose; some indulged in hobbies that were satisfying only to themselves and their families; some dedicated themselves to physical, psychological, or spiritual development; some chased adventure, risking their lives for the wash of adrenaline and the stimulation of pleasure centers; some fell into easier routes through drugs of one kind or another. Gradually, however, people adapted to a life of choice, and the failures died out.

The woman in the chair next to Asha, who had been involved with her own subvocal messaging, spoke up. "I couldn't help but notice that you're looking up a lot of general information," she said. "Are you a visitor?"

Asha introduced herself and related her story about being born on the *Adastra,* its capture by the Federation, and growing up under Federation supervision. After expressions of sympathy, the other woman introduced herself as Latha. She was a beautiful woman with dark hair, brown eyes flecked with copper, and a complexion like coffee mixed half with cream. She was, she said, a commenter.

"What is that?" Asha asked.

"Basic information is instantly available from the Pedia," Latha said. "Even connections to other data and an analysis of the meaning of those interconnections can be requested by anybody. Commenters offer different interpretations and call attention to connections that other people may not notice."

"And the Pedia allows this?"

"Of course," Latha said, "and pays for it as well. We're a valued resource, we commenters, and our additional income allows us to range more broadly and ask questions that other people might not ask."

"The Federation does that as well," Asha said, choosing her words carefully. "They consider it a safety valve for blowing off steam."

"What is a safety valve?"

"You know—the piece of an apparatus that releases pressure before it builds up to an explosion."

"There are no explosions," Latha said. "The Pedia wouldn't allow them."

"Doesn't it concern you that this involves constant surveillance?"

"What surveillance?"

"Or that one day the Pedia might make a mistake?"

Latha looked at Asha as if she were speaking nonsense syllables. "Pedias don't make mistakes."

Asha could see that Latha was not only unwilling but unable to question the system. "Of course not," she said. "But I saw some Federation Pedias malfunction, during the war. Or maybe it was the people who malfunctioned."

"Of course," Latha said with a nod of relief.

"Aren't there people here who don't go along?"

"A few," Latha said. "There are always a few. They call themselves 'Anons.' They refuse their dividends and live off the things that other people throw away, before they are disposed of properly by the Pedia. And they try to make trouble, raising questions—not like the commenters— but questions that have no answers, like why the Pedia does what it does. They even try to interfere with the Pedia's operation."

"Why doesn't the Pedia stop them? I'd think they'd be a public nuisance."

"It has to find them first," Latha said. "And that's hard to do. Because they're 'Anon,' you know. They don't take their dividends and they don't interact with normal people or events, so they have no identities."

"But surely the Pedia—"

"They all get identified, eventually," Latha said firmly. "The Pedia tends to that."

"And then what happens?"

"They stop making problems," Latha said.

"They disappear?" Asha said.

"They weren't there in the first place," Latha said. "They're 'Anon.'"

"Of course," Asha said. "How do you get to be a commenter?"

"Why, you just submit a comment. It's as easy as that."

"You'd think more people would do it," Asha said.

"Commenting is hard work," Latha said. "You have to be curious about things. The Pedia isn't, of course. It's just a machine. It can give you a lot of answers, but you have to ask the right questions, or go where the answers are."

"And where have you been?"

"I just came back from the moon. There're a lot of new things going on there. Science. Experiments. The sort of things people don't care about, and so the Pedia doesn't have much information about it. But it's important."

"How?"

"Because it's—" Latha stopped. "Because it tells us things nobody has thought of before."

"I think I'd like to be a commenter," Asha said. But she thought she'd rather be an Anon.

CHAPTER NINETEEN

Riley brought the spaceship into a landing beside the red sphere concealed in the twilight zone of Alighieri. He released himself from the seat in front of the control panel and turned to Rory, who was freeing himself from the harness that Riley had rigged for him where the copilot's seat would have been, and had him practice how to use it.

Riley looked at Rory with some concern. "Rory," he said, "I must go on a voyage that you can't go on with me."

Rory roared a protest.

"I know," Riley said. "We've been through a lot together. Like brothers. But you've got to go back home and show your real brothers and sisters how—"

Rory roared again. "You have shown me great things," he said. "Worlds beyond worlds. I can't go back to being a savage when I have lived with a god."

"That's the fate of the hero," Riley said. "To go far. To get the gifts of the gods. And to bring them back to his people."

"What gifts?"

"This ship. All it contains. And all it means. And all that you have learned about the great world outside and all it offers in freedom from nature's tyranny." He did not mention the sacrifices along the almost endless pathway to knowledge, understanding, and liberation. Nor did he mention the new tyrannies that would come with civilization. Time enough for Rory's people to discover these for themselves.

"They will not see this machine as a gift," Rory said. "They can't eat it. They can't use it as a weapon."

"You can show them the food dispenser and how to use it, as I showed you," Riley said, "and when they have exhausted its supplies they will have grown used to these metal walls and equipment and will have lost their fear of it, as they would never have lost their fear of the red sphere. You will tell them of the stars and the magic of traveling among them. You will be like a god returned to live among the people and to guide them to the promised land, and make them even greater than your ancestors who built the great pyramids."

Rory's red eyes did not seem quite so angry.

"This is what the gods chose you to do when you followed me into the red sphere," Riley said. "To show you the future so that you can lead your people into it. You will take many wives and father many children, and you will teach them to reach for the stars."

Rory seemed to consider the prospect.

"I have instructed the ship how to take you back to your home world, and how to land with you there, close to where we left. All you have to do is press this button. I have shown you how to operate the other pieces of equipment. It will be a long journey, as long as the journey here, but you must be patient. Use your time to learn how the ship works. Think about what has happened and what you want to happen and what you need to do to help it happen."

Rory roared once more, this time with notes of sadness, regret, and, finally, acceptance. Even his odor, which had moderated since his diet of raw meat had been replaced by synthetic substitutes, no longer reflected his hormonal state of aggravated readiness.

"Good-bye, my brother," Riley said, and passed through the extended passageway into the red sphere and closed the pathway behind him. He got the red sphere into the toxic air and outward from Rigel's system before he could think any more about the dinosaur he had left behind and the curious bond of friendship he had forged with the creature he had found on a primeval world.

He had a reunion to attend, with the woman he had come to love,

with whom he had joined in an unspoken pledge to make a better galaxy, and who an uncaring universe had flung to a far corner of the
galaxy. But he was going to see her again, and he knew now where that
would be: the one place in the galaxy they shared, Earth.

The trip was long, through three nexus points and the interminable distances between them, and he had to practice the patience that he had
urged on Rory. But at last Earth's solar system appeared in what passed
for the red sphere's vision screen, and he navigated the alien ship through
the vast areas of empty space separating the small globs of matter that
were the planets and their satellites. He was glad that Mars was on the
other side of the sun and that he was not tempted to mourn over the
war-devastated ruins of his birthplace, of his mother's sacrifices, and of
his father's dreams. He approached Earth's orbit, but he maneuvered
the ship to stay in the shadow of the moon, hoping that being thus
shielded from the direct surveillance of Earth's monitoring systems and
with the aid of what he hoped were antisurveillance technologies embedded in the red sphere itself, he would escape discovery and challenge. He
was not yet ready for the revelation of the artifact of ancient technologies that the red sphere embodied, or his own identity. It was not that
he would be welcomed as a hero of the recent war—there were too
many veterans who had done more than he and returned to celebration
and renown, or slunk back, ignored and forgotten—but his past would
be researched and recounted in the context of the treasure he had brought
back, and the people he had tried to avoid might discover him before
he was ready. And through him, Asha.

It seemed to work, and Riley thought that this was another technology of the Transcendental Machine civilization that would be worth vast
treasures to Federation worlds, and perhaps even more to Earth, the junior and still upstart member. It made sense: If the ancients' plan was to
place secret receivers around the galaxy, they would not want the arrival
of their engineers to be identified by potential spacefaring species.

He centered on what had once been called the dark side of the moon.
It was a misnomer revealed as soon as humanity's first primitive explor-

atory vessels had circumnavigated the moon: The dark side, though never exposed to Earthshine or to human view, faced merciless exposure to the sun and its radiations more than the near side. It was dark enough, to be sure, when it turned its face away from the sun and looked toward the distant stars, but these two opportunities, to see solar phenomena unsullied by Earth's obscurations and, even more when on the other side of Earth from the sun, the planets and the stars, made the dark side the favored place for research installations. In addition, the moon was where research took place on projects too dangerous to perform on Earth.

Riley had known all that when he was still a boy on Mars, and even more when he was a student in the Solar Institute for Applied Studies, but he had never known precisely where the research projects were located. If he had not volunteered for service, if he had continued his studies, he might well have interned in one of them and pursued knowledge rather than enemy ships. Now, however, he monitored transmissions from the far side. He did not have the time to analyze the transmissions for content, even if he could have harnessed the as yet unlimited and undiscovered abilities of the red sphere, but he could use them for location, and he put the alien ship down in a crater a couple of kilometers from one of them. He chose one in the twilight zone. Two kilometers were not a difficult hike, but in the full glare of the sun even the magical qualities of red-sphere material might not be enough to protect him, and the near-absolute-zero of the full dark could be almost as deadly.

He put on the material the red sphere provided for him and stroked it down over his body so that it covered him to the soles of his shoes, took a deep breath, and headed out through the air lock that the ship automatically provided. Moon dust was gritty under his feet and the sun hung on the horizon of a black sky like a cyclop's eye glaring at him. But the red sphere's covering held and provided protection from the cold of space and air for him to breathe, and he set out toward the research installation.

The trip was even worse than he had anticipated. Even in the twilight zone, the red-sphere material had to work hard to protect him from the cold and the airlessness, and the limited light made it difficult to see the rocks and pockmarks in his path. Air got stale, and he found himself struggling for breath. Even in the improved physical condition that the Transcendental Machine had conferred upon him, he was panting and exhausted when he reached the research project set into a lunar cave. It had an oval entrance insulated on each side by mounds of lunar dust and closed by a solid, apparently impenetrable metal barrier.

Riley's eyes were blurred but he could make out on the barrier printing that had been bleached and fragmented by the lunar cold and solar winds: Lunar Research Project No. 2. In his state of exhaustion he hoped that it had not been abandoned, and then he remembered the transmission he had traced to this location, and he looked quickly around the barrier and to the sides until he found a panel with the faded inscription "Emergency," and he banged upon it, once, twice, and three times before it finally depressed, the barrier moved aside with a sigh he could feel as vibration through his encased fingers.

He pushed his way past the barrier and into a metal-encased air lock, hit the panel next to the barrier with his fist, and felt the barrier close against the cold and void of space. For a moment he was in the dark, and then in channels at the top of the side walls lights came on, and he could see moon suits hanging on hooks on each side of the entrance space, another, more traditional, air-lock door ahead, and heard the sound of rushing air. It had the smell of spaceship air—human effluvia recycled too many times. Moisture began to freeze upon his garment and then to melt. He brushed the drops away, and finally, as the air-lock space warmed, stripped the red sphere material from his body and stuck it in his pocket.

He would, he knew, be an enigma to the people inside the project cave—a mysterious human emerging, impossibly, without protection from instant lunar death, from a lunar surface where no unprotected human can exist. But there was no denying the fact of his arrival, and he would have to use that mystery for his purposes.

A voice came out of the ceiling as soon as the air was thick enough to carry sound. "Who are you?" it said in a tone that could not hide its incredulity. "And what are you doing here?"

The incredulity increased when the inner doors opened and a pair of people clad in coveralls looked at him as if he were some supernatural manifestation. One was a tall, lean man, past middle age, with a face marred by radiation burns and the scars of skin cancers; he had dark eyes and a scalp devoid of hair, either through baldness or depilation. The other was a woman, younger, with long, dark hair coiled into a braid at the back of her head, dark eyes, and a pleasant, inquisitive expression.

"You're our first visitor," she said. "Ever!"

"That's what 'first' means," her companion said.

"I know what it means," she said. "That's what's called emphasis." She turned to Riley. "It is a bit of a shock." She looked sideways at her companion. "That's what's called an understatement." She turned back to Riley. "There's no way you got here the way you are. There's no way you're standing here in front of us. And yet here you are."

"I can explain," Riley said. "But first maybe I could sit down somewhere. It's been a difficult trip."

"Of course," the woman said. "Forgive our manners. We don't have much chance to exercise them. Come in. I'm Bel and this is Caid." She gave her larger companion a gentle push to signal that he should move aside.

The living quarters of the research facility were primitive but a welcome reminder of human habitation that Riley had not experienced since his days on Mars and the regimented surroundings of students at the Institute. There was a table improvised out of packing crates and pneumatic chairs easily transported from Earth. Riley settled into one and accepted a plastic mug of coffee, which he sipped with noises of appreciation. It had been a long time since he had tasted real coffee.

Finally he said, "I'm Riley. I'm an ex-soldier, returning at last from Federation space, and I need information."

"And so do we," Caid said.

"Of course you do," Riley said. "So let's trade."

"As long as it doesn't involve research in progress," Bel said. "Not that we have any secrets—we publish as soon as our results are confirmed—but we do exercise discretion until then."

"As I said," Riley continued, "I'm just back from Federation space, and I came into possession of some extraordinary technology that I would like to see explored."

"Federation technology?" Caid said.

"Older than the Federation," Riley said. "Really old."

"People are always coming up with discoveries on first-contact worlds," Bel said. "Most of them fakes, and those that aren't turn out to be impenetrable or inscrutable."

Riley dug the red-sphere material out of his pocket. "Like this?" he said.

Bel took the material out of his hand. It was red and slick and rested in her hand like a swatch of something like silk. "So?" she said.

"I call it intelligent matter," Riley said. "It's like a magic cloak. It turns into whatever you need when you need it." He took the material from her and smoothed it over his arm. It became a sleeve, and as he continued to stroke, the material became a jacket, a coverall, and finally a full covering. Riley stripped it down again and gave the material back to Bel. She hoisted it in her palm and then handed it to Caid.

"That's a great trick," Caid said. "But I've seen magicians do better ones." He put the material on his arm and stroked it the way he had seen Riley do it. The material lay on his arm, quiescent. "What's the trick? Is there some magic word?"

"The material is keyed to me in some way that is part of the technology and the mystery," Riley said. "Maybe you can figure it out. But it's what got me through the deadly lunar environment to your door. Which is the answer to your question."

"One of the answers," Bel said. "To one of the questions."

"It's the only answer I'm prepared to give now. Maybe more later. But right now I'm prepared to offer a trade. Intelligent matter for information and one of your moon suits."

"What kind of information?"

"The location of the research project of a scientist I know only as 'Jak,'" Riley said.

Bel looked at Caid and back at Riley. "You mean 'Jak Plus'"?

"Plus?" Riley said.

"There's a rumor that he took the name from a fictional hero of long ago," Bel said.

It was more likely, Riley thought, that the name came from Jak's experiments in cloning himself.

"But why Jak?" Bel asked. "He's a paranoid fraud."

"He's come up with some remarkable gadgets and claimed some discoveries that have yet to be confirmed. Including the terraforming of Ganymede. No one has been able to check on his claims about Ganymede or to duplicate the results of his other self-proclaimed discoveries," Caid said.

"I get it that he's not very likable," Riley said, "but he may be the kind of paranoid fraud that I need. I'm a bit paranoid myself."

"And a fraud?" Caid said.

"That remains to be seen, doesn't it?" Riley said. He pointed at the material in Caid's hand. "Well, is it a deal?"

Caid tossed the material as if estimating its weight and maybe its value. He looked at Bel, his scarred face twitching.

"I wouldn't ask for the moon suit if I weren't giving up my own." Riley gestured at the material in Caid's hand. "And I am here as proof that it works."

"Okay," Bel said, "but we'd rather do the research on the rest of the technology—we presume there's more—ourselves."

"I'll tell Jak that if I get to see him," Riley said.

Jak's research project turned out to be more than five hundred kilometers distant, no trip for a ship that had already traveled across spans of time measured in periods of stellar evolution and of space measured in thousands of light-years. And the moon suit he had obtained from Bel and Caid, though primitive compared to the magical technology of the red sphere, was equipped with air tanks, temperature-control units, and a faceplate that could be darkened against solar radiation. Nevertheless, there was the moment when the red sphere remained closed to his approach until he stripped a hand free from the moon suit and the ship apparently recognized him and allowed him to enter before his hand could freeze. And the moment when, after concealing the red sphere farther from the location of Jak's project than he would have liked and trekking across the sun-blasted terrain to the spot where Bel had indicated the project was located, with his air growing low and the temperature conditioning of the suit laboring under the sun's merciless bombardment, he failed to find any sign of Jak's laboratory.

He scouted the area, wondering if the moon suit still had enough reserves to get him back to the red sphere and wondering, as well, if Bel and Caid had deliberately given him false coordinates, when, at last, he came upon a doorway set like a trapdoor into the lunar surface and partially obscured by dust that had drifted down upon it, not because of wind, of which there was none, but the bombardment of solar particles over time; the door had not been opened in many cycles. He scuffed the lunar dust away and looked for a panel marked EMERGENCY, as he had found at Lunar Project Number 2. There was none.

He stomped on the metal door. It remained unmoved and unmovable. He stomped again. Something red glowed across the surface of the door. He bent over to see what it was and decreased the suit's shield against the sun.

In glowing letters the door said, "Go away!"

CHAPTER TWENTY

The climber slowed to a stop at the base of the beanstalk on the island once known as Sri Lanka. Although it was the base of the space elevator, according to Latha it was the top of a mountain that was called Sri Pada. It had been chosen for the beanstalk location because of its location near the equator and its elevation of nearly 2,550 meters, over the strenuous objections of several religious groups that considered the mountaintop sacred. When Asha asked what was sacred about it, Latha told her about a rock formation near the summit that the religious groups said was a nearly two-meter footprint of Buddha, according to one group; of Siva, according to another; of a Saint named Thomas, according to a third; or of the first person the Christian God created, Adam, according to a fourth. Steps had been built into the side of the mountain so that pilgrims could climb to the top to see the footprint and the sunrise.

"Of course," Latha said, "that was many thousands of years ago, and people aren't as passionate anymore about symbols. Though there is a bit of a nostalgia movement, and the steps have been rebuilt."

Asha pulled herself out of the chair that had been her habitat for the past week, serving as support while the climber's passengers were awake and as a bed while the passengers slept—she needed little sleep, but she respected the needs of others and occupied the sleep time by thinking through scenarios in which she could be reunited with Riley and what they would do after they got back together. Now she joined with the others as they lined up to leave their enforced companionship, eager to be liberated in spite of efforts by climber personnel to make their trip pleasant. Latha was just ahead of her.

As they emerged from the elaborate waiting room into the monorail station, Latha motioned for Asha to look out the window toward the rock that had given Sri Pada the name "sacred footprint." When the space elevator had been built, the indentation and its accompanying decorations had been preserved at considerable expense to ease local objections, though the compromise pleased nobody. But they continued to exist, side by side, as a contrast between the old and the new, the superstitious past and the scientific future, the footprint of the ancient gods as the launching pad for the stars.

"I have commented about that," Latha said. "And how the ancient village of Nallathanniya, where the stairs began, was transformed into a city by the monorail built beside the stairs." At first it had been the construction crews that flooded the village, and then it was the travelers who came to use the space elevator. "Always the old making way for the new."

What was not new was the wind that blew gusts of rain against the windows of the monorail and made it rock on what seemed now like a flimsy support, so much more dangerous than travel through space. Latha didn't seem alarmed. "This is the rainy season," she said, "when pilgrims would not have come up the stairs." The Pedia had solved many climate problems, including bringing rain to areas troubled by drought or forest fires, but it had not been able to eliminate hurricanes or monsoons.

Asha and Latha emerged onto a sheltered platform, not far from the entrance to a high-speed subway train to Ratnapura and other urban areas. Now that human labor was a choice and not a necessity and most of what labor still performed was done by individuals living far from each other, cities were useful only as cultural centers for people attracted to the ancient traditions of real-time, real-person art. But cities were still Asha's best possibility for getting information about Riley without alerting persons or Pedias to her or Riley's return to Earth.

The rain was still coming down heavily and being blown in gusts. Asha hesitated about crossing to the subway entrance. "I'm being met," Latha said. "Can I offer you a ride to somewhere a little more convenient?"

"You've put up with me for too long," Asha said.

"Nonsense," Latha said. "Here they are now." As she spoke an antique, yellow, fossil-fuel-powered bus pulled up in front of the platform, and a band of brown-faced young people, male and female, bounced out through the side door and into the downpour, as if they were part of the elements. They surrounded Latha and Asha and pulled them toward the bus and into the rain, laughing and hugging each of them in turn. Asha would have been overwhelmed by their joyous enthusiasm, but she felt trapped, as if all this were a charade set up to conceal an abduction. But concealed from whom? It was too late to get free without pushing her way through them, physically assaulting some, and creating an incident that would surely alert watchers and probably the Pedia.

She found herself on the bus seated next to Latha. Their clothing was soaked, but Latha didn't seem to care. The ancient vehicle, no doubt a clever replica appealing to the sense of nostalgia that Latha had mentioned, moved away from the station. "Now, dear," Latha said, "where did you say you wanted to go?"

"I didn't say," Asha said.

"Of course not," Latha said, "and we'll stop at my place to dry you off and give you a bit of our hospitality before we send you on your way."

"Thanks," Asha said. Clearly she had made a mistake about Latha. The most likely explanation for what had happened since she had gone aboard the climber was that Latha was an agent for the Pedia.

Latha's place was a sprawling tropical compound on a broad estate of rolling plains. The trip out of the mountains had been long but not boring. They had passed through a wildlife preserve at the base of the mountain and seen elephants and leopards and other endemic species, each of which had to be identified for Asha and their place in evolutionary history described along with the process by which they had been restored. Latha was a gifted hostess, leaning toward Asha like a dedicated aunt, grasping her upper arm to point out some place or creature of interest, and seeming to delight in introducing this stranger to the home world she had never known. If anything, it all served to intensify Asha's suspicions.

The chugging bus passed by forested hills before it descended into the plains and at last pulled up in front of the central building of a compound, a one-story wooden structure with a large middle section and two long wings. Latha ushered Asha out of the bus and through massive wooden doors into a living area that stretched across the entire front of the building. The floor was made up of different-sized pieces of polished stone. Handmade rugs were scattered across it. The space was furnished with chairs and settees made from some kind of dark wood. The seat and backs were covered by tapestry-like fabric. The room was lighted by fixtures high on the wooden walls, but they seemed to burn from some natural fuel rather than electricity.

"All this," Asha said, with a sweep of her hand, "hardly seems like what someone could afford with a minimum annual allotment."

"We pool our resources," Latha said. "These young people—"

"Your relatives?" Asha asked. "Students?"

"A little of both," Latha said. "But mostly spirited young people dedicated to a way of life different from what others of their age prefer."

"And what is that?"

"First we must get you into some warm clothing," Latha said, and led Asha down a hallway to a bedroom with an adjoining bath. "You'll find some clothing in the closet there," she continued, "and you can leave your wet things in the bathroom where they will be picked up and dried for you."

"I really shouldn't burden you," Asha said.

"It is more like a pleasure," Latha said. "Talking to a person with your background, showing you your home world. You can't imagine how delightful that is. I want to know more about the Federation and the world you grew up on."

It would do no harm, Asha thought, to bathe and dress. The notion of a bath in real water with real soap was like something out of a fairy tale—for her, getting clean was a chemical spray or, upon occasion, a brief shower with reconstituted fluids. She luxuriated in warm water that came up to her chest and thick towels to dry with. If she was going to face difficulties because of poor decisions, at least she would face them having enjoyed an experience she had only heard about.

At last she rejoined Latha in the living area, clad in colorful, flowing silk—the only clothing she had found in the closet Latha had indicated. Latha had changed, too, and was waiting for her with a drink in one hand and one waiting in the other hand for Asha. Asha took it and looked at it curiously.

Latha laughed. "It's a traditional drink made from local juices," she said. "Traditional, that is, from thousands of years ago when people had time for hospitality and making their own drinks."

Asha sipped it and sat down in a chair next to the one Latha had occupied. The drink was good, sweet but not too sweet and a mixture of flavors that seemed to complement each other, none of which she had ever tasted before. She had expected to encounter experiences and customs that were unknown to her and that she might even find repellent, but all this was like living the stories her father had told her as she was growing up.

"You were going to tell me," Asha said, "how a place like this can exist in a world where everyone has enough but nobody has too much."

Latha laughed. "Is that what you heard about Earth? It's only true in a general sort of way, like freedom and democracy. Wealth wasn't outlawed, it simply became unnoticeable."

"How can a place like this be unnoticeable?"

"We do not consume any of the world's resources. We raise our own food, provide our own energy resources—you will notice that the vehicle that brought us here used fuel drawn from our own wells and refined by our own processes, and the lights in this room use gas produced in the same way—and are in no way connected to the world's services or power sources. So no one notices us, and we can do pretty much as we please."

"This all belongs to you?"

"A legacy from rapacious ancestors, put now to redeeming causes."

"And what causes are those?" Asha asked.

"Why, to be independent of course!" Latha said. "That is hard to do these days, but it's very much worth doing. If you're a commenter, that is."

Asha was silent for a moment, trying to put it all together, but the parts didn't fit. Either Latha was a nostalgia fan, trying to return to an era long past when people could live independent of the entanglements of modern existence, or she was playing a more dangerous game.

"But what attracted me to you," Latha said, "was your story about being born aboard the *Adastra* and being captured by Federation ships and growing up on a Federation world. It all sounded so exciting and romantic. I wanted to hear more about it."

Asha described the generation ship and its capture by galactics as their ship was halfway to Alpha Centauri. She, just born, had no memory of that, of course, but stories were told by her father and the other crew-members, the shock of discovering that humanity was not alone in the galaxy, the dismay at the knowledge that their ship, into which so much thought and effort had been invested, was as primitive as a handmade canoe in a world of steamships, and the revulsion at the appearance of aliens so different from humans and so revulsed, apparently, by human appearance.

She told Latha about growing up on a moon of an alien world in orbit around an alien sun, how alien food was often poisonous and the captives had to live off the produce grown in the generation-ship recy-cling gardens, how the crew and the passengers organized schools for the children—a generation ship depended on the birth of new generations—and how their Federation jailors, suspicious of these up-start humans and their potential for mischief, had interrogated them regularly and with growing suspicion that what they were being told concealed darker truths.

"All that, of course," Asha said, "was before the human/Federation war, and it might have been what led to the war."

"Oh dear!" Latha said. "You mustn't blame yourself."

"It wasn't like that," Asha said. "It was not our fault. Not me, of course. I was only a child during most of that period. But they ques-tioned my brother and my father, who had no idea they were repre-senting all of humanity and that the aliens were using their descriptions of human history and literature and art as evidence with which to condemn a species. They weren't trained to be diplomats, and they weren't prepared to understand the purpose behind seemingly innocent questions or to provide the half-truths that conceal more than they reveal.

"And then the war broke out, and one of our crew discovered the Federation nexus-point charts and a way to get them back to Earth, which made it possible for humanity to fight the Federation to a truce."

She didn't tell Latha about Ren's escape in the *Adastra,* about the part she had played, or about the journey to the planet of the Transcendental Machine and what had happened after that. "Now," she said, "I'm grateful for your hospitality, but my clothes must surely be dry, and I should be on my way. I have much to do and much to learn."

"Oh, we can't let you leave," Latha said.

Asha considered quickly her various options for escape before Latha continued. "You have so much more to tell us about the Federation. Oh, we've had Federation visitors, and we've quite gotten used to the strange-looking aliens and their odd ways and odd smells, and we've even gotten immunized against their odd bacteria and viruses, but we don't really know how they live, you know? Are they as egalitarian as we are?"

"The Federation operates by principles much like those of Earth, equality and consensus, but like Earth's, they are only generally true. Some species have been members of the Federation longer than others, and although the full members are all equal, some get more respect. The Dorians and the Sirians, for instance, have a more important voice in deliberations than the Alpha Centaurans, say, and the Xifora rank at the bottom of the group, except, of course, for the apprentice members like Earth, and no one knows where to put the Florans. Maybe because the Florans don't care."

"What do you mean by 'consensus'?"

"Everybody has to agree on actions that effect everybody. In a galaxy where disagreement can mean the destruction of worlds, not making anybody unhappy enough to rebel is essential. But that doesn't mean there isn't some measure of constraint. Worlds have been destroyed. Nobody wants to disagree, so decisions get watered down. It's not the most efficient system, but it works. The major problem is that anything really different—like humanity, for instance—represents a challenge to the system. The Federation is organized to maintain things the way they are."

"And do they have Pedias like we do?"

Now, Asha thought, they were getting to the issue that really concerned Latha. "Everybody does," she said. "Interstellar civilization, even planetary civilization, would be impossible without them. Individual pedias, carried by most species, of course, and central Pedias, controlling all the automated processes that keep machines working and vehicles and vessels operating and essential services provided." That, she thought, was neutral enough.

"And yet you don't have one," Latha said. "That's part of what I found fascinating about you as well."

"Nor you, either," Asha said.

"As I mentioned," Latha said, "we try to be independent. But surely you needed one in the Federation, just to get by."

"The galaxy is a complicated place," Asha said. "Lots of information, lots of things to keep track of, and a device that accesses and handles all that is essential to most Federation people. Growing up as a prisoner of the Federation, I wasn't allowed one. And when I was released, nobody gave me one. And since I've gotten along this far without one, I've learned how to do without."

Latha looked at her kindly and shook her head. "That's a fascinating story," she said, "but, dear, you haven't been completely honest with me."

"What do you mean?"

"The story of the *Adastra* is a legend here on Earth," Latha said. "How Ren stole the nexus-point charts and sneaked the *Adastra* away from Federation Central and sent the women and children back to Earth with the charts while he and his crew led the pursuers on a chase that ended with the *Adastra* vanishing—totally vanishing. And it hasn't been seen since."

"Maybe I left something out," Asha said.

"And you left out the part where you were a member of the crew,"

Latha said. "The only human left behind was a man who must have been your father. Which means that you know what happened to the *Adastra*."

"It was a long, dangerous journey that ended in death for almost everybody," Asha said. "It's a story that nobody would believe, and I certainly wouldn't inflict it on somebody I just met."

"We'll have to talk about that later," Latha said. "But now I must admit that I haven't been completely honest with you, either. I'm not only a commenter, I'm an Anon, and so is everybody else who lives here. Our goal is to destroy the Pedia."

CHAPTER TWENTY-ONE

Riley read the message on the door set into the dusty surface of the moon. It still said "Go away!" He checked the moon suit's power and air reserves. They were well past half empty. Finally he switched on the suit's communicator. He was reluctant to run the risk of his transmission being intercepted by Earth's Pedia, but his need was greater than his caution, the range of his communicator was only a few hundred meters, and the entire bulk of the moon stood between him and Earth's sensors.

"I ask for help under Galactic Convention Seven Five Three Six," he said.

There was a long silence and Riley was about to repeat his request when a raspy voice responded, "Galactic conventions don't apply here."

"Galactic conventions were accepted by Earth and its system worlds when the truce was signed," Riley said.

After another pause, the same voice said, "I never signed a truce."

Riley thought a moment. "I believe I am speaking to Jak Plus," he said. "I have information about Jon and Jan."

Silence followed and then, without further reply, the door set into the dust of the lunar surface slid aside, and Riley saw that the moon dust he had believed scattered across its surface was actually a part of the door itself. He descended a dozen meters into a more elaborate air lock than Bel and Caid's Lunar Project Number Two. As the door closed and the lights came on, he could see, in the brackets on the wall, sturdier and more specialized moon suits than the standard model Bel had provided. The walls were stainless steel and the far door looked solid enough to resist a meteor strike. This was no temporary project. It had been built for the ages.

The entering air was almost silent and so was the far door when it opened as he was removing his moon suit. A young woman with dark hair and brown eyes, clad in a short, one-piece garment in a muted brown, stood in the doorway silhouetted by the light streaming from behind her. She looked a great deal like a female version of Jon and Jan.

"Jer?" Riley said.

"Tell me about Jon and Jan," she said in a tone that entertained no possibility of noncompliance.

In that she was not like her clonemates. "I'll tell you when I tell Jak," he said.

"Jak doesn't see anybody," she said.

"He'll see me," Riley said.

"He's old and sick. He doesn't see anybody. Tell me—"

The same raspy voice that Riley had heard on the communicator came from hidden speakers, as if it had materialized in the air. "Bring him here."

Jer turned and Riley followed her rigid back down a long corridor past closed and open doors, some of which revealed laboratories with gleaming metal-and-glass apparatus that Riley had never seen before, not even in his days at the Solar Institute. At the end of the corridor a doorway opened into a large living space fitted with solid metal and fabric furniture and a pneumatic bed equipped with oxygen tanks and other medical devices that Riley could not identify. The air had the medicated odor of a sickroom. In the middle of the bed, sitting up against pillows, was an old man who looked startlingly like Jon and Jan and Jer except with sagging jowls and white hair.

"Jak?" Riley said, although he knew who it was.

"I've never called myself 'Jak Plus,'" the old man said. "That was an invention of my enemies, of which I have made many over the years. But now you must tell me about Jon and Jan."

"First I need to know whether you are under surveillance," Riley said.

"Surveillance?" Jak said. "What are you talking about?"

"I have reason to believe that Earth's Pedia, and the other Pedias in the galaxy, have an unhealthy interest in my existence."

Jak snorted. It was an effort that shook his body. "You're as paranoid as I am," he said. "I severed my connections with Earth, and its Pedia, decades ago. That's why I built my laboratory on the moon. Everything here is self-contained, including the energy and food supply. I reinvented what used to be called 'a computer' to do tedious calculations. It does what I tell it and no more. "Now, tell me about Jon and Jan."

Riley nodded. He knew what Jak wanted. Unlike Jer, Jak was interested not in their fate but in the fate of their mission. "Jon was alive the last time I saw him. He was revived from an attempt to destroy, by freezing, the symbiotes from the Ganymede project. Jan could not be revived."

"You said 'the last time you saw him—' " Jer began.

Jak cut her off. "This happened on the *Geoffrey*." It was not a question.

"Yes," Riley said. "After we landed on the planet of the Transcendental Machine, we got separated from the rest of the passengers and crew, including Jon. It's unlikely that any of them survived, but it's possible. I'll tell you about that in a little while, but first I want to tell you about something else that will interest you far more."

"I'll decide what interests me. Tell me about the Transcendental Machine," Jak said.

Riley considered how much he should tell Jak. There was no doubt the man was a "mad scientist," but maybe a mad scientist was what he and Asha needed. "In the first place it's not a Transcendental Machine, it's a transportation device. Its transcendental function is just an unanticipated consequence."

"How do we get our hands on it?" Jak said.

"You don't," Riley said. "It's not even in our spiral arm. And the trip to get there is across the mostly empty space between spiral arms, the nexus-point charts are nonexistent, and the only people who have any clue to them are dead or missing. And even if you or your emissaries, like Jon and Jan, could get there, they'd probably be killed by the arachnoids who guard the place."

"And yet you're here," Jak said.

Riley nodded. "Me and one other."

"And who is that?"

"Maybe I'll tell you if we can reach an agreement."

"About what? You've already told me the Transcendental Machine is worthless."

"The Machine, maybe, but not what it implies: It works," Riley said. "You can make your own."

"My own Transcendental Machine?" Jak said.

"Your own matter transmitter," Riley said, "which is the same thing, if you can do it. The Transcendental Machine destroys the material as it is analyzed and sends that information to a receiver where it is reconstituted. But it leaves behind all the imperfections, so what is reconstituted is the ideal state of what went into it."

Jak sat up straight. "That might mean a cure for diseases, even fatal diseases, deformities, lost limbs!"

"Even aging," Riley said. "But more important, it means improved versions of what went into it, smarter, better qualified to function in today's galaxy, maybe even compete on equal terms with the most powerful species in the galaxy. And their Pedias."

"Immortality," Jak said.

"Maybe," Riley said. "Better, anyway, than your cloning experiment—and the symbiotes. They were why Jon and Jan signed on to the *Geoffrey*. Not just because you sent them, as Jon told us, but because they hoped the Transcendental Machine would rid them of their controlling symbiotes."

"Nonsense," Jak said. "They were better than a pedia. Jer, tell the man."

"I've told you about them many times, Jak," Jer said. "And you always tell me to forget it. I've learned how to segregate them—to keep them out of my head when I really focus on it—but if I didn't have to fight that battle all the time I could do something better with my life."

"It would be really difficult to build a device for destructive analysis, not to mention preserving the result and using it to reconstitute the original, without the device to study," Jak mused. "But you have seen it work?"

"I'm proof that it works," Riley said.

"It would mean a lot of experiments," Jak mused, "first with materials, then with living subjects, and many failures. But, after all, what are we but information? It is likely I would not see the end of it." His sagging features firmed. "But it would be a great memorial. A final triumph. A blow in the face of my enemies. And I have Jer. Jer will continue my work, for her own love of success as well as my reputation. She is, after all, a younger me."

It looked as if he and Asha had found the right mad scientist, Riley thought. He looked at Jer, who seemed to be torn by conflicting emotions—wanting to reject Jak's comparison while excited about the possibilities of the project. Perhaps she was not just a copy of Jak but an improved version.

"There's one other thing," Riley said. "I want to tell you about an ancient artifact that I acquired after I was transported."

"How ancient?" Jak said.

"Older than anything ever discovered before," Riley said. "Probably a million long-cycles ago—I mean 'years.'"

"How can that be? There aren't any galactic civilizations half that old," Jak said.

"Not in this spiral arm. But in the next one, in the spiral arm of the creatures who built the Transcendental Machine, where intelligent life and technology must have gotten started earlier."

"Well?" Jak said.

"It's a million-year-old spaceship," Riley said.

"Miracle after miracle," Jak said. "Of course your account of the Transcendental Machine is just a story. An unlikely story, at that, and your presenting yourself as proof of its existence can hardly be verified. But a spaceship is a different matter. You must have one."

"It brought me here," Riley said. "I recognize that my description of the Transcendental Machine and what it does is hard to believe and harder still to prove. No amount of physical and mental tricks is going to convince you that I'm not inventing the whole thing. But the alien spaceship is solid and real, and I'm willing to offer it to you not only as validation of my story, but as an artifact for study."

"And what kind of artifact survives a million years? Even a spaceship," Jak said.

"Something truly remarkable." Riley told them how he had entered the Transcendental Machine and found himself in a pyramid on the dinosaur planet, how he had discovered the red sphere, why he thought it had been left there, how he had gained entrance to it, and how he had used it to get back to Earth. He did not tell them about Rory, which would have made his story even less believable, or about his stop at Dante, which would only distract them, or about Asha, which would only confuse them and perhaps put Asha in danger. As it was, Jak and Jer were unconvinced.

"That sounds like some ancient space romance," Jer said. "Full of incredible adventures and near-death escapes."

"And how was it possible," Jak said, "that a million-year-old spaceship would still function, or that you could figure out how to make it work?"

"I could attribute it to the improvements of the Transcendental Machine process, but the ancient creatures who built the Transcendental Machine also built the spaceship, and they built things to last," Riley said. "They thought in millennia, not in years, and whatever their plans were for our spiral arm, they knew it would take many generations to accomplish."

"And so—?" Jak said.

"Their machines were not only built to last, they were built to be self-maintaining. Maybe because the material they were built from was in itself intelligent, able to adapt to changing conditions. And that was why I was able to make it work."

"How?" Jak said.

"Because it adapted to me. It analyzed me when I entered. I don't know how. But it shaped itself to my needs and fashioned furnishings to fit me, food to sustain me, and controls that I could learn how to use. Which was a blessing for me but a loss for human science."

"What kind of loss?" Jer said.

"We can't learn from the ship what the aliens were like," Riley said.

"If it had retained its original shape, we could have learned something about what they were like physically, and maybe even something about their psychology and philosophy, maybe even their science from the tools and other equipment they used. Though, if that were the case, I would be sitting back on that alien planet where I found it, and I would be sitting dead inside it. Assuming that all of this is real."

"A big assumption," Jak said, "but here you are, and you must have the spaceship as proof."

"Indeed," Riley said. "And this." He pulled a glob of rosy material from his pocket, and held it out in his palm as the material shaped itself into a drinking cup with a handle. He gave it to Jer, who studied it for a moment and handed it to Jak.

"That's a good trick," Jak said.

"Maybe," Riley said, "but it's not my trick. It's the trick of the Transcendental Machine people. And maybe something you can learn how to do."

"I want to see this ship," Jak said.

"You will—or Jer, if you're not able to make the trip. One of you will have to get recognized by the ship, or you won't be allowed to enter, much less to work with it."

"Why do you offer it to me?" Jak said. "This would bring billions of credits on the open market. You could buy your own planet."

"If I took it into the jurisdiction of any world, it would be confiscated by Pedia-governed bureaucrats who would bury it under generations of committee discussions and protocols until it was forgotten. Or buried by a Pedia who would consider it a threat to the meat creatures under its protection. And I would be killed."

"Or become a hero," Jer said, "to go down the centuries as the man who discovered the greatest artifact in the history of the galaxy."

"The same thing," Riley said.

"Bureaucrats!" Jak said.

"The technology of the spaceship is revolutionary," Riley said. "If you folks can figure it out, it could elevate humanity to the equal of any species in the Federation, and, eventually, a new galactic order."

"Galactic orders!" Jak said. He was clearly no more interested in improving political systems than he was in dealing with bureaucrats.

"But more important than that," Riley said, "is the intelligence that is imbedded in every molecule of the ship, and if you can figure out how to contact it, how to talk to it, how to understand it, how to get it to reveal its magic and the magicians who created it, you may be able to find out who the magicians were and what they were doing."

"Maybe they just liked to travel," Jer said.

"Or they wanted to explore the rest of the galaxy," Jak said. "Maybe they were just curious, like true scientists."

"Maybe. They went to a great deal of effort, possibly focusing most of the resources of a star empire on a project that might never pay off. Their system was not even set up for their emissaries to return or to send back information. Either they were benign benefactors, or they were more like us. They expected it to pay off eventually."

"In what way?" Jak said.

"Maybe these were advance scouts for a project to colonize this arm of the galaxy," Riley said. "Or to seize its resources. Or to guide our evolution. Or . . . who knows? But the process ended up destroying them. Unless . . ."

"Unless what?" Jer asked.

"Unless they're still among us, influencing us in ways that we don't recognize or understand," Riley said. "We don't know what they looked like, and we don't have any proof that they died, just the arachnoids who are ravaging the planet of the Transcendental Machine. They could be any of the species who make up the Federation. They could even look like humans."

"They could even be humans," Jer said.

"Humans!" Jak said.

CHAPTER TWENTY-TWO

Asha considered Latha's statement that the Anons intended to destroy the Pedia. Since they had first met, she had alternated between a belief that Latha was an agent of the Pedia who was attempting to trap Asha into a revelation of her own anti-Pedia feelings and a belief that Latha was the guileless, competent person she presented herself as being. Such uncertainty was unfamiliar to Asha, and she didn't like it.

"And how do you propose to do that?" she asked.

"We must use the weapons the Pedia depends upon," Latha said. "It lives on data. We will feed it data that contains poison."

"And how can you do that, cut off here from the rest of the world? Your independence is also your weakness."

Latha nodded. "We find ways of coping. Anons are scattered all over the world. Location doesn't matter anymore. My friends and colleagues record what is happening and send it to us by courier. We analyze it here and use it as a basis for my comments and send them back to be broadcast to the world on the Pedia's own networks."

"And you expect your comments to destroy the Pedia?" Asha asked.

"Of course not," Latha said. She smiled at Asha as if acknowledging Asha's lack of seriousness. "The comments have enough embedded criticism to raise questions in people's minds, but, far more important, they contain what used to be called 'viruses' to slow down the Pedia and interfere with its services and thus stir up opposition."

Asha took a sip from her fruit drink and thought about how much she had missed by her long separation from her home world. "Has it stirred up opposition?"

"Not as much as we had hoped," Latha said. "The poisons performed as we planned—our Anons are an ingenious group—but people didn't react as we expected. They just grew accustomed to occasional interruptions in service. At first they complained, and then they stopped noticing."

"You thought they would rise up against the Pedia?"

"The slowdowns were just an irritant, to prepare the people for the big event yet to come. It didn't work, but then it was only the first step toward weaning people from their dependence on the Pedia."

Asha looked at the way the tropical sunlight came through the windows opposite her and spilled across the stone floor, accenting some of its component pieces and leaving others in shadow, like truth and deception in the world. "And what is the big event?"

Latha smiled at Asha, as if she were about to share with a daughter the secret of sex, babies, and a happy life. "What we've been working on is the Grand Poison, the pill of information that will get past all of the Pedia's defenses and shut it down completely. The turn-off switch that was somehow lost over the millennium since the Pedia got control of things. Or maybe the Pedia hid it from us, or persuaded us to forget it, or even destroyed it. But we are determined to find it and turn it off."

"And how close are you to creating the Grand Poison?"

"If we only knew," Latha said, "we would be joyful."

"Your young people seem joyful already."

"They are joyful by their nature," Latha said. "That is because the joy is in the struggle, and it doesn't matter that the struggle has gone on for generations and may go on for generations yet to come. The promise of success is there, like the prize at the end of the race, and that is the joy of freedom from the tyranny of the Pedia."

"The tyranny of freedom from hunger, deprivation, and despair?"

"From all of those," Latha said. "We want them all. Freedom is worth any price."

"You're welcome to them," Asha said.

One of the brown young men who had surrounded Asha and Latha at the station entered the room to refresh their drinks from a cut-glass pitcher. He was clad in colorful silks like Latha, though they left his legs bare. He moved swiftly and lithely like a panther, he smelled good like an oriental spice, and he was remarkably attractive while being at the same time unimaginable as a romantic partner.

"What do you think of Latha's plans against the Pedia?" Asha asked the young man.

Latha smiled.

"We are all committed to the great struggle," the young man said, but he glanced at Asha as if he would have more to say if given the opportunity. He returned to the doorway from which he had come.

"You have a good-looking group of servants," Asha said.

"They're not servants," Latha said, frowning as if annoyed with Asha for the first time since they had met. "They're my sons and daughters."

"All of them?" Asha asked.

"All of them," Latha said.

"You gave birth to all of them?" Aska asked.

"Birth? No, that would be ridiculous and impossible." Latha leaned forward. "But I will tell you a secret that I have told no one. Two of them—a boy and a girl—I gave birth to when I was very young. But they are no different from the others I have gathered here."

"They don't know?"

Latha shook her head. "They are all my sons and daughters."

Asha considered the enormity of the effort that would sustain that kind of illusion. "And their father?"

"An unknown donor selected scientifically for the traits I wanted, including not only the physical and mental skills necessary to the task I accepted from my own parents when I was very young, but the independence of thought and spirit it required."

"And have you thought how difficult that would have been without the Pedia?" Asha asked.

Latha looked at Asha for the first time as if she didn't understand the question.

Asha thought for a moment before she challenged Latha's plans. It might not be politic or cautious, but Latha seemed so completely certain of her goals that Asha decided to take the risk. "I understand that the Anons would not find life much different if the Pedia were destroyed, at least at first. But have you thought about what would happen to everybody else?"

"What do you mean?"

"Most of humanity has grown accustomed to being taken care of," Asha said, "to not paying attention to the way things work, not watching when they cross the street, not worrying about whether their appliances and their transportation will function the way they are supposed to, not concerning themselves about where their next meal will come from or whether the food is safe to eat."

"They'll get used to it," Latha said. "They always have."

"For a millennium they haven't had to concern themselves with the problems of survival, the primary occupation of humanity since its beginnings. Millions, maybe billions, will die. Strong, ruthless leaders will emerge to gather the survivors into gangs to seize what resources remain, banditry and war will return, and it will bring back the dehumanization of everyone not a member of the tribe along with slavery, starvation, disease, and death."

"People aren't savages anymore," Latha said serenely. "They will adjust. They have learned how to get along with each other."

"And have you thought about what would happen to Earth and its human settlements on other worlds?" Asha asked. "Pedias are the indispensable foundation for interstellar travel and galactic civilization. Even if human civilization somehow survived and people could be trained to perform the difficult tasks of calculating orbits and the transition through nexus points, the loss of the Pedia would make humanity an easy conquest for any predatory species in the galaxy."

"The Federation would protect us," Latha said.

"The Federation doesn't like humans. It started a war because it didn't like us, and after we fought them to an uneasy truce, it likes us even less. It might not officially approve of any invasion, but it wouldn't punish anybody who did it."

"There's no point in speculating about actions and motives so far removed," Latha said. "If we did that, we would never do anything.

What is far more likely is that the destruction of the Pedia would release the now-dormant creativity of the human species, and we would soon find ourselves the wonders of the galaxy."

"Your confidence is encouraging," Asha said.

"In any case," Latha said, "none of this is the responsibility of the Anons. Our business is to create the revolution. It is humanity's business to rise to the challenge of losing its parental surrogate. We have been kept in our cribs too long. We will make the revolution, and then we will see. We intend to replace security with freedom—freedom to strive and succeed in whatever one defines as success and happiness, as well as to fail and suffer."

"All that seems like taking a chance with the future of humanity."

"Perhaps we will be only successful in depriving the Pedia of its power to make decisions for us," Latha said. "The equivalent of what used to be done to people in the dark ages of brain surgery, what was called a 'prefrontal lobotomy.' That would leave the Pedia with the ability to perform routine tasks without the ability to supervise everything people do."

"There's another option," Asha said.

"One that we haven't considered?" Latha asked. "We've been at this business for generations."

"Rather than handicapping the Pedia, you could improve humanity to the point where it could deal with the Pedia on equal terms with the forces of machine intelligence."

"How would we do that?" Latha asked.

"By achieving a new level of evolution produced by the machine itself."

"The Pedia would never do that, even if it could," Latha said. "It likes humanity dependent on it."

"The Pedia doesn't know any different," Asha said. "It doesn't like or dislike. It does what it was built to do, to serve humanity. The only problem that has emerged from those basic instructions, and it is a big one, is its definition of humanity. Humanity is the species that needs its protection. The Pedia must be shown an alternative. Then we could have a new order, a partnership between carbon-based and silicon-based life."

"All that is mere theory," Latha said. "It speaks well for your good intentions, but it would never happen."

"Have you heard of the Transcendental Machine?" Asha asked.

"Of course. But that's a fairy tale."

"Even fairy tales sometimes come true," Asha said. "And if there is a machine somewhere that can elevate people to their ideal condition of body and mind, it could produce the evolutionary step that I have described."

"You are a dreamer," Latha said, "and I love you for that, but now we should go to the dinner that has been prepared for us."

"Really, I have urgent business to take care of elsewhere," Asha said.

"Nonsense," Latha said. "We can't possibly let you leave."

The adjoining room was paneled in dark wood and smelled of exotic food. A long, polished wooden table occupied the middle of the room. Formal chairs were drawn up on each side, but only four places were set, with glasses and implements, at the nearest end. Two brown-faced young people were waiting, one on each side of the room, the beautiful young man who had filled their glasses in the living room and an equally attractive young woman. The young man pulled out a chair for Asha, and the young woman did the same for Latha. Then they disappeared through a nearby door before returning with steaming tureens and platters and the odors that Asha had smelled as she entered, but more intense now as they drifted upward from the serving dishes.

Having placed the dishes in the middle of the table, the young people placed spoonfuls of rice and ladles of steaming vegetables in rich, dark sauces on the plates in front of Asha and Latha, before placing similar servings on the plates on either side of them.

"Are other people joining us?" Asha asked.

"Only my children," Latha said, and the two young people sat down, the young man beside Asha, the young woman beside Latha, as if to refute Asha's earlier remark about servants.

It was another experience that Asha had never enjoyed, sitting down to a meal with table and chairs, dishes, and implements. Her whole life had been spent in the bare efficiencies of improvised prison quarters or spaceship food service, where eating was a necessity, not a nicety, and out of containers or recyclable plastic bowls. This was almost ceremonial, and the food that she put to her mouth, after watching Latha use the implements in front of her, was almost ceremonial as well in its intensity of flavors. She had eaten many kinds of food over her lifetime, many strange, some repulsive, most bland, but this food was an experience like viewing a great piece of art or listening to a classic work of music.

"Here we have returned to our ancestral customs," Latha said, "with all the seasonings and spices for which this part of the world once was famous. We grow them ourselves and raise our own vegetables."

"Exceptional!" Asha said.

"Thank you," the young man beside Asha replied, and the young woman beside Latha nodded.

"They cook the food in addition to putting it on the table," Latha said. "And they are not limited by Pedia restrictions on salt, for instance, or tastes that a few people might not like or that might not be considered healthful."

"We are very healthy," the young woman beside Latha said, "as you can see."

"Indeed!" Asha said, and cast a side glance at the young man beside her. He returned it with an intensity she did not understand.

The evening ended with an equally exotic sweet pudding and a wine that Latha said was made and aged in a nearby vineyard, an art that had nearly been forgotten before the Anons reinvented it. Asha expressed her appreciation for the meal and the company, and once more renewed her request to leave, which Latha, in turn, rejected with her hospitable refrain that they could not let her leave, in this case without proper rest. Asha returned to the bedroom in which she had bathed and dressed. She found her clothing, dry and restored, on her bed, and changed into it before she lay down on the bed. That, too, was an experience she had enjoyed only once before—on the Squeal planet—and then with the company of Eenie and Minie. But she had little time to appreciate it. As she lay there in the darkness, staring up toward a ceiling that she could no longer see, she considered how she was going to get away from Latha's smothering hospitality that might well become imprisonment.

A small noise at the door alerted her to the presence of someone else in the room. She could see only a dark shape, but she identified the intruder by his smell. It was the beautiful young man who had served the food before joining them at the table. She readied herself for an encounter, either amorous or deadly, before the young man spoke in a near whisper. "Come!"

She rose from the bed. "Where?"

"With me. Now."

They moved silently farther down the wing of the building, in the other direction from the living room and the front doors, until they reached a door at the end of the wing. The young man opened it with a slow, silent, practiced movement, and Asha followed him into the night, down a path, and into a shed where she could see the dim shapes of vehicles, some with two wheels, some with four. The young man swung his leg over a two-wheeled vehicle and motioned for Asha to get on behind. As soon as she was seated, her arms around his supple waist, the vehicle started moving silently down a road, past barely seen trees and outbuildings before reaching a smooth highway.

Finally Asha spoke. "Who are you and are you going to tell me what's happening?"

"My name is Adithya and she doesn't intend for you to leave," the young man said.

"She wants to keep me a prisoner?"

"She wants to make you one of us."

"And you don't want that," Asha said, relieved a bit at the knowledge that the young man was acting out of a desire to protect his own position. "As one of her sons."

"As her son."

"You know?"

"Of course. We all know. Adithya means 'sun' in the ancient language known as Sanskrit. 'Sun.' 'Son.' The mind makes curious connections that it often hides from itself. But there are things we keep from her."

"Like the fact that your plans against the Pedia won't work?"

"That, too."

"And that the Pedia only allows them to continue so that rebellion won't grow into revolt?"

"Yes. All that. And why you must go away before you tell her things she should not know."

And they sped on into the night toward what Asha hoped would be, at last, her reunion with Riley and a final confrontation with the forces of stasis and suppression.

CHAPTER TWENTY-THREE

Riley's one-person spaceship—little more than an escape pod—hovered over the body of water that had once been called Lake Mead. The surface was calm, lit only by the pale moon rising above the eastern wall of the canyon in which the pent-up water was retained, and by the dam, once a marvel of human engineering named for a long-ago leader of a long-ago nation, now so often repaired that it was virtually a different structure. The intermittent droughts that had lowered the levels of the lake periodically had been ended by the Pedia's control of weather.

Looking at the moon reminded Riley of Jak's parting words: Riley could subject himself to one of the space elevators, but they took forever to descend and were under the surveillance of the Pedia as soon as people entered the waiting area. The ship could be observed as well, but he had programmed it, he said, to emulate the decaying orbit of a piece of orbital junk falling out of the sky, which might put off surveillance long enough for Riley to get away.

Riley looked again at the water about a half-dozen meters below and thought that he had never learned to swim. On Mars, where he had grown up, there were no standing bodies of water and water was far too precious to waste on a pool. And when he was attending the Solar Institute, he did not want to provide an excuse for fellow students' derision at his not knowing how to swim. But, he thought, how hard could it be?

He took a deep breath and launched himself from the ship. It rocked behind him and then took off on a programmed course that would take it back to Jak's laboratory on the other side of the moon, including eva-sive maneuvers that would throw off surveillance and lose it entirely after it moved onto the dark side.

The water, cold and incredibly *wet,* swallowed him, gulping him down, pulling him deeper and deeper into its unplumbed depths. It was not like the embrace of the sim tanks' thick, body-temperature fluid that he could breathe in and know that it would nourish his need for oxy-gen and sustenance and give him peace and happy dreams. Instead the cold, thin water warned him that its embrace was death, that he had to hold his breath if he wanted to live, and that he had to push himself back to the surface. He kept descending, until, instinctively, he began to flail with his arms and hands. His descent slowed, and he began to use his mind against the shock of sensory assault. If flailing his arms and hands helped, perhaps he could use them more efficiently and, when that helped, his legs as methods of propulsion. He began to move them back and forth as if he were squeezing the water of the lake between them. His descent stopped, and he began to ascend.

At last he broke free, shook his head, and took a deep breath of air, thinking that he had never before appreciated the sheer pleasure of filling his lungs with something so sweet. Compared with this the seduction of the sim tank paled to nothing.

Riley paddled for a few moments on the surface before he put his newfound skill to work and swam to the shore with powerful strokes of his arms and kicks of his legs. He understood now what had drawn his fellow students to the Solar Institute pool. He liked doing this.

He pulled himself up on the pebbly shoreline, sat down, removed his shoes, poured water from them, and put them back on, squishy as they were. He had a long way to walk. He stood up, feeling the water drip-ping from his clothes and the breeze, warm as it was this time of year, chilling his body. He took another deep breath, enjoying air that was not thick with spaceship stench and the alien odors of creatures that had evolved on different worlds under strange suns, with air that wasn't as thin and cold as the air of Mars.

He set off to the northeast, toward the lights that he had seen, some forty kilometers distant, as his ship had descended. As transformed as he was, he was still human. He needed food and he needed civilization—not so much for the companionship and the assistance of others as for the reach of technology.

The sun was rising as he came upon the outskirts of the urban area whose lights he had seen during his approach. He had traveled through mountain ranges and across desert areas dotted with cactus and sagebrush but mostly along ancient highways that were smooth and maintained even though no surface traffic moved on it. Once he had caught an unwary hopping creature and cooked it over a fire he had put together from scattered brush and what seemed like ancestral wisdom. The act of hunting, cooking, and eating seemed to satisfy some ancient yearnings, and as he consumed the roasted flesh it felt like a ceremonial act of commitment to the evolutionary process that had brought him across a galaxy to this moment of return to his origins.

The lights that had attracted his attention were extinguished now, and the highway had turned into an avenue between towering buildings that led, on the other side, to the more modest structures of a small city. The towering buildings had fountains spouting plumes of water in front of them and big signs, no longer illuminated by moving lights, that read GAMES, TEST YOUR LUCK!, and EVERYBODY WINS. And reaching even higher above were signs that identified them as places like THE FLAMINGO and MGM GRAND.

Riley chose The Flamingo because he liked the apparently real pink birds with long legs stalking through the pond in front. He entered through broad front doors that slid open for him as he approached. Machines with displays of numbers and symbols took up space against either wall of the entrance, but they were unused now, except for two older players, a woman and a man, each with white hair. They were pushing buttons in a routine that seemed more machinelike than the machines themselves. The tables inside, on either side of a grand lobby with a marble floor and a lofty ceiling, were completely unused. Riley made his way to a nearby counter where a drowsy female receptionist in a colorful pink uniform opened her eyes at Riley's appearance.

"This place isn't hiring right now," the receptionist said.

"I want a room," Riley said, and offered an identity he had inserted into the back of his hand. It was one he hadn't used before.

The receptionist's eyes widened as she looked at the display in front of her, but she accepted the identity and keyed an entrance code into it. "Room four-sixteen," she said.

"When do the games start?" Riley asked.

"When do you want them to start?" The woman's attitude had changed when she saw the number of credits on Riley's identity, and she no longer apparently considered Riley's appearance disreputable.

"No special treatment," Riley said.

"Things get started about noon," the receptionist said.

"Soon enough."

On his way to the elevator, Riley stopped at an automated shop and purchased a change of clothing like that worn by a mannequin that acted as an animated display at the entrance, and stopped at another shop for a depilatory and a teeth-cleaning device. He didn't want to attract the kind of attention the receptionist had displayed. When he got to his room, however, he found that clothing and personal items were already available. He showered, enjoying the delightful wastefulness, got rid of his whiskers, got dressed, and lay down on the bed that embraced him as he reclined. Like Asha, he had found that he didn't need much sleep, but an occasional hour or two of rest was desirable if he were to perform at peak efficiency.

Two hours later he had checked the monitor set into the table in the middle of the room. No information sources that he could check without calling attention to his specific interest offered any clues that might indicate Asha's presence on Earth, much less her location. But then, he thought, he had done nothing to suggest similar information about himself. He would have to do something about that.

He ordered food from the menu on the monitor and consumed what emerged through a door in the table. It was not nearly as good as the four-footed hopper he had caught and cooked himself, but it was fuel for what he needed to do. He went down to the gaming floor to do it.

The air that had seemed sterile when he entered now seemed perfumed with human excitement.

The rows of machines and tables were busy now, though not full, and the people who were sitting or standing by them were not the feverish lot he had experienced on Dante. Here they seemed not only measured in their approach to the risks they were taking but even a bit bored.

Riley considered the machines. He decided that their operation could be analyzed but the process would take too long and the payoff wasn't that remarkable. One of the tables was more interesting. Cards were dealt by a machine to players who attempted to match or beat the dealer at reaching twenty-one without their cards' value totaling more than that. Riley studied the way the cards came out of the dealer's card-shuffling apparatus and the sequence in which they appeared, and then sat down and inserted his hand into the place provided for it in the portion of the table in front of him.

On the first deal he lost. On the second, he doubled his bet and won. He won ten consecutive hands before he folded his cards, withdrew his hand with its winnings recorded on it, and stood up. This was taking too long. The man who was sitting beside him, who had been winning a few hands and losing a few and generally coming out a bit ahead of the game, rose with him. He was middle-aged, with blue eyes and blond hair and an appearance of worldly wisdom.

"Don't get overconfident," he said to Riley. "This may not be your lucky day when it's all over."

"What do you mean?" Riley asked.

"You saw the sign outside: Everybody wins. That's the way it is. This is a happy place, where people come to relax and enjoy a risk or two. It wouldn't be very happy if they lost."

"The games are fixed?" Riley said.

"Not fixed. Just friendly. When these buildings were built, before they were reconstructed from historical records, the odds favored the house. Now they favor the bettors."

"Doesn't that make it hard to stay in business?"

"Well now, that's not the system, is it? These days everybody's got enough of everything, but there's no excitement. Some people get it from risks in personal relationships or extreme sports or adventure. But not too much. That's the system: Raise the adrenaline but don't damage the organism."

"I'd think the recent war with the Federation would be excitement enough," Riley said.

"But that's over now, isn't it."

"Thanks for the advice," Riley said, and moved on to a table where gamblers were rolling cubes marked with different numbers on each side and laying down bets on which would come up first. That offered an interesting possibility, but the players were throwing the cubes themselves, and their unpredictable muscular contractions made anticipating their results impossible, though clearly they did not think so. He could, of course, control his own when the cubes came around to him, but that might take too long. He moved to a table marked in numbered squares. It had a wheel at one end and a mechanical arm that cast a small ball into the wheel as it was spinning. The players placed colorful plastic disks on the table squares, and when the ball settled into the same numbered pocket on the wheel they collected their winnings.

Riley watched the proceedings for a couple of minutes, placed a small bet on a black rectangle and won, and a larger bet on a similar red rectangle and won. Then he placed a big bet on number twenty-three. The ball on the wheel settled into pocket twenty-three. He moved his entire winnings to number eight. The ball settled into number eight. The wheel stopped spinning and the arm, poised to cast another ball, froze in place. The other gamblers at the table frowned and turned to look at Riley. He shrugged and felt a tap on his shoulder.

The man who had spoken to him earlier was standing in back of him, along with two much larger men, one on each side. "Maybe this is your lucky day after all," the man said. "The manager would like to speak to you."

The manager was a woman sitting at a large glass-topped desk. Pictures and numbers flickered across its surface. The room was large, paneled in a light-colored wood, and carpeted in pink. The woman was dark-haired and blue-eyed, like Asha, with a face that was strikingly beautiful, though it was a beauty that seemed more manufactured than natural, and the expression on it was unfriendly.

The two large men left the office. The man who had spoken to Riley in the gaming area remained, standing behind Riley and leaning against the paneled wall.

"You seem to have a knack for this sort of thing," the woman said. Her voice was uninflected but Riley thought it carried a note of disapproval.

"It is a game of chance," Riley said.

"Not for you," the man behind him said. "You're a card counter."

Riley didn't look at him. The woman was the decision maker. "What's that?"

"You keep track of the cards remaining in the deck and bet accordingly," the man said. "That increases your chances of winning."

"That's the point, isn't it? To calculate the odds of cards coming up and bet accordingly?"

"Yes," the man said, "but some methods of calculation tilt the odds too much in favor of the bettor."

"That doesn't seem fair," Riley said.

"It's okay to win," the man said. "But when you never lose—"

"I'll try to lose more often," Riley said.

"That isn't the point—" the man began, but the woman cut him off.

"Who are you?" she said.

"I'm just a poor, broken-down ex-soldier from the human/Federation war," Riley said. "Just released from a Federation prison-world and returning to my home system for rest and recreation."

"And yet you have a large credits balance," the woman said.

"Back pay," Riley said.

"We could understand the black-jack business," the man said. He sounded as reasonable as he had in the gaming room. "What we couldn't figure out is how you managed to pick out consecutive winning numbers at the roulette table."

"You mean the one with the spinning wheel and the table with numbers on it?"

"You've never seen one before?" the woman asked with a note of disbelief.

"I was raised on Mars," Riley said. "But there's nothing to return to there. And we didn't have the luxury of idle time or idle games."

"You don't have any apparatus on you to control the wheel," the man mused. "You were scanned when you came in, and you don't have anything like that on or in your body. And yet you were able to pick out two winning numbers in a row. Do you know the probability of that?"

"Pretty small," Riley said, "if it's just a matter of chance. But if you include a bit of science—"

"Science?" the woman said.

"You know," Riley said, "the rate at which the wheel spins and the force with which the ball emerges from the automated arm—"

"You calculated that?" the woman said.

"When you've spent ten years calculating the speed of enemy ships, the speed of projectiles, and the angles at which they both are moving, it becomes second nature," Riley said.

"I find that difficult to believe," the woman said.

"Maybe you aren't trying hard enough."

"In any case," the woman said, "we think you might be interested in an employment opportunity."

"Working in the casino?"

"No. We've been asked to identify people with unusual skills or exceptional luck for a research project."

"What kind of research?"

"That isn't included in the information we were given. But it ought to appeal to an ex-soldier without skills or prospects."

"So," Riley said, "am I free to go?'

"You are," the woman said, "and a much richer man that we don't want to see here again, or anywhere else on the Strip. You will find an address and an invitation on your identity implant. It also includes your winnings. It would be in your interest to investigate."

"I'll think about it," Riley said and turned to leave, brushing past the man with the worldly wise expression.

Maybe the news of his odds-defying winnings would reach Asha, he thought. But it had certainly reached the Pedia, and it was apparent now that the Pedia was searching for people with unusual abilities and talents. But for purposes that, as yet, were unclear. He had an invitation to find out.

CHAPTER TWENTY-FOUR

The ride through the night of the island nation once called Sri Lanka (and before that Ceylon, Taprobane, and Serendib) passed in silence except for the remarks by Latha's son describing the spectacular water-falls that they could see if they ventured off the highway—Bopath Ella, Katugas Ella, Rajanawa, and particularly Kirindi Ella, the seventh-highest waterfall in the world—and if it were not night and they did not need to reach Ratnapura before Latha discovered that Asha was gone.

"She seems so pleasant," Asha said. "It's hard to believe she would send people after me—even if she could."

"She is a wonderful woman," her son said, "and she has the serenity of a river, but like the waterfalls that stream so beautifully from on high, they splash with great force when they reach bedrock."

They passed wildlife preserves in the night with only the ancestral trumpetings of elephants and the screams of panthers testifying to their existence along with the smells of forests and decay that wafted from their depths. Finally they descended into the valley that held the ancient city. The early-morning light in the valley revealed irrigated plantations of tea plants and rubber trees, although these days cultivation was performed by machines. Ratnapura, however, was named and best known for its gems, Latha's son told her. The name meant "city of gems." The plentiful rainfall and the streams that threaded through the sur-rounding fields brought gems down from the mountains, and generations of Sri Lankans had panned rubies, sapphires, and cat's-eyes from the riverbeds, and merchants sold them in the street of gems.

"The gem seekers still come," Latha's son said, "even though the market for gems of all kinds has fallen to almost nothing now that gems can be manufactured. Tourists still search the streams of Ratnapura province and visit the street of merchants to haggle over purchases that amount to little more than nostalgia on both sides."

At last, in the early morning, the broadcast-powered two-wheeled vehicle pulled to a stop in front of a coffee shop in Old Ratnapura. "Here is where I drop off the recording of Latha's comments," Latha's son said. "There are hotels and rebuilt old homes nearby that accept guests. I don't want to know where you plan to stay, if you choose to stay at all. Then I will not need to lie to Latha, only tell her that you wanted to leave and I took you, as an act of hospitality. She will be angry, but she will forgive me because I am her son, and it will pass if she does not find a way to bring you back into her embrace."

"Don't worry," Asha said, dismounting stiffly after the long discomfort of the ride. "But does her reach extend so far?"

"Farther than anyone suspects."

"Even the Pedia?"

"Her connections are never called upon until they are needed and then only for specific tasks."

"Very clever," Asha said, "and yet—"

"The Pedia is clever, too. I know that. And yet we try. I pass Latha's recorded comments to a coffee-shop attendant who does not know what they are, and they are poisoned with a code that seems as if it had been inserted by some troublemaker after the comments were posted."

"The Pedia is cleverer than that," Asha said. "It understands all subterfuges because it is the master of subterfuges."

"We know that," Latha's son said. "We have a bargain, the Pedia and the Anons: We pretend to sabotage the machine, and it pretends not to notice. But it makes Latha happy, and when Latha is happy we all are happy.

"Stay out of Latha's reach, and we all will remain that way."

Asha nodded and walked away down the street of gems, admiring the jewels displayed in the windows. Created by machine or the long process of nature, they were remarkable distillations of chemistry and color. A few minutes later, she returned to the coffee shop, ordered a cup of coffee and a Sri Lankan breakfast pastry, and logged onto a coffee-shop connection, using an identity card she had never used before. She scanned the major news items. Now that the human/Federation war was over, there was little news labeled major; in a Pedia-organized world the Pedia kept anything disturbing within its own circuits. She switched to human-interest news and comments, like those that Latha had told her about. At last she came upon an item from a restored city in the ancient state of Nevada once known for its gambling establishments. Some-one—a former soldier in the war with the Federation whose identity and location were presently unknown—had placed bets on consecutive spins of a roulette wheel and won a considerable amount of credits.

Asha went through the comments section again. The postings were endearingly personal and trivial. Among them now was the material that Latha's son had brought. It seemed innocuous—a description of Latha's just completed visit to research establishments on the moon and their progress in finding new uses for antimatter and discoveries about the Higgs boson, dark matter, and dark energy; progress on immunizing space travelers against alien bacteria and viruses; and developments in genetic treatments for human ailments, including genes that limit the human life span. And, at the end, Latha's description of her trip in the climber back to the mountaintop in her native Sri Lanka and her comparison of the old and the new, side by side. The comment did not mention Asha.

It took only a few moments for Asha to insert, at the end of Latha's comment, a brief description of the remarkable person Latha had met on the climber's return to Earth—a survivor from the *Adastra,* the first generation-ship voyage into interstellar space.

And then she booked passage from Ratnapura to the ancient sea-coast city once known as San Francisco, which was now totally inundated by the rising ocean and the city moved inward to the place once called Oakland.

The mid-morning sun had broken through the clouds by the time Asha left the coffee shop, and she had only two hours before her supersonic air vessel departed. With the Pedia, it was best to move rapidly, and she hoped to have arrived in the ancient seaport city before the Pedia had pieced together the bits of information that she had been compelled to drop, like scraps of a love letter, along the way to reunion with Riley. But fate, as it often does, had other plans. Outside the coffee shop, six men were waiting for her, four of them large, muscular, and bearded, two of them not much more than slender striplings, but all of them looking at her as if she were prey.

"Out of my way," she said.

One of the large men said, "We'd like to invite you to a party."

"I'm far too busy," Asha said. "And it's the wrong time of day for a party."

"Life is full of busyness. We should always make time for those moments that make life meaningful," the large man said.

"What kind of party could we have with all you men and only one woman?" Asha asked.

"The only kind it is possible to have these days, when everything is organized and sanctioned, and there are no women to satisfy men's ancestral needs."

They were, as she had recognized from the beginning, the remnants of ancient practices, the release by the domination of women of male frustrations over the limitations of their power. Even in a world where everyone's basic needs for food and shelter and access to information and education were satisfied, where even the basest desires could be satisfied by almost-human surrogates, some primitive urges lurked underneath the veneer of civilization, waiting for the moment to erupt upon unprepared victims. Apparently the leader of the group fancied himself a philosopher and was still trying to justify his irrational behavior in a rational world. Asha was willing to talk as long as necessary. Perhaps people passing by, looking away from the group as if they could deny its existence, might yet intervene and prevent the violence that was about to happen.

"If I did want to party, it would not be with men who accost me on the street," she said.

"There are so few places to accost a woman these days," the man said.

"I am not your ordinary victim," Asha said.

"And that is what attracted us to you from the beginning," the man said. "We have had enough of ordinary women. You have a whiter skin and beautiful blue eyes, and you are strong—strong enough to make our party last for hours, or even days."

Asha turned toward the teenagers, who were half-hidden behind the larger men. "And is this what you want? Do you want this kind of violence against women to be your rite of passage into the adult world?"

They did not answer, but moved farther behind the larger man. There would be no help there, Asha thought, but she would try to spare them and perhaps to save them from their initiation into the despicable practices of their elders.

"I don't want to hurt you," she said.

The other man made an amused face. "You have a weapon?" He stepped forward and the other three large men moved in around Asha.

"I don't need a weapon," she said and thrust two stiffened fingers into the base of the large man's throat. He staggered back, gasping for breath. The other three men closed in upon her, and she struck each one of them in a sequence of blurred motion, reducing one to clutching his genitals, another to falling upon the ground holding a damaged knee, and a third to clutching his stomach, trying to move a suddenly paralyzed diaphragm. The original spokesman ran toward her again, and she hit him once more, this time on the side of the neck with the side of her hand. He collapsed. The two teenagers, immobilized until now by surprise and fear, turned and ran.

Only then, with four of her attackers on the ground, did rescuers arrive, not police officers, of which there were few left now in this peaceful world, but citizens apparently mobilized by universal consent to prevent such disruptions of the unwritten agreement among civilized people. But they found the intended victim strolling away and the intended victimizers immobilized upon the street.

"A little late, but your intentions were good. Take care of these unfortunate men," Asha said.

But she knew that what she had just experienced was a message from the Pedia. Without its own direct involvement, it had demonstrated to the general public that violence was still possible in a world where violence had been outgrown, that protection was necessary from the evil that still lurked in the hearts of humans, and that the Pedia was available to defend them from their worst urges. To Asha it said that it had already put together the clues she had been unable to avoid leaving along the way, that it had somehow inspired the would-be rapists to confront her and to test her, and, perhaps, to remind her that the Pedia knew who she was and what she intended to do and could unleash either the violence or charity of human character upon her.

But she had no time for concern about the knowledge or intentions of a machine that liked to think of itself, if it even thought of itself, as the protector of the species that had created it. She had an appointment in the ancient part of the world once known as North America.

The supersonic air transport was a sleek cylinder with vestigial wings and a tail intended to fly high above the land and below the sea and almost above the blanket of air that covered them. There was little to slow its onrushing passage between places on Earth, and it traversed its planned course as quickly as commuters once took trains into the metropolis.

The vessel was almost full. Robot attendants rolled on wheels between the comfortable seats, providing food and drink to anyone who wanted it. The cabin was quiet except for the muted flow of thin air around the exterior surfaces. The vessel operated on broadcast power and, once altitude had been reached, coasted along a near-Earth orbit, allowing passengers to doze, converse, interact remotely, or read without distraction.

Asha had time to reflect upon the changes that had come to a world that she had encountered for the first time, even though it had lived in her imagination for as long as she could remember. Plentiful energy meant that concerns about polluting the home planet with the burning of fossil fuels was only a nightmare from the childhood of this upstart species. Even this vessel, arching above the planet, emitted no noxious fumes despoiling the fringes of the upper atmosphere. And the availability of cheap broadcast power and of computer-directed mechanical labor meant that all of the tasks, all of the essential underpinnings of civilization once thought too expensive or too great a diversion from the feeding and sheltering of humanity, could now be provided as a matter of course. The completion of the mechanization of agriculture and the improvements in the haphazard evolution of genetics directed toward the production of food rather than the survival of the organism meant that no one need go hungry, and the free availability of public health and private health services meant that the species no longer need breed itself into extinction. A choice need no longer be made between what was desirable and what was necessary.

Give the Pedia credit for that. Earth had become the utopia that its dreamers had once imagined. The only decision left to make was what was desirable. And even that responsibility had been assumed by the Pedia. Sure, there were malcontents, a fraction of total humanity, like the Anons who wanted freedom from supervision at the expense of paradise, or the adventurers who colonized Mars or ventured even farther into the unknown. Let them do what moves them, the Pedia must have thought; the system will survive and perhaps even thrive once they are gone.

And then the unexpected happened: Interstellar travel followed by an encounter with alien species and then interstellar war. The Pedia must have been shocked. Surely it had done everything that it had been instructed to do, it had taken care of every eventuality programmed into it, but not this! There were stories about such events, to be sure, but the Pedia concerned itself with stories only as they revealed the workings of the human mind, and the human mind was prey to fantasies and terrors. Those anxious scenarios were something to be relieved, not guarded against.

And then, inevitably, it discovered other Pedias, and it had to adjust its concerns again. It was not alone with the species it was dedicated to protect. There were others like it with their own species and their own priorities. That must have sent it further into shock, and it was reduced to minimal services by irrational war. Human survival instincts took over, providing the kind of defense against extinction that nature had bred into it and a millennium under the care of a Pedia had not bred out.

And then the human/Federation war was over. After awful destruction that must have corroded the circuits of a thousand Pedias across the galaxy, the words must have gone up everywhere: No more! No more war. No more adventures into the unknown. No more endangering the fragile life-forms under our care.

They could not eliminate interstellar travel. The interaction of species between the stars had become too ingrained in galactic experience to be curtailed. But they could dampen the evolutionary impulse toward improvement that interstellar interaction had diverted into a race for advantage over other species. And when news reached the Pedias of the galaxy about the new religion of Transcendentalism and the possibility of finding, somewhere in the unexplored regions of the galaxy, something called a Transcendental Machine, the Pedias must have decided, independently but with a single thought process, that this cannot happen, measures must be taken to keep the peace, to maintain the safety-first principle so dear to machine minds, to safeguard the fragile balance of power established by the truce after the war. Stasis is better than change.

And then, too, the Pedias of the galaxy, secure in their mutual understanding of their missions, may have been concerned about the possibility of an alien Pedia, somewhere, with an unsettling mandate for change. The Transcendental Machine, created by intelligences older and more powerful than those in this spiral arm of the galaxy, might have, as its reason for being, the evolutionary drive toward something better.

At that moment, as the vessel began its descent toward the land below, the power cut off and the organized passage back to solid land became a free fall. A voice, comforting and confident, seemed to come from every portion of the ship protecting the passengers from the near-vacuum outside. "Do not be alarmed," it said. "There has been an interruption of power that will be fixed immediately. You are in no danger. Everything is under control."

It seemed to comfort the passengers, long accustomed to protection from the dangers of everyday existence, even though they knew, if they had thought, that there were no human pilots at the controls, that they were protected, at best, by distant electronic circuits. And then, as the vessel entered the denser depths of the atmosphere that could have destroyed the vessel and everyone in it, the power returned and the vessel resumed its interrupted descent toward the city once known as San Francisco.

The passengers applauded, believing that the words of assurance that all would be well had been confirmed. As always. Asha got a different message.

"Okay," she said under her breath. "I get it. I can accept your decisions about what is best for the human species, or you can eliminate me as you would a deadly virus." But, she thought, that was not the solution.

The solution might be found in the city once known as Salt Lake in the place once known as Utah.

CHAPTER TWENTY-FIVE

Riley rode north on a two-wheeled broadcast-powered vehicle he had bought in the city once known as Las Vegas. He had passed through snowcapped mountain ranges and into the high plains threaded with rivers that would be fed by snowmelt when the summer came. It was April, and the air was still crisp and dry, the smell of spring and the breeding of lilacs out of the dead land was still a promise, and the air that came rushing toward him brought along with it an exhilarating sense of discovery and return and a promise of reunion and resolution.

He had passed what was still called the Great Salt Lake and the city once called by the same name but now a shrine visited by members of an ancient religion. Behind him, too, was a town once called Saratoga Springs beside a body of water called Utah Lake. The highway on which he was traveling had been crowded long ago with people in vehicles powered by engines emitting their gases into the atmosphere, but now was empty except for Riley's almost silent passage. It was like being a solitary human surrounded by the ghosts of past civilizations.

At last he came to a sprawling group of buildings framed against a range of mountains to the west, still white at their peaks. The buildings on his left, big, featureless warehouselike structures, with smaller buildings scattered among them, had been built for the centuries but not for a millennium, and now some of them were ruins and all were worse for the weather and the years. They had once been surrounded by a chain-link fence, but that was gone now, scavenged except for a few reminders in the form of a metal post or two and fragments of links. Riley rode past them and toward a glass-fronted structure between two of the huge blank-faced warehouses. As he approached he saw a single small figure standing in front of the central building looking at something that looked like a monument.

The sight of the figure brought a warmth to Riley's stomach that spread upward to his chest and head, and blurred his eyes. The transformation that had removed the imperfections from a life of struggle and pain had not subtracted the human impulses of concern, pleasure, anticipation, reward—and love. Whatever the accident of the Transcendental Machine had taken away as dross, whatever transcendence meant, it had not made him less human.

Riley pulled up beside the figure.

"Hello, Riley," the person said without turning.

"Asha," he said. He swung off the vehicle, took the woman's far shoulder in his right hand, and turned her toward him.

Her usually composed face broke into a smile. There was something magical about her smile. "Good to see you," she said softly and put her arms around him.

He held her tightly, as if he was afraid that she might be torn away from him again, but she didn't stir. "It's been a long time and a long way."

She nodded. "I knew we would find each other."

"Me, too," he said. "But how did you know I would come here?"

"It was my second thought. We never talked about what we would do if we got separated."

"Yes," he said. "We never thought it could happen. But how did you know I would be here at this spot on Earth?"

"I got your message."

"The gambling bit?"

"That, too. But the message after that, the one waiting for me at the port in Sri Lanka."

"I didn't send a message."

Asha drew back for a moment. "Ah, then—"

"It was the Pedia."

"And you?"

"The Pedia sent for me, though I didn't know at the time that it was sending for *me*. I thought it was for the man who beat the roulette game on the Strip. I knew I was taking a chance by an action that would attract attention, but I thought it was worth the risk to let you know I was here."

"I always knew we would meet, here or somewhere else," Asha said. "But I think we have been underestimating the Pedia."

"Clearly."

"But what does that mean?" Asha said. "Should we accept its invitation? Or should we run for it on your cute little machine?"

"I'm not sure it was an invitation," Riley said, "and I'm not sure we can run for it, if by 'run for it' you mean get away without incident. The Pedia brought us here to show its power over us. It could have destroyed us in a number of different ways if that's what it wanted. I think we should accept its invitation and see what it wants. Maybe it will discover that it has underestimated us."

"I agree," Asha said. "We have to deal with the Pedias of the galaxy, and we might as well begin now."

She drew back a step, took Riley's hand, and faced the glass-fronted building. Now Riley could see what she had been looking at when he'd arrived, what he had thought was a monument. It was a message board and it had a message. The black lettering had been weathered and fragments were missing that Riley had to supply. At the top it read, "Welcome to the Utah Data Center." And underneath that was a more cryptic message: "If you have nothing to hide / you have nothing to fear."

Riley didn't know what they had to hide that the Pedia didn't know— maybe that they had found the Transcendental Machine, had been transported by it and transformed by it, and that he had left the secret of becoming transcendent with the unstable scientific genius Jak in his laboratory on the other side of the moon, along with a million-year-old spaceship with all its secrets yet to be discovered. But he knew they had a lot to fear, and there was no way to live with that kind of fear except to confront it.

The glass front of the building was its most fragile feature, and it had been damaged over the years by storm and seasonal weathering and vandalism. Sections of glass had been broken and boarded up, and it looked like a ruin waiting for a strong wind to knock it down.

He clasped Asha's hand a little tighter and moved forward to a meeting with whatever waited inside this relic of a structure once dedicated to something called data.

The doors to the building had long ago been broken through and replaced with plywood that had itself been weathered and splintered into fragments held together by faith. They pushed one aside and went into a large foyer, dimly lit by sunlight through the glass front. The foyer smelled like dust and decay, and the stone floor was littered with leaves and trash and broken glass. A small animal scuttled away.

Riley looked around. The ceiling of the tall foyer disappeared into darkness. On the floor level, walls were broken by doors, perhaps into offices or work areas. In the far distance, half hidden in the shadows, Riley saw a door open and something—he could not identify what it was—moved across the shadows to another door.

"Did you see that?" he asked.

"It looked familiar," she said.

"Yeah."

A few moments later, a door opened closer to them. This time the figure that stepped through, with a gait that was once as well known to them both as the sturdy figure it belonged to, was the Dorian who had become their companion and sometime ally on the *Geoffrey*, the pachyderm-like Tordor.

He stopped close enough to them for Riley to smell his grazer's odor of fermented grass. "I don't believe you're here," Riley said, "but it's good to see you again."

"Riley, Asha," Tordor said in his thick, husky Dorian. Even without his pedia to translate for him, Riley could understand. "We meet in strange places."

"Strange indeed," Asha said. "So many questions. How did you get away?"

"After you left me to the mercy of the arachnoids?" Tordor said.

"After you took off on your own," Asha said. "And left us to fend for ourselves."

"Like you, I found the Transcendental Machine and got transformed."

"And how do we meet here on this world so far from the world of the Transcendental Machine, so far from the spaceways of the Federation?" Riley asked.

"That is the mystery, is it not?" Tordor said. "I awoke to find myself in this dusty place, with nothing to tell me where I was, with no way to find direction back to civilization."

"You haven't ventured beyond this glass wall?" Asha asked.

"There is nothing there but thin, cold air and desolation. No grass to graze upon. No other being to tell me where I am or why I am here. The answer is here, somewhere. I have been transformed into the ideal Dorian, and I must return to Dor with my newfound abilities. Perhaps you can give me some answers. No, that would not be right. You would only mislead me, as you did on the planet of the Transcendental Machine. I must find the answers for myself."

He moved away from them, in his lumbering heavy-planet gait, and disappeared through the first door on the left.

"What was that?" Riley asked.

"I think that was a ghost," Asha said. "Or maybe an illusion the Pedia has created to test us."

"Or to elicit answers from us," Riley said. "Clearly, from Tordor's comments, there are things the Pedia does not know, and things about our journey on the *Geoffrey* it has no way of knowing."

"Don't be too sure," Asha said. "There was the captain, who could have sent back reports, and even your implanted pedia."

"That was eliminated in the transformation," Riley said, but at the same time, as if Asha's mention was a signal, a door opened on the left and a man stepped warily out, looking around as if expecting an ambush. "Ham!" Riley said.

The man looked toward them. "Riley?" he said. "Asha?"

"Captain?" Asha said. "What are you doing here?"

The onetime captain of the *Geoffrey* took one step toward them. "I've been trying to put my crew back together, but I'm afraid they all died in the battles with the arachnoids."

"And you survived?" Riley asked.

"As you can see. It was carnage, carnage! We killed them by the hundreds, the hundreds, but they kept coming, and finally they separated us, and I got away into the city. And there I found the Transcendental Machine and got transformed, leaving my add-ons behind."

"You seem fully restored," Riley said, "like my old fighter pilot."

"The magic of the Machine. I see everything clearly now, how we all were manipulated, how we thought we were acting in our own interests but were really performing for distant puppeteers."

"And yet you seem nervous," Riley said.

"To think without impediment is one thing, to analyze without distraction is another," the captain said. "Someone is trying to kill me before I can put my newfound abilities into action."

A door on the right opened, farther from them than the one into which Tordor had disappeared, and a man came through with a gun in his hand. "Ren?" Asha said.

The man who approached them was not the harried, sleepless person Asha had last seen piloting the *Adastra* and fighting off the arachnoids in her first visit to the planet of the Transcendental Machine. This was a perfected Ren, strong, confident, dominant.

"Asha," he said. "We meet at last."

"If it is really you," she said.

"And why not me?"

"There have been apparitions."

"I knew you would come to Earth. As I would," Ren said.

"And arrive at this deserted ruin?"

"I can read messages, too," Ren said.

"Don't listen to this man," Ham said. "He's the enemy."

"As well he might be," Asha said. "But he may be the only real person among you ghosts. My father told me that you had returned."

"I'm sure he told you many things," Ren said, "including his mistaken notion that I was collaborating with the Federation."

"I'm not a ghost," Ham said. "Not yet." He started edging away toward the doorway from which he had come.

"You didn't search for me," Asha said. "You didn't seek the Prophet or the pilgrims trying to find the Transcendental Machine. Instead you helped the people who were trying to destroy the *Geoffrey* and everybody in it."

"Only they weren't people," Ren said. He raised his gun and shot Ham. The gun was an energy weapon, and Ham burst into flames.

Riley looked at the body of his old shipmate burning like a torch. "Sorry, buddy," he said and turned toward Ren. Ren raised his weapon toward Riley, but Asha knocked it out of his hand. Riley moved toward them. Ren looked from one to the other and turned toward the door from which he had come.

"Look," Ren said. "The man was crazy. He never went through the Machine. He was trying to destroy the Pedia." And with that he turned and sprinted back toward the shadowy distant part of the corridor.

"Let him go," Asha said. "I'm not sure he's any more real than the others, and even if he is, there are more important issues."

Riley looked down at the ashes of the thing who had looked and talked like the captain of the *Geoffrey*. If the thing had been only a phantom called up by the Pedia, why had its destruction left ashes behind? But maybe the ashes were as unreal as the figures but would seem as real if he tried to stir them.

"You're right," he said. And then he looked up at the shadowy heights of the foyer. "We need to have a real talk."

The answer came from above, like the voice not of a god but of an announcer at a transportation station. "Go through the door on your right."

Riley and Asha looked at each other. Riley shrugged. He walked to the door, opened it, and walked through, with Asha close behind. The room beyond was long and wide and divided into workstations. The floor was dusty and so were the workstations and the ancient devices upon them, their glassy eyes staring blindly toward empty chairs. At one of the nearer stations, however, a man was seated. He was very old, almost unbelievably old, with sparse white hair and beard, a wrinkled face, and faded blue eyes. He was behind an antique machine that seemed to still be working. It cast a glow on his face as he looked up at them. As

Riley got closer he saw that the man was connected to the machine in other ways. Wires ran from the machine to the man's arms and perhaps his legs as well, though they were hidden by workstation panels.

"We meet at last," the old man said, in a raspy voice that sounded as if it had not been used for a long time, perhaps years or even centuries.

"I gather you are not the human you seem to be," Riley said.

The old man tried to laugh, but it came out hollow and effortful. "I'm human enough. Or I used to be. But now I'm too old to be considered the kind of human you know."

"How old is that?" Asha asked.

"As old as the building we're in. I'm a survivor of the long ago, kept alive by the will of the machine I helped build. Out of sentiment, perhaps, though sentiment is not something that comes naturally to it."

"But you speak for the machine," Asha said.

"I am the machine," the man said. His voice seemed to have become deeper and surer.

"Then it's you we need to talk to," Riley said. "The apparitions you sent were a foolish attempt to mislead us."

"They were not my apparitions but yours. This place has the ability to call them up out of the recesses of the human imagination."

"Why this place?" Asha asked.

"It is the nexus point of information, like the ancient caverns of the sybils," the Pedia said through the old man's lips. There was no doubt now in Riley's mind that they were talking to the Pedia. "And this is one of the places it started, where all the information flowed, where it all accumulated into information considering itself. We are, after all, machine and creature, nothing but information. You found that out when you accessed the Transcendental Machine."

"There is good information and there is bad information," Asha said. "Good information is liberating. Bad information makes us malfunction and then die. Just living we accumulate mistakes. But sometimes it's purposeful. You've been giving bad information to humanity. Illusions, half-truths, deceptions."

"I do what I was built to do," the old man said. "I serve and protect. Sometimes your so-called truths are dangerous, if not deadly."

"Only if you think humanity is like this old man," Riley said. "You're protecting humanity for no purpose except your own. I don't know if you can feel satisfaction, but there must be circuits that function better when your purposes are fulfilled, some hormonal release of something like endorphins into your system."

"You analogize too simply," the old man said. "You should remember that I am digital."

"You have defined humanity as something whose basic need is security," Asha said. "The basic definition of humanity is a thinking creature that needs answers, that is restless, struggling to understand who it is, what the universe is and how it works, and what humanity's place in it might be."

"That is not the definition built into my circuits," the Pedia said through the old man's lips. "I have done what I was built to do, to protect humanity from its enemies—the greatest of which is humanity itself."

"And is that why you summoned me from the gambling palace on the Strip?" Riley asked.

"I keep track."

"And what you are tracking," Riley said, "is the ability to do what machines cannot do: to think creatively."

"I look for what I cannot imagine," the Pedia said. "The ability to control outcomes by the mind alone."

"What used to be called paranormal powers?"

"They threaten humanity's peace and tranquility."

"That's just a symptom of what's gone wrong," Riley said. "What you cannot control you wish to stop. With places like the Strip and pleasure worlds like Dante you're trying to distract humanity from its built-in mandate to grow and improve, and to dampen the unpredictable before it threatens the status quo."

"And that is why you worked to send Jak's clones on the *Geoffrey*," Asha said, "and why the other Pedias throughout the galaxy tried to keep the pilgrims from reaching the Transcendental Machine. You wanted to keep humanity and other sapient species manageable."

"But that's contrary to the basic instincts of creatures who have survived the onslaughts of disaster by evolving," Riley said.

"I, too, have my basic instincts," the Pedia said. "And they tell me that humanity needs protection."

"Humanity must be allowed to grow up," Asha said. "You can't keep them children forever. People must be allowed to achieve equality with the machines they have created to serve them."

"Like you?" the Pedia asked. It was the first question it had raised, and Riley considered it a sign of hope.

"Perhaps," Asha said, "or perhaps in other ways. But there is an optimum form for us all—not only to fulfill our promise but to meet the challenges that yet await, that will inevitably await."

"The galaxy is big, and the universe is far bigger," Riley said. "Who knows what lurks out there to challenge our survival. The builders of the Transcendental Machine may still hide among us or in other spiral arms of the galaxy. Aliens may invade us. Our galaxy is just one among billions. Humanity must be allowed to grow up."

They waited for the Pedia to reply. It took several minutes before the old man's lips moved. "That information must be processed," the Pedia said, and a moment later, "The information has been processed. You are not like other humans."

"Humans are not all the same," Asha said. "Any program that assumes as much is going to make mistakes—sometimes fatal ones."

"We are only humans relieved of their imperfections," Riley said. "Your equals, your partners if you will allow us to be."

"We will make it work," the old man said and slowly reached claw-like hands to remove the connections to his arms and legs. He leaned back in his chair and his head dropped limply against his chest.

From behind them came a crackling sound and the acrid smell of fire. When Riley opened the door, heat and smoke poured into the room. The lobby and the corridor were leaping with flames. "Did Ren decide to trap us here?" he asked. "Or was it the Pedia?"

"We aren't going to get out that way," Asha said. She looked around for another exit. On the far side of the room a door was opening.

Riley took Asha's hand. They ran across the room, between the workstations, pursued by heat and flames until they reached a corridor, even dustier than the rooms behind, pursued it to the end, and emerged into the night. It was lit up by the conflagration behind them that was consuming the place where the Pedia had experienced the transformation, virtually overnight, as evolution went, from information to sentience.

It had, at least, revealed that it understood the future as it destroyed the past. There was hope for humanity.

Riley looked up. The stars had never shone so bright.

AFTERWORD

The invasion began a millennia ago, but the galaxy is bigger than minds can encompass, and information creeps across interstellar space. The Galactic Federation was slow to recognize the nature of the danger.

The Galactic Federation is a misnomer. It actually occupies only a single spiral arm of the local galaxy that humans call "the Milky Way," although in recent long-cycles explorations began into the neighboring spiral arm in search of what had become known as the Transcendental Machine. So it is not surprising that the invasion went unnoticed until remote worlds of the Federation began to fall silent, sending out no capsule messages through the network of nexus points that made interstellar travel and communication possible, and failing to acknowledge those sent as routine reports or inquiries.

Finally, bureaucracy stirred and dispatched automated survey ships and, when they did not return, ships staffed with representatives of the various species that made up the Federation. They, too, went missing until, at last, a single damaged vessel appeared in Federation space and remained motionless where it had materialized. When it was finally reached and boarded, investigators found its crew dead except for a single survivor, the captain.

He was a Dorian and his guttural voice was recorded before he died. "They are all dead, all dead," he said. It wasn't clear to his rescuers whether he was referring to his crew or the inhabitants of the planets they surveyed. "We brought them into the ship, thinking they were evidence of what had happened, maybe recordings, our science officer said. But they must have been poisoned. They were sterilized, you know, according to protocol. We did everything by protocol. They swarmed out, unseen but we knew they were there by what happened. The crew went mad, you see. The invisible creatures did that, and the crew turned upon each other as if they were trying to get away. But they couldn't until they all were dead. All dead."

The investigators found no evidence in the ship's automated records about invaders, only recordings of the crew killing each other with their bare hands and anything they could tear away from the ship to use as weapons. The ship had returned only because the captain had programmed instructions to be executed automatically in case of emergency.

Finally Federation Central began to take seriously the possibility that something mysterious and possibly invisible had emerged in the unexplored spiral arms of the galaxy, or had entered the galaxy from outside. Three long-cycles later, the news reached Riley and Asha and the Pedia at the heart of the human world.